CONTEMPORARY AMERICAN FICTION

LADIES' MAN

Born in 1950, Richard Price was just 24 when his first novel, *The Wanderers*, caused a literary sensation upon its publication in 1974. *Bloodbrothers*, *Ladies' Man*, and *The Breaks* soon followed, establishing him as one of the finest writers of his generation. Over the past few years, Richard Price has made another career as one of Hollywood's premier screenwriters; *The Color of Money* (an Academy Award nominee) and *Sea of Love* are two of his credits. His most recent novel is *Clockers*.

D0988536

LADIES' MAN

Richard Price

BLOOMSBURY

First published in Great Britain 1995

Copyright © Richard Price 1978

The moral right of the author has been asserted

Bloomsbury Publishing plc,
2 Soho Square, London W1V 6HB

A CIP catalogue record for this book is available
from the British Library

ISBN 0 7475 1529 8

Printed in Great Britain by
Cox & Wyman Ltd, Reading

To Laurie Sammeth with love

*To John Califano for two more years of
growing pains, shared lights, love and friendship*

To the memory of my grandfather, Morris Price

_____

*I would like to thank the Yaddo Foundation
for the time and the place*

"You have no idea what it's like to be me!"
— PETER LORRE in *M*

MONDAY

So there we were. Me, I was doing my usual hundred and fifty sit-ups. My feet were jammed under the couch for leverage and I was holding a five-pound barbell behind my head like an iron halo. La Donna was in her black Danskins sitting by the wall doing dancercizes. I had a stomach that looked like six miniature cobblestones. La Donna was so limber that standing and without bending her knees, she could work her head down between her legs and kiss her own ass. How very nice for the both of us. She was a twenty-eight-year-old bank clerk would-be singer; I was a thirty-year-old door-to-door salesman and we both walked around all day like Back to Bataan.

When I was doing my sit-ups I liked to watch TV — Lucy or Fonzie, whatever reruns I could get a hold of. That was not allowed when La Donna was around. She needed silence to stand there, pull one foot backward, up over her shoulder, and tap the base of her skull with her heel. I could have worked out when she wasn't around, but six weeks before, on a Sunday morning after she finished her dancercizes, she came over to where I was doing sit-ups and just sat on it. There are aborigines in New Guinea who have been squatting by an air strip since 1943 because a plane once landed and dropped off food. Six weeks ain't that long. Meanwhile, if I needed extra money I could do exhibitions, have two-ton semis drive over my stomach at state fairs.

La Donna walked past me on the way to the bathroom, a thumb-pinch of tush peeking out over each thigh. My stomach queered and I couldn't do another sit-up. I lay flat on my back and stared upside-down at the wall unit across the room. I followed her into the bathroom. She was hunched over the sink spitting out toothpaste. I stood behind her, dropped my gym shorts and got into the shower.

"Comin' in, babe?"

She looked up at me with a werewolf froth of toothpaste and spat into the sink again. "I'm gonna work awhile."

The shower curtain had a box design with alternating white and clear plastic squares and I watched her wash her face. When she finished she started to work her dusty black leotard down her shoulders and thumb-hook it below her hips to her knees so she could pee. She had tits the size of fists, hard and muscular with long, rubbery, dark brown nipples. That was unusual because her skin was as pale as dough. She sat on the pot and wiggled her toes which still had weird bumps and corns from when she had been trying to make it as a dancer. I leaned against the wall in my soap overcoat and pulled on myself.

Love. We fought like the U.S. Marines, and the only pleasure we ever got with each other was the hour between the end of a fight and sleep. That was the only time we really talked or fucked. The rest of the time we walked around afraid of each other, not really understanding or appreciating each other; what I found funny she thought pathetic or mean and what she found funny I usually considered a major yawn. I loved good balling and good movies. She was into modern dance and nightclub-type singing.

On the other hand, she had this cute big head with matching big ears. She never smiled and always had an incredible serious look on this outrageous baby face — round, with round gray eyes and a Danish nose, broad but upturned like Hitler intended. But I knew how to get her laughing, and when she did, that serious baby face broke up, went east and west, and she would cover her mouth and touch the tip of her nose with her index finger like a high-class Japanese hooker and she was a kid and she was human and I loved her. She needed me. I knew she needed me. And I wasn't stupid or shallow. I knew all about sexism, and productive relationships and growth, but I'm talking about love. I'm talking about irrational, illogical passion. And you can go to all the forums on meaningful concepts, you can have all the shared interests you want, but the bottom line with what I'm talking about here was how her arms felt wrapped around my neck when she was coming, how she looked at me when I made her laugh. And how I knew she needed me, how I felt in my heart she needed me. The rest was all good and well, but it wasn't from the gut and it wasn't love.

"Kenny? When you come outa there I wanna run down 'Feelings' a few times, okay?"

"Sure, babe."

She got up, flushed, pulled her leotard back up to her hips and left the room. I waited until I was sure she was dressed before I came out of the shower.

"Anytime you're ready, babe." I didn't feel like listening to her sing again, but she had the showcase that night and it was important. She sat cross-legged on the living room floor back against the wall frowning and staring at her nails.

"I wanna wait awhile, Kenny, okay?"

"Sure, you mean like a few minutes?"

"Awhile."

"You want some coffee?"

"No thank you."

It was a small apartment and the living room was off limits now. I went into the bedroom and turned on the TV low, but the room was blasted with sunlight and it made me feel like an invalid to have the box on. I turned it off and scanned the titles of books on the shelves. I had a million books. I loved books. My father loved books. I rebrushed my hair in the closet mirror. I could hear La Donna breathing through her nose in the living room. I felt like a big cat in a cage at the zoo. I had taken the goddamn day off to be with her, to be supportive. It was high noon. I couldn't take her goddamn depression, her goddamn isolation. I paced, fists on hips, then walked into the living room ignoring her, snagged a book from the wall unit and returned to the bedroom. She never looked up from her nails. She was frowning so hard her eyebrows were touching. I threw the book on the bed and changed my shirt. She never even thanked me for taking the day off. I didn't make money when I took off. I didn't make money, she didn't take singing lessons. She got paid in peanuts at that bank. After taxes she didn't even have enough money for a 45 let alone singing lessons. And she wasn't very good either. That fucking music teacher Madame Bossanova or whatever the hell her name was told her she was the next Liza Minnelli, but if I stopped forking over for lessons all of a sudden she'd hear the truth from that old Russian cunt, and the truth was that she couldn't goddamn sing. I put on my coat and headed for the door.

"See ya later," I mumbled.

"Okay."

Now she was biting her nails.

I stood by the elevator feeling like a class A pud. Where the hell was I supposed to go? She didn't even ask me when I was coming back, where I was going, nothing.

We lived between Broadway and West End Avenue on Seventy-seventh Street. I walked to the deli on Broadway, sat at a window table and ordered coffee so I could have a few cigarettes. It was a windy sunny nothing of a February Monday. There was nobody out on Broadway except bag ladies and street whacks. In a way it was just as well I took the day off. Door-to-door really bit on a cold day. Fuck the job. That job sucked in any kind of weather. If I had any balls I'd quit, go back to school and get a teaching degree. I'd teach English. Books. Books were bitches. I always had this fantasy of teaching English in some little ivy-covered brick schoolhouse in New England — running down Jack London to all these blond little plumpling dumpling kids. Or it's Halloween and the leaves are turning and I'm sitting up there on my desk reading them *The Legend of Sleepy Hollow*, or *The Monkey's Paw*, and maybe some of them have nice, blond, thirtyish divorced mothers and fourposter beds and heavy patchwork quilts and dream on. Maybe next lifetime. I would have been a bitch of a teacher though. I could talk about books like nobody's business. Hemingway, Baldwin, Stephen Crane, Poe, Richard Wright — you name it, I read it, and I could talk your ass off about it too. Talk. Talk, talk, talk. Cold days with nothing to do always brought me down. I liked the night better. It was too dark to notice the weather. I liked night life. I thought of the evening to come and I swallowed a lick of panic. She was going to get butchered. Every Monday night this joint over on the East Side, Fantasia, had an amateur night. First twenty people off the street got ten minutes on-stage. If you had talent they invited you back the next week. About one in ten thousand went on to become famous entertainers, but the management milked the legends of those people for all they're worth and every week twenty clowns with dreams of Johnny Carson shows, Vegas and all went onstage and got massacred by audiences who made the Roman Colosseum fans look like humanitarians. And that night one of those clowns was going to be La Donna.

And didn't she know it. She had to know it. I didn't care

what her goddamn singing teacher told her, she had ears, she
was intelligent. I thought of her sitting in the apartment staring at her nails. She knew it. And I knew me. I wasn't going
to say dick. I couldn't. In the beginning we could say anything to each other, but now it was too dangerous; if we started
cracking on each other with truths at this point we would
inevitably get to the bottom truth, which was that we had no
damn right being together anymore, and I for one was scared
to death of the alternatives. So I settled for the bullshit low-
key rage of two people going through the motions of a relationship, a life; and I would let her humiliate herself at Fantasia
in the name of not rocking the boat even though the boat was
capsizing fast, and I would even have the stones to call it
being supportive.

"Kenny? When I finish I want you to tell me if I look better
if I bow my head" — she slowly dropped her chin to her
chest — "or if I should just close my eyes and keep my head
up. Please don't smoke."

I ditched my cigarette and spread my arms across the top
of the couch. La Donna stood five feet in front of me.

"Feee-lings, no-thing more than . . . fee-lings, try-ing to forget . . . my fee-lings of loove . . ."

She was bad. Not real bad; she could carry a tune, but
every note bordered on clinking. And she was standing in
front of me as if she were singing in the front row of an
Episcopalian choir. No movement from the neck down. She
wouldn't look at me. She was singing to some point three
feet over my head.

"Fee-lings, Wo wo wo feee-lings, Wo wo wo fee-lings . . ."
She ended with her chin slightly upturned and eyes closed as if
waiting for a kiss on the forehead.

"That's nice, baby. I like that better with the eyes closed.
Just relax a little more and you'll be outa sight." I reached for
another cigarette, then stopped myself. La Donna stood there,

hands on hips, nervously chewing off shreds of dead skin on her lower lip. She was staring in my direction but her eyes were glassy with thought.

"Okay." Her eyes were still unfocused. "I wanna run it through once with the Spanish lyrics."

"Fire away, kid."

"La Di?" She was in the shower and I poked my head into the bathroom and stared at the floor. "What time that guy say to get there?"

"Five, but I wanna get there at four. What time's it now?"

"It's three now," I warned.

"Oh Christ," she said through clenched teeth.

I went into the living room and started flipping through the records. I pulled out *Cabaret* and put on "Tomorrow Belongs to Me." When I saw the movie all those cute little Nazis singing in the beer garden had made me cry. I wasn't into Nazis or anything, there was just something beautiful about that scene that got to me. I always felt a mixture of pity and envy for kids. Childhood was hell, but I swear I'd give anything to start all over again.

"*Pleeze* don't play music." La Donna was dripping nude at the far end of the living room. "You . . . *know* . . . what . . . other . . . music . . . does . . . to . . . my . . . concentration." She sounded like she was trying not to lose her patience with a retard, her eyes wide with anger, her hair plastered with water over her left tit. I didn't move. If I told her she was beautiful, that I wanted to ball, make love, whatever, it would be my death by radiation. I didn't move for a few seconds until she realized I was defying her. It was like Russian roulette. Maybe I wasn't horny after all, just thrill crazy.

We arrived at Fantasia just about four o'clock. The sun had begun to go down about three and it was as cold as a snowball's ass. Even though they didn't take sign-ups until five

there were already about ten of us yo-yos in what looked like
a bread line. Everybody was hunched down into winter coats,
hands in pockets, faces pinched in pain. We got on the end
and watched everybody on Third Avenue watch us. La Donna
was wearing a big fur coat and too much make-up. She held
a manila folder between her elbow and ribs containing a
8-by-10-inch studio picture of her dressed in a Suzie Wong
side-slit number with LA DONNA printed below the photograph
in bamboo letters. She also had a letter of recommendation
from Tony Randall, the story behind which kept changing
every time I heard it.

"Well, you know, if you don't believe in yourself, if you
don't have confidence in yourself, nobody else will."

"Oh, I have confidence in myself."

Some black kid standing in front of us in aviator glasses
and a long coat with a fake fur collar was lecturing to a
blond chubby teen-ager carrying sheet music for "September
Song."

"I believe in myself. I really do." The blond kid sounded
like he was trying to convince the jury. The black kid seemed
skeptical, arching his eyebrows with self-importance like He
Really had self-confidence. I slipped my hand under La
Donna's collar, grabbing the nape of her neck. "You got self-
confidence?"

She hissed and turned her head away. No sense of humor.

"I'm gonna smoke, okay?"

"I'm not your mother," she said, still looking away.

I dropped my hand from her neck.

"Why don't you get fuckin' Tony Randall to stand on line
with you?" That I muttered to myself.

In front of the two kids, an older guy in a gravy-colored
raincoat was leaning against the building. He was short,
fiftyish, blubberized and toupeed. His nervous darting wall-
eyes made Peter Lorre look like a squinter. Every time a cab
honked he started blinking in spasms. In front of him, two

other guys were talking. One guy was tall, dressed in baggy chinos and a lightweight dungaree jacket. He had the longest, pointiest head I'd ever seen; it was shaped like a slip-on pencil eraser. His hairline began a good two inches above his temple as if his hair had been glopped on like whipped cream on Jell-O. He wore bottle-bottom glasses, the heavy black frames held together with rubber bands at the joints, and his elevator forehead was sprinkled with pimples. The guy he was talking to looked like Rasputin's dwarf — a Mad Russian. About five feet even, scrawny, dressed in a pea coat, he was balding but combed his hair forward in sparse bangs over his eyes like Moe of the Three Stooges. He held one arm across his gut supporting the elbow of the other arm, which was slowly stroking a goatee that looked more like a collection of long chin hairs than a beard. As the guy with the glasses talked, the Mad Russian kept massaging his chin and staring up at him with hungry gleaming eyes as if trying to figure out how to knock out that big turkey so he could cook him in a pot.

"I — I feel kinda good today." He had a meek voice. "I wrote a new joke. My cousin is so dumb" — he pushed his glasses up his nose — "my cousin's so dumb he had to take a color-by-number course in graffiti."

The Mad Russian didn't laugh, only smiled wolfishly licking his lips and rhythmically tugging his chin hairs.

The comic shrugged, embarrassed. "I don't know, I kinda like it, and I also picked up this." He took a switchblade out of his back pocket, shook it in front of his face and out snapped a comb. The fat popeyed guy jumped, but nobody noticed. He started combing his bird's nest as if to illustrate further that it really wasn't a knife.

La Donna stared at all of them, horrified and ashamed. She looked like she was ready to walk. I felt sorry for her and put my hand on the back of her neck again, but she shook it off. A hefty-looking Jewish chick emerged from a taxi, shouted at the taxi driver, "Remember, twelve noon New Year's Eve nineteen seventy-nine behind the soccer stadium in Istanbul. Be there!" and ran across the sidewalk to the end of the line, which was us. She briskly rubbed her hands and made a loud *brrr* sound. "This train go straight out to Montauk, or do I have to change at Babylon?"

La Donna looked away like don't fuckin' bother me. I smiled, jammed for a comeback line. La Donna's rudeness pissed me off to no end. I could never stand people who couldn't even transcend their own shit, just for the sake of politeness if nothing else.

"You a singer or a comedian?" She pointed a nose as big as a shark fin at me.

"Neither." I shrugged. "I'm a lion tamer. I used to gig with Terrytoon Circus."

"A lion tamer," she whispered behind her hand to an invisible third party on her left. She raised her eyebrows and gave a short uh-oh whistle. "Well, how you doin', Lion Tamer, what's your name?"

I felt embarrassed telling her my name, as if it didn't count.

"Kenny Becker." I extended my hand.

"Mona Nucleosis."

Even though La Donna was making a big point of being disinterested she choked a snort over that one.

"You a comedienne, Mona?"

In response she whipped out a Plasticene tear sheet from her shoulder bag. It was the front page of the second section of a six-month-old *New York Times*. "The Big Apple's Ladies of Laughter — Top 15 Comediennes." She was number thirteen.

"Hey, La Donna, look at this!"

She turned, glared at me and glanced at the page without focusing her eyes. A big solid blond dude came up behind Mona. He was built like a fullback and wore a black vinyl, lightweight, wet-look jacket over a floral body shirt open to the sternum. He had enough chest hair for a national park and six strands of gold chains were crisscrossing under his collarbone. He stood there with a permanently arched eyebrow rolling his shoulders and absently high-stepping in place like a boxer waiting for ring intros. He was dressed for the wrong time of year, but snow or no, the look on his face was, hey, fuck weather. His dark brown chest fur clashed with his metallic blond hairdo. The guy was heavy into Streaks 'n' Tips.

He caught my eye as I was checking him out and thrust his arm toward me. By reflex I raised my shoulder to block a punch but he only extended a paw.

"Jackie di Paris." He said it like he was answering the question "Who the fuck are you?"

"Kenny Becker." The handshake was of course a bone-popper. Mona was gawking at him, her tongue hanging out like a club tie.

"Jackie, this is Mona."

"Hey, Mona!" He winked. "You a real moaner or what?" He laughed, squeezing her shoulders. She made a strangle face and popeyes for my benefit.

"Awright, Mona the moaner!" He laughed. "Yeah." Letting her go and breathing into his fist.

La Donna turned slightly, gave him the once-over and turned back. My stomach slipped a few inches. I didn't want him to notice her. "Hey, I saw that." He pointed at her, grinning in triumph. He rocked side to side, rubbing his hands and blowing into his fists as if he was waiting for the 6:00 A.M. shape-up down at the longshoremen's hiring hall.

"Jackie di Paris, huh?" I figured him for a bouncer trying to be a singer. "That your real name?"

"John di Marco, di Paris is my stage name." He squinted at me. "You're from the Bronx, right?"

"Yeah."

"You Jewish?" like a polite accusation.

"Yeah." What about it, douchebag.

"Oh." He shrugged like it wasn't serious. "Where you from?"

"Burke Avenue."

"I'm from Belmont Avenue. You know Belmont Avenue?"

"Sure, I know Belmont. You don't live there no more, do you?"

"Now? Nah, I'm over here now. Up on Eighty-sixth Street, Germantown." He nodded uptown.

"You sing?"

He shrugged and pouted, "I'm tryin', you know? I got nice pipes. I got stage presence. I used to be a bodyguard for Peter Lemongello . . . it's all fucking bullshit. What kinda work you do?" He squinted.

"Me?" Brain surgeon. "I'm in sales."

He laughed. "What the fuck does that mean?"

"Whata you mean, what the fuck does that mean?" I snapped, pissed and embarrassed.

"Sales could be anything, right?" He shrugged. "You a VP or a clerk?"

"Neither." I turned away.

"Myself" — he poked my arm — "I'm now in communications." He waited for me to turn back to him, his head cocked, chin pointing to his shoulder, a smirk plastered on his lips. "I sort mail for the post office."

All the difference in the world. I lightened up, dipped my head in acknowledgment, "Door-to-door."

Mona started talking to the guy who came on line behind Jackie.

"You know, I'll tell you something, you never know who's going to make it doing what in this world." He put his hands inside his rib-high jacket pockets and scanned the street. "And the God's honest truth, I don't know about you, you know, door-to-door, but I put in forty fuckin' hours a week in that goddamn PO. That's forty hours working with every low-life bastard that can pass a multiple-choice exam to get a federal

job. Punching out a time card to take a crap, vending machine
coffee with every meal." He dropped his voice, still staring out
at the street. "Getting chewed out by some bullshit nigger
with two years' seniority on me. And I swear to God, if I
didn't believe I was destined from some fuckin' greatness for
something a hell of a lot better . . ." He rubbed his mouth.
"I dunno, so we'll see. I'm feelin' pretty good tonight, so we'll
see. You a singer, too?" He raised his chin in my direction.

"Me? Nah, I'm down here with my girlfriend, she's a
singer."

"Who, her?" He tilted his head back and to the right where
Mona was yakking away. He looked like he was in pain.

I jerked back and squinted too, like gimme a break.

"La Di." I turned La Donna around. "La Donna, this is
Jackie di Paris."

"Hey, now you're makin' sense." He held out both hands
palms up. "How you doin', baby." He leaned forward and
kissed her under her ear, holding the other side of her face
in the flat of his palm. Then he straightened up holding both
of her hands in his. "I'm sure you're a very fine singer, and
I'm sure you'll do very well tonight." He winked at me.

La Donna frowned and nodded awkwardly.

"Wha, you nervous?" He jerked back and looked outraged.
She mumbled "A little" and tried to extract her hands.

"What are you nervous about?" he sneered. "Don't fuckin'
worry, they're all fuckin' jibones out there."

"Thank you." She pulled one hand free. He let go of the
other one and drew me and La Donna into a huddle. "Also" —
he had his arms around our shoulders — "there's no fuckin'
competition," he whispered, raised his head, peered at the
line and ducked back into the huddle. "You ever see such a
line-up of freaks?"

At that moment a ripple of energy pulsed up the line. We
turned around; a tall, thin guy in a sealskin coat and a lamb's-
wool Cossack hat was working his way up to us, cradling a

clipboard and handing out yellow Community Chest Monopoly cards.

"Name?"

"La Donna." She straightened up, gave him all her attention, like this joker had the power. She tilted her head and read her name as he wrote it on the clipboard.

"La Donna what?"

"Just La Donna." She held her manila folder with her fingertips.

"Singer?"

"Yes."

"Okay." He handed her a yellow card. The number thirteen was written on the back in red Magic Marker. "You're number thirteen. Be here no later than nine. Any drinks you have at the bar you pay for. You got ten minutes up there, one song. If you want piano accompaniment you have to supply the music. If you're late you're out. Name please?"

"Nah, I'm with her." I took her by the elbow, waved goodbye to Jackie, who was getting his number, and ushered her across the street.

"What time is it now?" she asked.

"Ten after five. We got almost four hours. You wanna go to a movie? They got *Heart of Glass* playing at the Coronet."

She didn't answer.

"You wanna rent a hotel room and screw around?" Hah. "No, seriously, if you want we got time to go back to the house and fall out for a few hours."

"Please, I can't stand that house sometimes."

"So move out, bitch" — that too under my breath. Sometimes she would hurt me in such a way I always felt like a schmuck if I tried to bring it to her attention.

"You hungry?" We stood in front of an East Side deli; all I had had all day was wheat germ cereal and coffee.

"I'm cold," she winced.

"Well, let's get some soup or hot chocolate or something."

It was one of those Renaissance delis with chandeliers hanging from heavily spackled red ceilings, the walls plastered with gold-veined mirrors and oil paintings of clowns and sunsets with little price tags in the corners. The menus were quilted, plush and big as baby books. All that so they could jack up the price of a hot dog.

"Look at this joint." We sat across from each other at a booth the sides of which were shaped like curlicued sea waves. "The Borgias used to come in here for their pastrami." Across from us was the floor-length meat and appetizer counter. "Meanwhile they still got the slobs with the T-shirts and flabby chests slicing the whitefish, right?" I winked at her. Her hands were clasped in front of her face, elbows on the table, both thumbs pressed against the bottoms of her front teeth. On the bottom shelf of the meat display case sat three huge hors d'oeuvre trays of tightly rolled cold cuts and cheese laid out in a sunburst pattern under yellow-tinted cellophane like a food version of the June Taylor dancers. Each platter had a name and an East Side address pinned on the cellophane. I wanted to make some clever comment about the trays to La Donna, but she looked like she was waiting out a biopsy report. An old-time waiter, short, bald with salt and pepper sideburns and mustache, came by, order pad in hand. He wore a food-stained chest-high apron under a red monkey jacket.

"Whata you want, babe?"

"Just tea."

I didn't think we were allowed to order just tea.

"Look, I just want coffee now, we'll order in a few minutes, okay?"

He closed the order pad without writing anything down and, staring over our heads, slowly walked toward the coffee and hot water service station.

"You talk to your sister today?"

"No." La Donna slid her thumbs up to her forehead.

"La Di . . ." I cupped her elbows in my hands. "Listen, Mommy, you're gonna be fine tonight."

"I wish to God you would *stop* reassuring me, okay?" She didn't raise her head or move her elbows.

The waiter reappeared, a full cup in each hand, waiting for me to take my arms off the table. He was staring back toward the kitchen.

"Sorry." I leaned back against the booth. He walked away without asking us for our orders.

"Whata you want, La Donna, you want me to split? I'll split." I spit that out as offhand and abrupt as I could.

"No," she mumbled. I couldn't see her face behind her thumbs, which had climbed up to her hairline. She started to cry. "No." She pulled wetly on her nose, then flattened her hands across her face, shuddering silently. For what it's worth, at that moment I felt better than I had all day. I leaned over the table and kissed her knuckles, which were directly over her eyes.

"Everything is gonna be okay."

"Sit over here." She pouted and patted the Naugahyde next to her, hiding her eyes with the other hand.

I slid under the table and popped up next to her. She still wouldn't uncover her eyes. "Hold me. You haven't held me all day, you know," she said half-sulking.

"Oh, Mommy." I hugged her as hard as I could. I loved her badly. Madly. She laid her head on my chest and I was in heaven.

The waiter came back, and I opened one of the mammoth menus, rubbing my hands together as if to kindle my appetite. "God, *now* I'm starving! Whata you want, baby, you want a Vic Damone or a Joe Namath?"

"I'll have a tuna salad on rye." She wiped her eyes with her napkin.

"Yeah, and ah, I'll tell you, I'm torn between a Duke Ellington and an Albert De Salvo myself."

When the waiter split again, I moved my hand along her

thigh under the table, and I could feel her body downshift, relax against my arm. Closing her eyes, she rubbed her cheek against my shoulder. Slowly she moved the flat of her palm in a U-curve from the inside of my thigh over the bulge of my crotch to the other thigh. I was so surprised I almost pushed her away. If there had been a power failure, I would have taken her right there, under the table.

"It's been a long time, Kenny," she whispered, running her hand back along the same route.

"Eight days and six hours," I said.

She snorted softly. "Well, you're in trouble tonight."

"Is that a threat or a promise?"

"It's what it is."

We straightened up when the waiter returned with the food. I couldn't eat. My insides were one big sexknot.

After the deli, I talked her into going to see a movie which wound up being about depression in Los Angeles, a move which didn't win me any awards for cleverness. By the time the movie was over it was eight o'clock and La Donna was into her black dog funk again. We had a couple of drinks at a fancy Greek diner and returned to Fantasia. I had a nice buzz going, but La Donna just got more tense, if that was possible.

Fantasia was laid out in two rooms. The front room was an ordinary bar that led through a sliding plastic curtain into a cabaret.

The bar was packed, primarily with the people from the line clutching their Monopoly cards and waiting to be called on-stage by the T-shirted maître d', who was guarding the plastic curtain. Besides the entertainers, the only other people in the bar were out-of-towners making their way toward the maître d' and their reserved tables inside. Loud, suburban contractors and their wives, drunk Texans, Jap businessmen, medical students; assholes, all assholes. They all seemed to be giggling, too.

We grabbed two stools along the bar and ordered drinks.

The bar area looked like the day room at Bellevue. Twenty people aching for a break, comedians ranking everyone in sight, the singers doing nasal warm-ups or posing in their minds for album covers, high-pitched laughter, forced laughter, barking, fast talking, mumbling to walls, praying and pacing, everybody pacing. Any second I expected a nurse to come in wheeling a stainless steel tray with rows of Dixie cups containing pills. Every time the curtain parted people tensed, craned their necks to peer into the next room to catch a glimpse of the floodlit foggy stage. We couldn't hear the acts — the sound didn't carry — but we could see faces at tables, see if people were laughing, smiling or just talking to each other, ignoring whoever was dying from diarrhea up by the mike. Whenever everybody else would wheel toward the parting curtain, La Donna would wheel in the opposite direction toward the street.

"What number they up to?" She grabbed her elbow across her chest and hunched her shoulders.

"Four, five, like that. You got time, you wanna take a walk?"

"No." She shook her head at her boots, then suddenly looked up at me with them baby grays. "You really think I'm gonna be good?"

I fell apart with love again. "The best, La Di." It didn't seem to take much for me to fall apart. All she had to do was act like she needed me. "And you look fuckin' wild, kid." That was true. She was wearing a silvery gray embroidered peasant blouse tucked into a heavy, black wool, shin-length maxiskirt over brand-new, round-toed black Fryes. Her hair was swirled up in a bun and she had big half-moon mother-of-pearl earrings dangling almost to her jawline. "Just fuckin' wild."

"I'm bein' a bitch today, Kenny, I know." She winced.

"No! No!" I shook my head and frowned.

"Just bear with me till this is over, okay?" She touched my

bicep and kissed me softly on the lips. "I love you, Kenny."
If she had asked me at that moment to please go into the
cabaret and shoot the person onstage so her turn would come
faster my only question would have been if she minded if I
used a telescopic so I wouldn't have to stand up in front of all
those assholes.

"Hey!" A short, sweating, shiny, pink rollerball wearing
glasses grabbed the lapel of my jacket. "They sell new clothes
where you got this?"

His eyes were desperate and his breath smelled like cologne.
I laughed because I didn't want this guy to kill himself. When
I laughed he jerked back smiling, like he had just drawn to
an inside straight. He was bald but he grew his fringe hair
long and plastered it across the dome. He whipped out a
calling card that read: MY CARD. I laughed. Then he handed
me another: CHUCK STEAK. PRIME COMEDIAN. I laughed.
Every time I laughed he shook his head and laughed along
encouragingly. The maître d' called out, "Six! Number six!"
and Chuck Steak swung his head toward the voice so fast his
rooster gullet was quivering from inertia.

"I'm number eight." He stared at La Donna. "Hey! It's
Joni Mitchell! Don't start the peasant blouse revolution without me!"

Wrong target. I put my arm around his shoulder and turned
him around.

A big black dude in a cowboy hat drifted past us like a
killer whale in a bad mood.

"That guy's an actor." Chuck nudged me and waved at
the guy. "Loved your movie!"

The guy didn't hear him and continued to move through
the room.

"What movie?"

"*Planet of the Apes*. They saved so much money on
make-up with him they financed a sequel."

I snapped my head back in disbelief. "Hey, Chuck." I

laughed weakly. "Why don't you save 'em for the stage, okay? I mean, you know, like, you don't know who you're goofin' on over here. You pick the wrong person, they might tear your heart out and stuff it in your shirt pocket, you know? You know what I mean, Chuck? This is like a dynamite room right now."

He raised his eyebrows and peered at my arm across his shoulder.

"Thay, fellah, you're not my type."

He spied Mona Nucleosis and stared with malicious mischief at her beak. He walked out from under my arm and went back to work.

"Jesus! Durante lives!"

Mona didn't even blink but got right into it. "Actually, I was born with an Irish pug. It looked too much like a nose job so I had the rest added on last year."

They talked in spurts and their eyes never met. They weren't hearing each other, just running their riffs like so much testing testing testing into a mike. I couldn't listen to them. Part of me wanted to jump right in and riff them to death and part of me wanted to grab them by the chins and beg them to lighten up.

I turned to La Donna. She was glancing furtively at a moon-faced girl sitting by herself clutching a guitar case. The girl looked so tense she made La Donna seem like Marlene Dietrich.

The Mad Russian stood alone behind Chuck Steak fingering his Mandarin chin, scanning the competition and slightly smiling, like he knew the answer. Even though it was February, he was shirtless, wearing only a dirty rib-high suede hippie vest with foot-long fringes. That and a necklace made of chicken bones.

Chuck noticed him out of the corner of his eye, did a double take, a triple take, then nudged Mona: "Hey! It's Moscow's answer to Charlie Manson! Ivan Cutchapeckeroff!"

The Russian did a slow head turn to Chuck, grinned, raised his hands palms up and out, then flipped them knuckle side up. Without saying a word he reached behind Chuck Steak's shiny scrubbed pink earlobe and withdrew a razor blade held delicately between thumb and forefinger. Chuck patted down the back of his head. Mona gave one of her eyebrow-raising uh-oh whistles. La Donna was now standing by the nervous chick with the guitar case, but she was looking away like a guy edging toward a pickup at a singles' bar. I didn't know if they had talked or not.

"Number seven? Seven!" Thirteen guts sank. I noticed when customers made their way through the psycho ward to the curtain the amateurs were staring at them with this expression like the customers were somehow superior people, like the tryout comedians and singers were animals and these sporty schmucks were visitors at the zoo. That made me berserk. I felt like jumping up on the bar and announcing that the travesty was canceled. That everybody in that goddamn room should put down their cross. That there was a charter bus arriving in twenty minutes and everybody was going on a pleasure trip, lunch included, so let's blow this joint.

I made my way over to La Donna. I thought it would be good for her to talk to the guitar girl. I passed the black kid from the line. He wore a loud three-piece plaid suit with sleeves that were too long. They came down almost to his knuckles. He had an expensive stitched leather bag over his shoulder and constantly adjusted his gold-rimmed aviators. He was still talking to the chubby teen-ager.

"You know, in all honesty, I can't really call myself an *amateur* per se."

"Number eight!"

Chuck Steak plowed through the bar crowd to the curtain, holding his card high in the air.

"You know, in all honesty, I can't really call myself an

amateur per se," the black kid repeated; he lit a cigarette and smoked it clumsily, holding it down by the webbing between his fingers and bringing his whole hand to his mouth when he took a puff.

"Who's your friend?" I nudged La Donna. She glanced down at the girl as if noticing her for the first time. With the guitar case between her knees and the blood drained from her face she looked like she was waiting for the cattle car.

"Now" — the black kid punctuated his bullshit with a cigarette — "if you've ever studied Mathis' style, he just gets up onstage and runs his repertoire. He's not very comfortable with trying to personally *relate* to his audience."

The fat kid shook his head automatically, but his brains were all over the floor.

"Now *me* on the other hand" — he touched all ten finger-tips to his vest — "I like to *rap* to my audience, you know, set up a rap*port*."

"Shit," La Donna hissed.

"Hey, relax!"

"I hate fuckin' triteness, fuckin' phonies."

The black kid overheard her. His face collapsed for a second but instantaneously recovered as if he had decided she was referring to somebody else.

"C'mon." I moved La Donna back to our barstools.

The big, tall, knuckle-headed spade stood in front of us, about six-five in a sky blue three-piece suit, black shirt, black cowboy hat, red tie and a red cocktail napkin stuffed into his breast pocket like a handkerchief. He wore the thickest glasses I've ever seen and he looked as dumb and mean as a dinosaur. He had spent the last hour drifting from cluster to cluster saying stupid warlike things, totally misunderstanding whatever people said to him in response and in general making the whole room squirm. He faced both of us, looking like he couldn't decide whether to kill me and rape her or rape me and kill her.

"Wha's yo name?" He squinted at La Donna, mouth open a good inch and a half. La Donna refused to look at him.

"Her name's Linda," I said. It took this big dumb bastard a good five seconds to turn his head to me. "Ah dint *as'* you."

"Well, she got to save her voice now." I smiled. He chewed that one over awhile, then returned his gaze to her.

"You a singer?" He examined her like King Kong checking out Fay Wray.

"Yeah, she's a singer. I'm a singer too. Are you a singer?"

He just stared at me. I must have supplied too much information too fast. If he touched her I would have smashed my drink in his glasses.

"How come you won't talk to me? You afraid a black mayn?"

La Donna threw her eyes and shook her head sadly while still looking away.

"She's afraid of everything. Her mother got scared by an encyclopedia when she was pregnant." I grabbed his hand and shook it heartily. "Listen, I just wanna wish you the best of luck tonight. I'm sure you're gonna kill 'em out there." He stared down at the handshake like he couldn't understand how his hand got between mine. I have big motherfucking strong hands, bigger than his, and I gave an extra firm squeeze. When I let go he moved in slow motion toward La Donna.

"I wanna wish *huh* luck too." He extended his hand to her, and I quickly stepped between them and grabbed his hand again. "I want to thank you for both of us." I grabbed La Donna away and tried to find a neutral corner in that loony bin.

"That big yom start something with you?" Jackie di Paris stood over us now, his jaw cemented with rage. "I'm gonna kick his fuckin' ass before midnight. He's been breakin' people's balls all night." Jackie glared across the room.

"How you doin', doll?" He kissed La Donna on the cheek. La Donna patted his shoulder like "Downboy."

"What's your number?" he said, holding his own at arm's length as if he were nearsighted.

"Thirteen."

"Yeah? I'm twelve. Hey, tonight's only the beginning. Maybe me 'n' you'll become a famous duet like Tony Orlando and Dawn." He blew into his fist and rubbed his hands as if he was still outside, winked at me, gave me a sidearm shot in the shoulder and walked off.

I started to move La Donna around the room again when she shook my hand away. "Kenny, *cut* it. I'm not furniture."

"Hey, will you relax?"

"*You* relax! *You* go up there in twenny minutes and *you* relax."

"Hey, relax, La Di." I didn't know what else to say.

"Kenny." She held my hand and took a deep breath. "You wanna help me, right? Please don't be offended." She kept patting my hand for accentuation. "Go inside, get a table and watch me from in there, okay?"

"Nah, I'll stay with you."

"Kenny, please." She looked more weary than tense. "Please, Kenny."

I had to do what she asked. I felt so hurt I wanted to cry. I didn't understand what I'd done wrong. I felt like I had blown everything. "What about that big nigger?"

She smiled. "I'll scream for Jackie di Paris."

"I can handle that bozo. Why don't you scream for me?"

" 'Cause you'll be inside."

I gave her a tasteless kiss, told her chin up and eyes closed and walked toward the curtain. As I went in I saw she was standing over the girl with the guitar again, but still looking away like she had no idea she was there.

"Thank you, Chuck Steak, Charles Steak."

He stepped off the stage sweating like a steam room attendant. I was seated during the last thirty seconds of his act, a cheap-shot homo joke, but from the high buzz of table con-

versation and the almost nonexistent applause I assumed that
the funniest thing Chuck had in his head was his name. I sat
at a table against the back wall with two drunks and a non-
descript guy about my age with a tape cassette and ordered a
Chivas from the waitress.

"I wanna remind you people that *five* of tonight's perform-
ers will be invited back on Sunday evening at six for a special
showcase, the, ah, cream of the *crap* as it were." That got
some laughter, some awws. The emcee shrugged and raised
his hands in submission.

He was a fast-talking prep school Jew, thin, also wearing
aviator glasses, shag haircut, Bloomingdale's pullover, very
obnoxious. Life would go on without him "Okay." He read
from the clipboard. "Number nine, Leonard Wooley, a
comedian."

It was the big spade with the cowboy hat. He sleepwalked
up to the stage.

"Than' you." He tried to adjust the mike, couldn't and
wound up lifting the whole thing to his mouth. He stared out
over the audience frowning.

"Wow, man, you Jews are *wild*, man."

Grumbles. Immediately the emcee came back onstage, grim
and mechanically applauding, to grab the mike. "Thank you.
Thank you," and he ushered Leonard Wooley off before he
realized what was happening. "Leonard Wooley, Leonard
Wooley. Leonard had to leave early, his Hitler Youth bus
threatened to split for Hamburg without him. Number ten!
Number ten!"

Ten was a bad comedian. He got slaughtered. When the
kid's time was up he looked like he needed a transfusion. He
did not get one laugh in ten minutes. It was brutal. The joint
was a killing floor. If they had given me a week to get ready I
could have torn down the house. I would have them all laughing, on their knees, then, as a finale, sprayed the joint with
mustard gas.

"For those of you who just walked in, I'd like to welcome

you to Fantasia. I'm your emcee, Danny Rifkin. Is anybody here from New Jersey?" About one fourth of the crowd cheered and yelled. "I'll try to make you feel at home." Danny boy started crooning a few bars of *The Godfather* theme and broke off into a call for number eleven.

"Cathy Wilbur, Cathy Wilbur, a singer, guitarist and composer from . . . West Virginia!"

It was the deep-freeze chick with the guitar. I saw La Donna standing by the curtain watching her. Cathy pulled up a stool, hoisted her guitar up to her chest and got right into it. She had a voice like an Irish saint, beautiful and clear, the guitar sounded nice, but the whole thing was a big yawn.

> I'm searching for clar-i-ty
> A crys-tal clear re-al-i-ty
> uh huh huh, uh huh huh

She was putting everybody to sleep, but nobody heckled because she was so goddamn sober and sincere. Just as it seemed she was finished with the lyrics she broke into a hum. She started humming and dai-da-dai-ing the whole goddamn song over again. By the time she was finished, people were exhausted. She received a nice round of respectful applause, half appreciation, half relief. She smiled for the first time that night, revealing totally rotten hillbilly teeth.

I started worrying about La Donna: (a) in general and (b) her doing "Feelings." I couldn't tell what kind of songs the crowd would dig. Maybe "Feelings" wasn't "up" enough. Maybe they only liked dirty songs.

"And now, number twelve, twelve. Mr. Jackie di Paris. Jackie di Paris, a crooner."

Jackie swaggered upstage like Gorgeous George, his chest bursting out of the floral shirt, half-moons under the arms, his nuts bulging against his thigh. His pants were so tight, the seam of his crotch looked like it was halfway up his ass. He handed the house piano player some sheet music and began adjusting the mike. A Texas dude yelled out something about Lady Clairol. Jackie stopped fucking around with the pole, found the guy in the semidarkness and gave him a look like if the guy was anything more than pigshit it would have been worth his while to break his face. Jackie kept up the evil eye a good thirty seconds. Long enough to quiet the whole place. He removed the mike from its stand and, holding it like a weapon, stepped to the edge of the stage. He was wearing three-inch white-heeled platforms.

"I would like to sing a tune written by one of the *great, great* songwriters of today." The joint stayed quiet. Everybody was intimidated. He sounded like he was reproaching the place, like he was telling us off. "*Mis*ter Piano Man, *if* you please." The guy at the piano rolled his eyes, then hit some very familiar notes.

"Hey!" Jackie snapped. "Dim those lights, hah?" The lights were dimmed, people glanced at each other across tables and shrugged. "Again, please."

"Fee-lings, nut-tin more dan fee-lings." My gut dropped out my ass. La Donna was screwed. Also, he was fucking horrible. His phrasing made Leo Gorcey sound like Rex Harrison. The mood he conveyed was about as romantic as somebody poking a finger in your chest. He wasn't singing, he wasn't even talking, he was arguing. People started yakking immediately. He lost everybody from word one.

"Feelings like I nev . . . Hey! A little quiet, hah? I'm singin', okay with you? Like I nev-ver lost . . . Yeah! I'm talking a *you!* yah cracker bastad!" Jackie stepped to one end of the stage and pointed his mike at the drunk Texan who had made the Lady Clairol crack. The Texan, a six-foot-plus potbellied gray-haired dude in a string tie, tried to get to his feet, but his friends, red-faced from laughing, pulled him down. He collapsed in his chair and started laughing too. The whole joint was laughing. Jackie looked as if he could

kill the world. He slapped the mike against his thigh, nodding
his head in small up-and-down motions as though he had just
made a decision and seconded it. "Fuck you," he spat into
the mike. "You're all fuckin' slobs. Consideration, you ever
hear that word?" That doubled the laughter. He couldn't
think of anything else to say and finally dropped the mike like
it was infected, snatched his music off the piano — the player
had to duck — and stormed off the stage, pushing people in
the aisle out of his way and vanishing behind the plastic
curtain.

Danny Rifkin came jogging upstage, swinging the clipboard.
He picked up the mike and made wild eyes at the house.
"Thank you, thank you. That was the charming and talented
Jackie di Paris. Jackie di Paris. Jackie had to leave us a little
early, he just heard they finished cleaning his cage. Okay,
number thir-teen, thir-teen. La Donna, a sin-ger."

It was pretty cold in the room, but I was sweating. My
hands were shaking so bad my ring was clinking like castanets
against my glass. La Donna came trancing down the aisle
from the parted curtain like there should've been a chaplain
behind her droning the Twenty-third Psalm. She knew. When
she gave her sheet music to the piano player, she was wincing.
Danny Rifkin helped her adjust the mike, wound up giving
her an exaggerated once-over and jacking off the mike stand.
The place broke up. La Donna wasn't hip to what he did,
and I wanted to tear that smartass sheeny bastard from
Bloomie limb to Bloomie limb. I wanted to hug her, protect
her, save her, take her a thousand miles away.

"Excuse me one second." Rifkin scanned the back of the
room, shivering and squinting. "Is the thermostat guy here?
Why don't you lower the heat a little more, Larry, I wanna
hang some fuckin' *meat* from the ceiling, okay?" Big laugh from
the Texans. He almost knocked her over getting offstage. She
had to backstep to give him room. Cocksucking pig.

The piano player began and La Donna closed her eyes.

"Feelings . . ." It was all over. The place broke out in hysterics. People were on the floor. She could have sung like Streisand, been the ghost of Judy Garland, it wouldn't have made a goddamn difference.

"Bring back Jackie!"

"Duet! Duet!"

By the time she walked offstage she was crying. She had skipped two verses, forgot the Spanish part, and three quarters of what she did sing was drowned out by competing hecklers. But she did remember to lift her chin and close her eyes at the end, and she did plow through it like a real trouper — she might even have been good.

She wouldn't talk to me. We sat at the tail end of the bar. She stared at her drink like she was using X-ray vision. I wouldn't have touched her arm on a dare. Even though it was pushing 2 A.M., the barroom was still packed. All the amateurs were sitting around waiting to hear if they made the five-person Sunday showcase. The place was considerably quieter because most of the entertainers had made assholes of themselves and they knew it. Everybody was stewing in their own self-shit image. Jackie di Paris sat a few stools down from us, hunched over, glaring at his drink, tilting his glass back and forth. The guitar girl had resumed her pose, nervously fingering her guitar case as if it were a cello. Chuck Steak was riffing but nobody was listening; the more nobody listened the more urgently he riffed. Mona sat at the bar doing needlepoint and frowning. Nobody was even drinking. The last act of the night was on — the black kid with the Johnny Mathis shtick. Because of the relative quiet we could hear him. He had a pretty good voice. He sang "Nature Boy" to a nice round of applause. Ten seconds later he emerged through the curtains sweating and beaming. The maître d' appeared with the clipboard.

"Okay, people, here are the five we want back on Sunday.

You ready?" Chuck Steak suddenly grabbed his coat and left. "If any of you can't make it, tell me now because we want to announce the finalists to the audience, okay? Here we go. Roger Rector!"

"Yo." A squat kid with bulging cheeks and bushy eyebrows raised one finger and tilted it forward. He did Shakespearean monologues in Donald Duck talk. Got a lot of laughs.

"Chandu the Bizarre!" That was Rasputin. He nodded to the maître d', arms folded across his chest, still smiling his evil grin. He did ten minutes of razor magic out there and scared the daylights out of everybody.

"Annie Akins!"

Annie Akins collapsed against the wall in disbelief. A six-foot, two-hundred-pound hulk of a broad dressed like Daisy Mae Yokum. Barefoot, wearing a polka-dot blouse and cut-offs, she had sung "Jubilation T. Cornpone" in a voice you would have paid to stifle. She was so bad that the meaner members of the audience were screaming for an encore. I didn't understand what was going on here.

"Jackie di Paris!"

Jackie just sat there hunched over, examining his drink. When he heard his name, he snickered, shook his head grimly, slapped the drink down on the bar and got up. "Fuck you," he muttered halfheartedly and left. All of a sudden I understood what was going on and I prayed to God number five wasn't going to be who I thought it would be.

"La Donna!"

Shit on rye. La Donna didn't look up. She raised a slightly trembling hand to her face and slowly rubbed it across the bone ridge of her eyebrows. She exhaled noisily and briefly glanced at me. I couldn't tell if she knew what was going down. They wanted a freak show. They wanted back all the people who were either so out to lunch or so atrocious that they had to be seen again to be believed. If Jackie di Paris hadn't sung "Feelings" first, La Donna wouldn't have gotten her laughs, wouldn't have been picked. They were screaming for a duet, and they would get it. Heartless bastards. La Donna caught the maître d's eye and nodded okay. My jaw dropped, and I stared at her incredulously. She returned her gaze to her drink. Was she that stupid?

"What happened to di Paris?" The maître d' fretted. The kid who'd sung "Nature Boy" was holding his gut like he just took two slugs. Mona gave an uh-oh whistle, packed up her needlepoint and left. The guitar girl gingerly fingered her cheeks and stared straight ahead like she was Helen Keller.

"If di Paris don't show, we'll go with Ronnie Landau."

"Oh, thank God!" the chubby singer blurted, crumpling his "September Song" score to his chest. The black kid stared at Ronnie Landau with bulging eyes, as if not only was he gutshot but he had just gotten a ticket for jaywalking as he staggered to the hospital.

"C'mon, let's go. I got work tomorrow." I headed for the street. La Donna followed, silent. The street was dead and heavy with windless cold. The amateurs filed out behind us, walking slowly north and south. I flagged down a Checker. I sat in the far corner hoping she would, on her own, choose to sit right up next to me. Instead she sat in the opposite corner, staring expressionlessly out the window.

"Seventy-seventh between West End and Broadway." All the way home I watched her alternately chew her fingernails and bunch her hands into fists. Her eyes never came within 180 degrees of me. While we were zipping through Central Park she said, "I'm not doing 'Feelings' Sunday," and that was it. She had left her picture and letter from Tony Randall in the club, but I was afraid to remind her.

All I could think about was her hand on my crank in the deli, her promise that I was in trouble tonight. Forget it. Sometimes when I was a kid I would be promised a toy that was never bought. And I knew that no matter how badly I wanted that toy, if I badgered or whined, or even hinted, I'd get cracked in the face. And all that I could do was sit there and go over the conversation of the promise in my head, feeling tragic and wretched.

That was about the level of desperation I would get into about sex with her. I wasn't insensitive. I knew all about appropriate and inappropriate. I knew what La Donna was going through but what *I* would get into transcended logic, intelligence, compassion. I would get swallowed up in that childhood intensity, that self-centered ocean-sized feeling of life and death around sex. And it would happen anytime I was scared or felt hungry or needy around people. Anytime my brain would slip into a survival head the order from Central was STICK IT IN. When in fear, fuck.

Out of all the artichoke layers of bullshit that made up my life, the only thing that never switched up on me was my dick.

The house was cold. The spic bastard super didn't think people were awake after eleven at night, so he shut down the heat.

"Coffee, babe?"

"No." She went into the bathroom and closed the door. I made myself instant coffee and brought it to the dining table in the living room. I sat there fingering a vein of tiny splits in the fake butcherblock surface. Through the wall, I could hear her washing off her make-up. It was so cold I put my coat back on. I still wasn't sure if she was hip to what had happened. She came out of the bathroom, disappeared into the bedroom, finally re-emerging into the living room wearing only a tight tank top and panties. Her hair was down and her nipples stood out like little pointy noses. She stared at my coffee, oblivious to the cold. I took off my coat.

"I made a lot of stupid mistakes tonight," she said to no one in particular. "Never should have done that song. It's not right for my voice. I was very lucky tonight."

Lucky. I felt like a shit. I couldn't bring myself to give her the lowdown because I couldn't handle the chain reaction that would follow. I was afraid if I confronted her with the real story we would never fuck again. Her soft fuzzy bush bulged slightly against the white nylon. Over the summer, one hot night we trimmed her pubic hair into a heart shape. It was either that summer night or the night before we fucked on the fire escape. She sat forward on my lap and cupped my balls in her palms in front of her.

"Right now I think it's a mistake to wander off too far from Dionne Warwick." She paced the living room, arms folded across her chest. I stared at her toes.

In the beginning she would love to take it in the ass. We wouldn't even need Vaseline. She would even reach behind her and grab the backs of my thighs to force me in deeper. When I went down on her she would sigh so deep and soft I would shoot my wad with her cunt in my mouth.

La Donna padded into the bedroom. I heard the sheets rustling. "I'll be in in a few minutes." I raised my voice. She didn't even kiss me goodnight, even *say* goodnight. She used to jerk me off and kiss the tip of my dick as I was coming — loud wet smacks — her face covered with jizz as she turned her head from side to side, eyes closed, running the head across her lips. There would even be come in her eyelashes. I sat staring at my coffee, took pleasure from my cigarette — long slow drags, a real nightcap.

When I turned back the covers I was horrified to see that before passing out La Donna had taken off her panties. She was dead asleep on her side wearing only that tank top.

Whereas most people who sleep on their sides would sleep curled in, she curled out — her head and feet curved back toward each other and her hips and belly thrust forward like a cross between a drawn bowframe and a Pontiac hood ornament.

I slipped in bed as noisily as I could, but she didn't budge, wake up, nothing. Laying on my side I tried to conform to her spine, pressing my crotch into the crack of her ass, thrusting my belly into the small of her back, arching my head to avoid getting her hair in my mouth. I ground my cock a little into her buns and stared red-eyed at the digital on her night table: 2:47. My back was killing me. I draped my hand over her ribs and touched her nipples. She clucked in annoyance and, still asleep, flopped over on her belly. I rolled on my back and stared at the ceiling.

Sighing deeply enough for six generations of damned souls, I bounced a few times and got out of bed. Her breathing was even-steven. I went back into the living room, had half a cigarette, returned to the bedroom and stood over the bed, my guts grinding and aching so badly I felt like whimpering. I started to crawl back under the covers, stopped, walked over to the window and went through the motions of adjusting the venetian blinds. I rattled the blinds for thirty seconds. She began to snore.

I lay in bed staring at the ceiling again.

"Feed me" — more to myself than out loud. I could hear the grinding of the kitchen wall clock. The bed pulsed slightly with breathing.

"Feed me" — louder, a harsh whisper. A neck vein twitched hotly under my jaw. My eyes itched.

"Feed me, bitch." In a normal speaking voice. She slowly raised her face from the pillow and stared at me in the darkness. I thought I would die.

TUESDAY

got up at seven. La Donna was still sleeping and I slipped right back into the hunger. Anytime I got up before her I would lie in bed just in case when she woke up she might feel like it. She would always tell me she wasn't a morning person. I guess that meant opposed to an evening person, although I wasn't seeing much difference. I rolled on my side and started rubbing her back. Her skin felt toasty through her tank top. After a few minutes I rolled away from her as if I was playing hard to get. Since last night I'd rolled over so much I felt like a trained dog. I began drifting back to sleep when I heard her waking up. I rolled toward her. Her face was six inches off the pillow, sleep-smeared and dazed. She looked like she was just hatched. I rubbed her back again and threw my leg over her behind. She yawned, smiled, darted a kiss on my shoulder and did some rolling of her own — right out of bed. I watched her ruddy ass as she toddled across the bedroom to the bathroom.

Seven-twenty-seven. Work. I felt like crying. I had never shaken that elementary school dread of the morning.

"Up and at 'em, Kenny, it's seven-thirty."

I didn't answer. She started singing to herself. "I wish you bluebirds da da da," and headed for the kitchen.

Coffee, vanilla yogurt and a cigarette for me, tea, whole wheat toast with honey for her. "Do you know the way to San Jose," she declared, staring, hypnotized over her raised teacup, and absently blew the steam away from her face.

"Do I know what?" I tried to sound like don't bother me, I'm wrapped up in my own thoughts. She was in a good mood, and it pissed me off.

"Do you know the way to San Ho-Zay," she sang. "I think I'm gonna do that instead Sunday night. Or maybe this! 'If you see me walk-ing down the street and I start to cry, each time we meet, Walk on by-y-y.' "

I sulked harder. It seemed she had convinced herself that Fantasia was the greatest thing to come down the pike since sliced bread. It was like living with Blanche DuBois. But I didn't give a fuck anymore. I wasn't gettin'; then I wasn't givin'.

"You were right. Eyes closed chin up worked the best." She hunkered down in her chair rolling her assbones against the seat and smiled at me.

"Oh yeah?" I muttered, looking away.

She reached across the table and grabbed yesterday's *Post*. She whistled as she read. I couldn't even make her squirm and I wanted her to writhe.

"You gonna see Bossanova today?"

"Madame Bas*s*ova, Bas*s*ova." She looked up from the paper. "When are you gonna get that straight?" she asked with lightweight petulance.

"Sorry, sorry, Bas*s*ova, Bas*s*ova. I should know how to pronounce it by now, I guess. I write her name on enough checks, *that's* for sure."

Her head snapped up, and I immediately felt like a stone prick, subtlety up the ass, cards on the table, on the floor, in your eye. I tried to cover fast. "Is she doin' good with you?"

I grinned like a mule eating shit. "That's such a goddamned weird building, the Ansonia. They got more whackos than Creedmore. You know, there must be twenty-five guys that call themselves maestro or professor and I bet ten Anastasia Romanovs." No good. She looked hurt and furious at the same time and I felt my chest break out in a constellation of heat rash.

She stared at me deadeye and her mouth got square and ugly. My brains were screaming Sorrysorrysorrysorry.

"*What* is on your *mind?*" she asked in a hushed voice. I killed her mood, okay, and now that I was getting the chance for a showdown, all I felt besides two years old was apologetic and guilty. I felt sorry and convictionless — a self-centered bastard.

I sighed. "It's, I dunno. We, we don't make *love* anymore like we used to." I came down heavy on the word "love." I never called it making love in my life. She sat silent glaring at me with that cement face, her hands curled around her teacup. My shoulders slipped into a permanent hunch.

"You know, we used to be" — I sucked air through my teeth — "so *tight* around that, and, and I know you're going through whatever you're goin' through and you're close to a breakthrough and all that, but ah, shit, I dunno, I, ah, I need *sex* from you, I need some physical *attention*, you know?" I almost gagged on the word "breakthrough," tried hard not to coat it with sarcasm. In that moment I knew I was her enemy because I was lying to her, betraying her for a piece of tail for myself. She sucked as a singer, she was putting herself through agony for nothing, and that was the dead nuts.

"You know, La Di." I picked my words as delicately as I would have tiptoed through a cow pasture, even though I was already hip-deep in shit. "The need to get laid is an honorable need."

Silence, then a hoarse whisper from a death mask. "Well, then go out and get laid." Not even a blink.

"Baby, I don't want nobody but you," and that was the gospel truth. I relaxed slightly because I had said something honest. "I dunno." I shrugged and smiled weakly. "Maybe I'm just more sexually oriented than you."

"Well, I just guess the hell you *are!*" she hissed and charged into the bedroom. The door slammed like a stinging slap. I was in a comfortably frightened state of shock. I stared at my coffee; my fingers felt puckered and dry. I felt like my life would go on forever. Suddenly the door flew open and La Donna stood hunched over, face red, knotted fists at her side.

"I'm *very* sexually oriented!" she bawled and started crying so hard and bitterly that I thought she was going to vomit.

So, the day started off like shit. Once she began crying like that the worst part would be over, but the whole thing was starting to feel like a routine, the same goddamn soap opera every day. We hugged, kissed, I felt better, she felt better, I made promises, she made promises, I fell madly in love again. I didn't know what she was feeling on that score. For me the fight always had the same origin. She would make me feel undesired and I would want to bust her hump for it; then when I did I felt guilty and horrible, she got trembly and self-righteous, the tears, etc. Sometimes it wasn't even so much about fucking. I just wanted to feel like she considered me hot stuff. And I would sell our souls down the river for a taste of that feeling. But as I trudged down Broadway, dragging my sample case to the bus stop, I was never so clear on the monotony of it all. And the sad fact was that I realized one of the reasons I didn't change channels was because everything else felt like a rerun.

In the beginning it was the best. I hated to think about how good things used to be before this singing bullshit started. I used to go up to her bank, she worked at a Portuguese bank on Fifth Avenue, and surprise her with bag lunches. And in the lunch I'd hide a little present. Once I got crazy and put a pair of jade earrings inside the baked strawberry farmer's cheese and she almost cracked a tooth. And it was hard for me to come uptown because my turf was the Village, which during lunchtime traffic was not exactly around the corner.

And I got her to read. She was never a big reader, but I had the touch. Knew exactly what books to turn her on with. She was into women, so I threw her some Flannery O'Connor, some Shirley Jackson, a little Willa Cather. On weekends we'd go up to a friend's cabin in Lake Mohegan, grab groceries, jump in the sack and fuck like fiends. Weekend after weekend, watch a little tube, make a little fire, eat a little steak, read a little literature. With luck, the sun would never shine and we'd be surrounded by this cozy leafy gray for two whole days.

The last time we did that was October. Five months ago. Now it was too cold. I was too busy, she was too busy, who knows. And she hadn't cracked a book since then either. Nor had I, come to think of it. And now everything sucked. The bubble had popped once again like it always did. She was off playing Don Quixote of the cabarets while I was running ragy dialogues through my head.

I must have lived with four La Donnas in the last six years and sometimes I thought I was destined to have twice as many in the next six. I seemed to float from one bad, heavy relationship to another, like a trapeze artist swinging from one suspended bar to the next with no net below. And I wasn't saying I was any prize either. I would be just as bad for them as they would be for me. But as bad as all my La Donnas were, what preceded them was a hundred, a thousand times worse; the sad case of Kenny Solo — Kenny living alone. Two years of a howling loneliness, a hunger that wouldn't let me sleep, wouldn't let me relax. For two goddamn years almost every night I would go to bars, to diners, looking for ladies. That's not true. I would just go through the motions mainly so at some point I could go home satisfied that I had at least tried.

And that was seven nights a week. Every night I would drive myself out of the house with a crazy feeling of "I'm missing it. It's all happening *now*. She's out there right *now*, you jerk."

Before Kenny Solo, I was Kenny Groupo. I lived a year with guys. That was another nightmare. Purple walls, gummed stars on the ceiling, no toilet paper, Pork Chop Hill mounds of dishes in the sink. Communal towels that smelled like rat death and assholes; no privacy, no privacy.

And before that I lived with my parents.

I felt like I hadn't found it yet. I hadn't made my move yet.

Something was scaring me about getting down. But something was coming. Sometimes I would wake up high as a kite about some intangible something. Sometimes I would walk down the street and feel all of a sudden like I could burst out of my skin with joy. Little rushes, tastes in my mouth. Something was in the air with me. Something was coming for sure. Something had *better* be in the air with me; I was thirty goddamn years old.

Riding downtown I had a fantasy of coming home and La Donna telling me she was pregnant. "Kill it," I would say.

I was not in the mood to walk around all day, kissing ass, hawking room spray to shut-ins. And if I wasn't in the mood to do what I had to do I was a goner. My job would turn into a nightmare. One thing I had learned in the last few years was that people picked up where you were coming from immediately, and if you were knocking on doors with a look on your face like who flung it and left it you would have so many slammed doors in your kisser you'd get windburn. And I had a face like a neon sign, too.

The bus left me off by the diner. The minute I swung open the door I got hit with that diner smog and that pain-in-the-ass crackle-hiss soundtrack of frying eggs and home fries. I started down the narrow aisle between the red vinyl booths and counter stools, my sample case, like a bad conscience, smacking into my calf with every step.

"Kenny, you look like shit." Cheeseburger George the grill man looked up from pushing around his cholesterol disasters.

"Thank you, George, have a nice day."

The Bluecastle House boys were sitting at our table in the far corner. Al Fiorita, Jerry Gold and Maurice de la Creep, sitting there in their jackets and ties squinting and wheezing from a combination of cigarette and griddle grease smoke. They hadn't seen me come in. Fat Al was in the middle of a story. Charlene blocked my path taking an order from two ugly Catholic School girls in maroon stadium coats. I could see Charlene's bra and slip outline through her waitress whites. She was emaciated and tall. Sunlight blasted through the wispy ringlets of her teased hair. Charlene always reminded me of mummies — she had high cheekbones, pinched lips and weird middle-aged skin, taut and glossy, as if she preserved it in diaphragm jelly. I touched her back. "Excuse me." I leaned toward the girls. "Do you mind if I borrow your waitress for a few minutes?" I gently squeezed Charlene's shoulder. "I need to have sex with her." Charlene clucked, slapping my arm with her order pad. The girls giggled and snorted into their fists, and I moved on down the line.

"So anyways, I ast this guy if he got a couple of minutes, you know, so, ah, we could talk about this." Al winked up at me and continued. "An' he says to me, 'Bawh? Ah doan hayv tahm to shake mah dick after ah take a pee, an *you* wan a coupla minutes? Hayl no!' " Jerry and Maurice broke up. Al basked in their laughter, sat fat and sassy like a vanilla pimp in his Windsor knot, matching cuff links and tie pin.

"Hey." He raised an arm to me, still glowing, "Death of a salesman!"

"Death of a salesman you." I smirked sliding in next to Jerry. Some joke. I parked my case under the table and poured myself some coffee.

"Hey." Al nudged me. "Maurice got a joke. Maurice, tell him your joke."

Maurice chortled as he scratched furiously at his head, loosening enough dandruff to snow in Buffalo. Poor Maurice. He was the ugliest, grossest dude I'd ever met. Nose hair, face creases, and bad breath. Thirty years a Bluecastle House man. They sent him into neighborhoods with lots of half-blind, senile people. He was a living memo to me to find some other line of work, and fast.

"What's the Greek national anthem?" he gloated.

"How the hell . . ."

"Never leave your buddies' behind!" He almost screamed with glee. Al and Jerry started laughing again, not with Maurice, as the saying goes, but at him.

"Don't fuckin' tell *me,* tell Cheeseburger George." I nodded toward the grill.

"Cheeseburgers." Maurice chuckled. "When I was in Italy, all the whores called the white soldiers Cheeseburgers, the niggers were Hamburgers. They'd say, 'No cheese-a-boorgers joos a ham-a-boorgers.' They loved niggers."

"They only said that when *you* were around, Maurice." Al winked at us.

"No, they had a special name for Maurice." Jerry wiped his lips. "Alpo."

Maurice half-cursed, half-laughed, along with everybody.

"Kenny, guess what?" Jerry lightly slapped my arm. "You know that coconut room spray? I sold six cans yesterday to a synagogue on Essex Street."

"Okay, boys and girls." Al emptied two huge cardboard boxes of ketchup-sized foils onto the table. I stared with disgust at the familiar blue-green wrappers.

"Awright, what's the story here, cream sachet again?" I picked one up and flipped it back into the pile. "That shit don't move, whata they always givin' us cream sachet for?"

"It moves," Al said confidently. Fat Al. He was one of

those "successful" salesmen. He even had a magnetized plastic ivory dollar-bill symbol on his dashboard.

"C'mon, Al, I had two hundred a these last week. I think I gave away twenty. Whatever happened to those liberation Afro Pics?"

"Where you gonna go with Afro Pics in the West Village?" Jerry grabbed two enormous fistfuls of sachet and stuffed one in each of his sport jacket pockets. When he stood up he looked like a pack mule. It always amazed me how little people cared about their appearance. Especially in our line of work. It took such little effort to make yourself presentable. If you didn't think enough of yourself to look groomed, how the hell could you expect anybody else to dig you?

I laughed out loud and everybody turned their heads to the window to see what I broke up about. Less than an hour ago I was freaking out because my existence made me feel like a gerbil on an exercise wheel, now I was riffing with equal intensity about good grooming. Life was wild.

"Hey, death of a salesman!" Maurice gave out a horselaugh that would embarrass a horse and flipped a cream sachet foil into my lap.

When I dropped out of college all I had was twenty-five credits to go. I always wound up thinking about that on mornings like this.

"Let's go, head 'em out!" Al got up from the table with an exaggerated groan, lugged his green alligator case from under the table and we all followed him down the aisle like an executive road gang.

"George" — I flipped a cream sachet foil onto the grill — "you look like shit."

When we hit the street I was not in an up-and-at-'em mood. I didn't even think I could sell a blood clot to a hemophiliac but I lucked out on my first shot — scored for a twenty-dollar sale on Bank Street to a kind-faced old German lady in a

faded floral housedress. She had sandbag breasts and big red
hands. Those hands looked as if they were in raw meat all
day. She lived in a long, dimly lit apartment with clunky dark
wooden furniture, brocade covers over everything and about
six thousand prowling cats. We sat on facing sofas, me with
the case and her with those huge meathooks folded calmly in
her lap and a ruddy creased smile on her refugee face. She
bought everything I showed her — hand lotion, room spray,
an ironing board protector. She never said a word, just nodded
for "one" when I asked, "Now how many should I put you
down for, one or two?" When she bought a Car-Vac, my
portable car rug vacuum cleaner in a can, I knew she was just
buying all that shit so I would stick around and keep making
human noises. That stuff always tore me up. I would always
get those lonely older ladies who would buy anything I had to
sell just to have my company. If they ordered something, not
only would I have to sit there to sell it, but I would have to
come back the end of the week and deliver it. And they would
always have cats. Millions of cats. I was allergic to cats, too.
I hated them. I'd sit there on some overstuffed cat-hair couch
running my bullshit, sneezing my brains out, eyes like red
stars, and these poor ladies would be holding their own hands
nodding nodding nodding, smiling smiling smiling, sometimes
silent like the German lady, sometimes gushing out the spew
of their sad sad lives, getting up, bustling around with their
bookcase behinds, offering me tea, coffee, sponge cake, cheese-
cake, pound cake, cupcake, kugel, babka — you name it. And
half of them couldn't even speak English.

Anyway, after she bought the Car-Vac and introduced me
to seven or eight cats — and you have no idea what an absolute schmuck you feel like nodding hello to a cat — I had to
split. I felt as if there was a big hairy angora stuffed comfortably inside each lung and I wasn't so much breathing as
leaking air. I even started sneezing blood.

But I made her day. Every day on the job I made somebody's day. Made that human connection. There were more

lonely people in New York than in entire European countries. And every day I found at least one and pulled her back into the real world for thirty minutes. As much as I bitched about cats and crazies, making that connection hit the spot with me. I got a nice little high every time I scored a lonely. Without getting grandiose about it, it was a side benefit that sometimes made my work tolerable. But there was an element of half-assed compromise in that aspect of my life too. Because, despite the good moments, the bottom line was that I still had to sell them some bullshit ironing board cover or hand cream. And I spent a lot of time knocking on empty apartment doors or spieling to jerk-offs.

The German lady was followed by a half-hour of nothing, then two back-to-back sales on Greenwich Avenue and then I totally lucked out. I caught three housewives kibitzing in the home of a fourth. When I announced through the locked door that I was the Bluecastle Housewares man I heard one broad say, "I don't know about Bluecastle Housewares, but I can sure use a man." They all cracked up, the locks were unlocked and I was home free. I was the absolute master of the soft-core innuendo. I knew how to come on saucy but not smutty, naughty but not filthy. I could read a person's tolerance level for the risqué as fast as it took an expert to pick your watch while shaking your hand. I didn't waste any time with these four. I whipped out my foaming hand lotion and demonstrated it by rubbing it first into my hands, then into their hands. I said, "It's also good for a couple of other things, but I won't go into that," and gave an X-rated wink. I had no idea what the hell that was supposed to mean, but they had a group apoplexy. I walked out of there a half-hour later with a forty-dollar order and my gut sloshing with coffee.

So it was almost noon and I had written close to eighty dollars. That was a decent day right there. Usually I would try to write up seventy-five to a hundred dollars a day, pull a five-day week, take home two-fifty to three hundred, and I was happy. I was no freak for money. I wasn't going to Red China for a vacation or buying a brownstone. I didn't have kids, my place was within my means, La Donna chipped in some, I had nice clothes, so with an eighty-dollar morning I was very happy. If I scored for fifteen, twenty dollars more early in the afternoon I would knock off and go to a movie instead of busting my nates for the extra few bucks I might make over that. And that's the way I was. I didn't have it so bad. The job was okay. Better than most. And if I took a year out of my life and finished college? Then what? What was I supposed to become, a social worker? Would I go to graduate school? Would I become a $60,000-a-year ad exec giving blowjobs to the Cheerios account representative so I could keep writing jingles? Bullshit. And teaching was a nice little pipe dream, but unless I was willing to do the South Bronx, who was hiring? So big deal I read books. So did a housewife. Besides, I had the diction of a neighborhood bookie, and my degree was geared for business administration. So, later for that. I made more money than most college graduates, did more good for people, too. And I didn't feel inferior because I didn't have my degree. I was smart. I was one of the smartest people I knew. I didn't need a piece of paper to tell me that.

So I was feeling good. Feeling more like a person, a talker, I went back to the diner for lunch. I ordered good food. I didn't eat garbage. A nice strip steak, some cottage cheese and Tab. Kept myself good and tight, lots of protein. Fucking Al might have been King Shit when it came to sales, but I'd still be doing a hundred and fifty sit-ups a day when he'd be pushing up daisies. After lunch I sat, I relaxed, I had coffee and read the paper. Maurice came in. He sat down across from me, flipped his order pad on the table and twisted in the booth to flag down Charlene.

"Relax, Maurice." Charlene was wiping the counter and spoke to him with controlled distaste.

Grabbing his pad, I did a quick tally of his day's sales: sixty dollars. I won. One order caught my eye. It was for eight shower caps, paid in full.

"Hey, what's this?" I turned the pad to him.

"Eight shower caps," he chuckled.

"Yeah, I see that. Who the hell buys eight shower caps? Whata you doing, you workin' seniles again?"

"Nah, it was a girl. I showed her all the different colors she could get and she liked them all so she got 'em all." He laughed. "Char-le-ene," he singsonged, tickled with himself.

Anytime I felt low all I had to do was compare myself to Maurice. But sometimes I wondered what he had been like twenty years earlier when he was my age. Or better still, what was *I* going to be in twenty years? Well, shit, at least I wouldn't be like Maurice. But what did that leave, Fat Al? Maybe not that way either. But one thing I would be, if things didn't change, was a fifty-year-old Bluecastle Housewares man. No good. No good at all. The notion nauseated me, wrenched me out of the diner and back to work.

It was pushing three-thirty and I hadn't made one connection since lunch. I was in a rage, in a panic. I got into the nervous habit of squeezing my crotch, like I was applying a tourniquet. That afternoon became a disaster. I blew sales right and left. I was surly, impatient — as if it was *their* fucking fault that *I* had to stomp around in icy February weather selling that bullshit and the least they could goddamn do was *buy* the crap, for Christ's sake.

At a three-story brick building on Eleventh Street I finally decided that this was it, whatever I did in that building was it for the day. There was no elevator and the hallways were somebody's idea of the future. They were wallpapered with what looked like silver foil. There were only twelve apartments. No one was home in the first eight. A real nelly faggot came to the door in the ninth; a short, skinny, limp wrist with a sinus cold that gave him a nose like Rudolph the reindeer.

He kept schlepping on his beak while eyeing the contents of my case through the six inches the chain lock allowed. He closed the door on me without saying sorry or no thank you, and I was stuck with all my cans and boxes sprouting around my feet like mushrooms. I muttered "Faggot" louder than I meant to, but I doubt that he heard me, and I had mixed feelings about that fact.

The name on the next door was Gordon. At that point I wasn't expecting anything miraculous. Even though I felt sorry for myself, I was also feeling a little better because after two more doors I could go home.

"Just a minute."

She sounded young and I quickly tucked my shirt into the elastic band of my shorts to flatten my gut. Three chains unlocked, the door swung open, and hey hey there she was, about five-ten, long red hair like Rita Whatever and wearing, no lie, a nightgown. It was two-forty-five in the P.M. and she was wearing a nightgown.

"Yeah?" She was half-smiling as though she had just woke up from a nice dream, and she leaned her head sleepily on the door frame, totally relaxed, totally unparanoid about me.

"Hi! I've got a free gift from Bluecastle for you!" What a schmuck. I raised my sample case slightly and pointed my chin at the apartment door. "Mind if I come in?"

"Oh yeah? What kind of free gift?" She yawned and rubbed the heel of her hand into her eyes. " 'Scuse me."

"We ran out of whips and vibrators." I pulled out one of those shit-ass cream sachet foils from my jacket pocket and held it up casually between two fingers, like an ID.

"Hawaii Five-O, ma'am, mind if we come in and look around?" My best shot.

"That's not much of a gift." Her skin was lightly sprayed with acne scars and a vaguely sour morning mouth smell drifted over to me. Nothing turned me off like bad breath, but I knew morning mouth was unavoidable.

"It's a door opener; I got better stuff in here." I tapped my case. She wasn't that nice-looking. It felt very important to feel that. I kept thinking about morning mouth and how someday we were all going to die no matter what.

She slowly turned from the door and walked unsteadily into the living room. I followed her in. The light from the living room window revealed her legs through her nightgown, and I immediately got one of those boners that start from the heart. For a fast two seconds I rubbed my crotch viciously behind her back, clenching my teeth and looking like a psycho.

She sat down in a flimsy, white, slightly unraveled wicker chair and hunched over, elbows on knees, hands crossed to her shoulders like she was shielding her tits from me. I sat across from her on a burgundy fake velvet sofa and opened my case between my feet. I could tell she lived alone. Two gilt-framed pictures of her parents, lot of plants, tortoise shell window shades, a portable typewriter on a cheap one-piece molded white plastic table, a stack of *New York* and *Ms.* magazines piled on the bottom rack of a TV stand, a small TV with aluminum foil on the antenna—I could tell plenty. And I could see somewhat between her knees if I ducked my head a little.

She nodded toward the case, a smirk on her face as if she had read my mind.

"So let's hear it."

The sleep was gone from her eyes, which were light green. I preferred dark eyes.

"You like coconuts? Everybody likes coconuts, right?" I plucked out a small aerosol can of room spray and shpritzed briefly in front of her. I inhaled with my eyes at half-mast as if I was smelling baked bread. Her eyelids fluttered as she jerked her head back, coughing into her fingers. Her knees parted for a second and I saw thigh.

"What? You don't like that!" I looked stunned. "It smells like Pago Pago in here now!"

She waved her hand in front of her face as if to clear the air. She had intelligent eyes; they had character. I parted my legs a little. I wanted her to know I had a hard-on.

"Do you know who my biggest customer for coconut room spray is? And I'm not lying." I leaned back and squinted. "Take a guess."

"Somebody in your immediate family, I imagine." She pumped a cigarette from a matching unraveling white wicker lamp table next to her.

"Nope, Terence Cardinal Cooke." I narrowed my eyes and pointed a finger. "He *loves* the stuff and has instructed the custodian at Saint Patrick's to snag a dozen cans every time I come by the church. Next time you go in there, smell the air."

"C'mon, what else you hiding in there?" She arched her eyebrows, and I swear to God she stared right at my crotch. I brought my knees together and did a nosedive into my case, fumbled around like I had three hands and whipped out the foam lotion, flipping it up like a baton and one-handing it.

"Here" — I wriggled my fingers — "give me your hand."

I rested the cold, bony back of her hand in my palm, shook up the can and shot a thick jet of cream onto her lifeline.

"Am I getting a light trim around the knuckles?" That eyebrow arch again.

"Very humorous. You're very quick." I smiled while rubbing the foam into her palm and fingers with both of my hands. It began to break down into a jellylike lotion. As I worked my ten fingers through her five, slithering through the taut webs and swirling around the joints my groin started pounding like a marathon runner's heart. I ran my middle fingers up and down her palm. She had make-up on from the night before; a slice of earlobe peeked through her red hair. My knees parted company again and my Adam's apple started doing elevator takes in my throat. "How does that feel?" My voice came out like Andy Devine.

"Mmm." Her eyes were closed.

I couldn't bring myself to spiel. Screw the spiel. She started

weaving slightly and let her head hang back so her chin was
stabbing up at the ceiling. I grabbed the can and shpritzed
more foam on our hands to keep it going. For a split second
her fingers massaged mine and I thought my brains would
spew out my ears. I started grinding in my seat, staring between her knees. I squeezed myself with a greasy hand. No
panties. Oh, my fucking God, she wasn't wearing panties.
Suddenly the phone rang, and I jumped like I was snapping
out of a nightmare. I think I actually said "Aw!" like a kid.
She shook her head and smiled.

"I'll be back!" She got up and went through louvered
double doors into the bedroom. I started following her in,
hunched over and slobbering like Fred Flintstone on Spanish
fly, but pulled myself together and returned to the couch. I
gave myself five. This was it. This was fucking it. Finally,
after six years of door to door, I was getting some nut. I
jumped up and started dancing in front of the mirror. Screw
La Donna. She could sleep like the dead from now on. I
smoothed down my hair and shot my cuffs. I was bad. I was
slick. I looked like fuckin' Marcello. I thanked God my
mother was dark; the old man's side looked like anemic book-
worms. I pulled down my tie knot, then pushed it back up.
It looked better down and down it went. Made me look more
laid back. Up for anything. I sat back on the couch and
waited, patting my banana like I'd pat a Doberman I was trying to restrain. Twenty minutes went by. Thirty. Maybe she's
putting in her diaphragm. I could've done it for her. I put in
La Donna's diaphragm all the time. The double doors opened.

"Hi." She smiled. I stood at attention as if someone had
just announced, "Gentlemen, the queen."

"Hey look, I'm sorry I'm taking so long."

"No problem," I lied.

"Listen, this is gonna be a real long call. Maybe you could
come back some other time? I'm *really* sorry." She whirled
her head on "really." I could see the cranberry tips of her
nipples through the nightgown. I felt torpedoed.

"Well." I clucked my tongue. "You know I don't come around here that often." I pulled up my goddamn tie knot. "I can wait." It was all over.

"No, that's okay. Why don't you stop by whenever, okay? I'm really sorry."

"Right." I felt so down I thought I was dying.

"You can let yourself out . . . That hand lotion was nice." Another apologetic smile and she was gone, back into the bedroom.

I felt like pissing on her couch. It was three-thirty. I should have split right then, but I felt as if she owed me something and I started stalking the apartment like it was mine by right of rage. I wound up in her bathroom; cutesy big-eyed animal print wallpaper and matching shower curtain. Bright yellow plastic toilet seat. I swept back the shower curtain like I was looking for evidence. The bathtub was filled with stray hairs and a Japanese loofa sponge lay there like the corpse of a sunken ship in a drained ocean. A fat roach waddled across a thin bar of gold translucent soap in a bright yellow soap dish shaped like a seashell on the small sink. The basin had large bright green copper water stains under each faucet. The floor was covered with a cheap cut-it-yourself green rug. She had done a shitty job of laying it down; it was bunched and rolled around the toilet base at one end and didn't reach the edge of the bathtub at the other. Her medicine cabinet contained the usual shit. Nylon floral cosmetic bag, filled with eye shadow, pencil liners and lipsticks. A small jar of Vaseline on a shelf with supermarket-brand aspirin and a hair-caked leg razor. Antidiarrhea pills in an amber prescription bottle. *That* disgusted me. Hairs in the bathtub, the fat roach halfway up the wall, his antenna swishing in slow motion. The place was a pit and she was a slob. A big dark gold towel didn't match anything else in the room. It was damp probably from the evening before because she didn't take the time and trouble to fold it over the bar but just jammed it in the goddamn towel rack like who gives a royal fuck. I couldn't find

a diaphragm or birth control pills. I hated that bathroom. It
stunk of her privacy and I was up for heavy sabotage, demoli-
tion, but I couldn't think of anything to do.

I was staring at a stalactite of hardened green toothpaste
frozen from the topless tube to the white enamel of the sink
when I got hit with a frightening flash of not knowing where I
was. Dizziness. I got scared. I couldn't sense me. I panicked
for a second, then snapped out of it. Suddenly I didn't want
to get caught in there. She would eat me alive. I got out
fast. I felt like an intruder, which I was. Her double doors
were still closed and I split.

I did the last apartment.

"Free gift from Bluecastle."

"I can't take it" from inside.

"Good." I clomped down the stairs. "I can't take it either."

Home, James. I grabbed a cab and shot uptown. Once I sat
back and lit a cigarette I started thinking about a lot of
things I didn't like to think about. Like my job, for one. I had
to quit. Fuck it. I'd go back to college, finish up and do
something else. Anything else. Go on unemployment and
just think, relax for a while. I was pissing my life away. Maybe
I'd let La Donna support me for a change. No. Better yet, I'd
go on unemployment and tell La Donna to walk.

I didn't want her in my life anymore. Or maybe what
needed to go was just the bullshit. Keep La Donna, throw out
the bullshit. That could be wild. It used to be wild. We
were quite a pair once. We used to be really good with each
other. But maybe it was too late for that. Maybe all the good
times had been fired by infatuation, and that was long gone.
The only things left were my sex hunger and our rage. Cut it
short. Stop the dying. Cut La Donna. Cut door to door. Get
a degree. Teach. Make it work with La Donna. Cut La
Donna. Kenny on the fence. Make your move. Make your
move.

The sun had punched out about three, and the streets were

gray. Everything was the color of iron. Old snow, sidewalks, cars. The cab pulled up in front of my building. The super had taken the canvas canopy off the front of the building and the ugly frame skeleton looked like shit, too.

The minute I stepped out of the elevator onto our floor I smelled La Donna. When I was a kid living in the projects every floor had a distinct odor that I associated with the families living there. You could have taken me up an elevator, blindfolded, ducked my head into any hallway, let me sniff and I could have told you what floor we were on. So I knew La Donna was home. I hung out in the hallway, sitting on the interior ledge of the hallway window, which faced three sides of the building, and the square made a cold ten-story drop into an enclosed concrete courtyard. There was one foil left in my jacket pocket and I flipped it out the window like a baseball card. It spun over and over itself, slipped into a dead float and slapped the ground with a distant tinny noise. Next came me, knees bent, palms pressed together like I was praying, then springing up, arms out in a breast stroke. Neeearroww babooom! Not yet, at any rate.

"Yo! I'm home!" I put my case down in the foyer and locked the door. No answer. Big surprise, I was alone. But then I heard my electric razor from down the bathroom end of the apartment. What the hell would that mean? A guy? I got goose pimples. The bitch was with another guy. Another guy in my house. I turned to sneak out, then stopped myself. What the hell was I doing? I grabbed an umbrella out of the hall closet and holding it against my chest like a rifle I stalked down the hall toward the bathroom. My heart was pulsing like a frog gullet. Leaning against the wall, I caught my breath, then ducked in front of the bathroom, screamed "Yah!" and thrust the umbrella inside like a bayonet. The bathroom was empty.

The buzz was coming from the bedroom, leaking from under the closed door. Two plus two, it was the alarm clock.

Thank God. My pits were drenched. I opened the bedroom door and froze.

La Donna was lying on the bed wearing only a blue T-shirt. One hand rested behind her head, and the other was ramming a vibrator up her cunt. She was concentrating so hard she didn't even notice me standing in the doorway. Look up, bitch, c'mon, look up.

"Kenny!" She screamed like she was trying to shout me out of the path of a Mack truck. Her face went all Os and she grabbed the vibrator with both hands. I didn't want to see that long thing come out of her. I didn't know whether to kill her or fuck her.

"What . . ." I started pumping my head up and down like Jackie di Paris. "What's that?" My knees were shaking.

She was so goddamn freaked she couldn't even turn it off. She didn't even close her legs. I couldn't take my eyes off her hands, her thighs, the glint of white plastic coming at me through her fingers.

"Kenny." Pathetic, twisting her face in misery.

"TURN THAT GODDAMN THING OFF!" I had never screamed at her, but I did then. I kicked the corner of the bed. I felt like I wasn't allowed to move out of my spot. She covered herself with the blanket. Her shoulders jerked down as she pulled out the vibrator. The buzz was splitting my head. I threw the blanket off her, grabbed the goddamn thing out of her hands. It slipped out of my fist and fell on the floor, buzzing and revolving like a gigantic wounded fly. I stomped it. Killed it. I was afraid to look at her. Afraid that she didn't cover herself again.

"What's that!" I was never so scared of another human being as I was then, pointing at that thing and barking my ass off.

She sat up in bed, sweating, hunched over and feeling totally rotten. She didn't cover up and I was ready to jump out the window.

"You know what it is." Her voice came out in croaks.

"Yeah." My head bobbed again. "I know what it is, it's like you . . . It's disgusting." Finally I had her. Had the upper hand, and it terrified me. I didn't know what to do with it. I wheeled around to split and she made a motion with her arms to me, like to reach out for me. Like for me to get in bed with her. I clomped out of the bedroom and ran like hell, almost breaking my neck tripping over my sample case.

I turned in spaced-out circles in the hallway waiting for the elevator when suddenly I had this feeling that if I waited one more second my apartment would explode outward in a rolling ball of flame followed by La Donna screaming her head off and swinging a sword as big as Justice. I took the stairs four at a time down ten flights, got lost on the ground floor looking for the lobby and made it out to the street. The minute I hit the sidewalk my whole body felt licked by a damp chill. I had been sweating like a hog. The gray was disappearing into early evening and the apartment buildings on West End Avenue resembled a long row of giant dead cash registers. The hell with that. I didn't need more depression. I walked over to Broadway feeling unreal, either me or everybody else on the street wasn't quite human. When I was a kid my Uncle Nat used to say to me, "Kenny boy, you know your uncle's a magician? Every time I walk down the street I turn into a bar."

I didn't laugh then, and I wasn't laughing now, but it seemed like sound advice.

I went into the Sun Lounge. It wasn't bad, red lights, dark, tacky, a shitty juke box with too many ay! ay! ay! mariachi numbers, but it was cozy. My finger did a search-and-destroy mission inside my cigarette pack. There was one left, but I broke it poking around. I felt crushed, as if that were the last cigarette in the world. Then I noticed the cigarette machine and my heart soared. I was acting like an idiot. For a second I couldn't remember why I'd stormed out of the apartment in the first place. Then I remembered and I felt this horny horror, this loop de loop in my belly. What was she reaching out to me for?

Despite the cold, the two barmaids wore hot pants. One was nice. Lemon yellow pants, henna red flat hairdo, copper waves plastered across her forehead. Big, big tits. She was okay but in another five years she wouldn't be able to get that ass in those pants with surgery. The filigree pattern of her underwear showed against her shorts. Hot cha, hot cha. She slid a cardboard coaster in front of me.

"Vodka martini." I didn't even know what the hell a vodka martini was. I didn't drink as a rule. I used to drink a lot, but I stopped four years ago when a girl in a singles' bar came over to me, grabbed a fistful of flab over each of my hips, and said, "Love rungs, too much love rungs," and walked away. Since that night I stopped boozing, eating potatoes, bread, desserts. I started doing sit-ups every day and was forever more unable to pass a mirror without checking to make sure my chest bulged out farther than my stomach. If I ever run into that mysterious woman again I will thank her profusely, then kick her face in.

The vodka martini tasted like lighter fluid but it helped regulate my breathing, so I ordered another.

The other barmaid looked pretty good too. Blond. But she had plucked eyebrows, which made her look as hard as nails. She was at the other end of the bar doing dance steps to some disco shit coming over the juke box and gazing into space, oblivious to the ten sad sacks sitting around the bar leaning cheeks on fists in front of their drinks, staring hopelessly at her breasts, her crotch. I hated cockteasers. Power like that.

A vibrator. A vibrator. Mother of Christ. How would she feel if she came home and caught me socking it to some inflatable love doll?

February. We had started living together in mid-June. That

was just about nine months. And not once, not once did I ever ball with anybody else. I didn't even want to. Maybe if she was available to me I would be more turned on to other women. Things certainly seemed to work that way sometimes. I flashed again on her reaching out to me after I smashed her vibrator. I felt my heart break, and I wanted to go to her. Some damn fandango. I ordered a third martini and threw it back like I was washing down aspirin. The drinks were whipping my ass. When I got high I got friendly. I wanted to talk to somebody. Anybody. Make new friends. I turned to the guy sitting next to me, but he got up peeling off a payroll five and walked to the john. It was a pay toilet but Henna Red buzzed him in from under the cash register. I winked at her but she didn't catch my eye and I felt like a fool.

Sheesh. I lightly pounded the bar and stifled a belch. I was worried about some guy screwing La Donna and my real competition was Everready. Fuck it. She wanted to play around? Then me too. I was wasting my time with her. I was at the peak of my manhood. And I was good. And I wasn't just saying that the way every guy says it. I was goddamn good. And I was big. I was good, big and the best. And I was wasting it with her. Everyone said it. Every woman I was ever with told me I was the best. I knew how to move, how to groove and I was a handsome bastard too. I had a nice frame, about six feet even. Hundred and sixty-five. Straight hair, dark skin, dark eyes, sensuous mouth, so I heard. Maybe when I quit door-to-door I could be a gigolo. Somebody put something good on the machine for a change and I winked for a fourth martini. Henna caught it that time. I could've made her.

Another guy got up, walked over to the john. He didn't know it worked by a buzzer and dropped a dime in the lock. The door wouldn't budge. He looked around helplessly but was too embarrassed to complain to the barmaids so he sat back down.

There was a bulldyke two stools away. About fifty. Short gray hair combed back with a little swept pompadour. She was staring straight ahead, near as I could tell through her bulging wraparound shades. A shiner peeked out beneath her left shade and she mechanically moved her cigarette between the ashtray and her lips over and over again as if she was a life-sized coin bank. She wore a short-sleeved black sweatshirt and a black leather wrist strap with dull silver studs on one wrist, a Florentine gold ID bracelet with LUCILLE in gold oriental letters on the other. I would've bet I could've made her too.

I could've made the world. I could've, just that day, made Charlene in the diner, at least two of those broads from the coffee klatch and if I was really scrapin' that old but not *that* old German lady. That was four. Four that day if I wanted. And Gordon. Oh my God, Gordon. My heart took off around the rib cage. She wanted it too. She was in her nightgown at two-forty-five in the afternoon.

Outside it was dark. Nighttime. And nighttime was the right time. One seventy-five West Eleventh. Gordon. Time for love. I dropped a ten for the drinks and hit the streets. I was drunk. Piss me off. Not so bad I couldn't walk straight and not so bad I didn't know it, but still, I didn't dig boozy elation. I hailed a cab.

"Gordon."

"What?"

"One seventy-five West Eleventh."

Okay, what would I say? Hey! I lost your order. I thought maybe you could give it to me again. I lost her order. She didn't *give* me an order. La Donna, I could've, would've, given you the best. I thought of that vibrator again. Her thighs spread out like that. She had a beauty mark right between her asshole and her cunt. She told me her mother had said to her once when she was a kid that that was where God was marking a spot for a third hole when lucky for her he was called away on business. I had left my cigarettes in the bar. The cab pulled up in front of the brick building.

Just be straight, man. Tell her, listen, you know what was really going down this afternoon so disconnect the phone and let's *git . . . it . . . on!* Yes indeedy. I was almost to her door before I wigged. I couldn't say that. It wasn't my style. Go with the order story. Hey! I forgot the order! What order? Oh Christ, yeah, ha ha, you didn't order anything. Well, since you're here why don't you come in and have a drink? Ring the bell, chooch. Heavy footsteps.

"Yeah?"

A middle-aged guy in a T-strap undershirt, dress pants and slippers. His nose came up to my chest but his shoulders were a yard across. John L. Lewis eyebrows, fistfuls of black back hair like bear fur peeking at me over his shoulders. Heavy glasses and Maurice de la Creep face crevices.

"Help you?" An arm like a crossbeam against the door frame.

"Yeah, no, is this the Jacuzzi residence?"

I didn't even have my sample case with me. I heard her talking to someone inside. The apartment was smoky and smelled like someone was cooking garbage.

"Jacuzzi, uh-uh."

"Right, sorry." Down the stairs and out into the night stone sober and into another bar. It was a gay bar. Twenty guys in crew cuts and RAF mustaches turned their heads when I breezed in. I did a quick 180 degrees and headed out the door. And they didn't even know what they just missed. Because not only was it big, it was as thick as a woman's wrist.

I headed for another bar but changed my mind. Enough was enough. I tried walking around a little but it was too cold. I didn't have my gloves or a scarf. I went to a coffeehouse down by NYU that looked like something out of the House of Usher. Ten-watt bulbs, carved-oak tables and chairs,

miniature busts of Dante and Beethoven and hanging on the
walls large portraits so old and dingy you couldn't even tell
if they were men or women. The guys hanging around were
dead ringers for William Shakespeare. Two Arabic women
in Gucci army fatigues yakking over cannolis. A girl reading
a paper in the corner kept glancing up at me without raising
her head, giving me the once-over as if she were wearing
bifocals.

I almost sat down at her table but was too beat to get into
anything more. I ordered an espresso with lemon peel, no
sugar thank you, sat back, closed my eyes and tried to get my
bearings. Seeing La Donna in the sack like that scared me.

That whole vibrator thing was very confusing to me. The
more I thought about it the more stupid and embarrassed I
felt. Big deal she was jerking off. If she was just fingering
herself without the help of Con Ed, would I have wigged?
Damn, I jerked off more than a monkey. But I wouldn't if
she was into . . . What's the difference. She was alone and
trying to get off and I blew in there like some heavy nineteenth-
century wop and now she probably would have trouble coming for the next six months. Nice going.

It was sexist of me. I didn't wanna be sexist. I felt much
calmer — the only thing I couldn't or didn't want to think
about was her *buying* the goddamn thing. Going into a drug-
store and asking for it and *paying* for it with *my* money while
I was whining and kvetching about having to fuck a milk
bottle because my quote unquote girlfriend was having a hard
time with sex.

But on the other hand, the other hand, the other hand.
Sitting in that dinge among the busts and the oak, I was beginning to feel like Hamlet. The fact of the matter was she
was probably crying in bed alone uptown. I always promised
her I would be there when she needed me, and I wasn't. She
was under strain from Fantasia. I was under strain from
chasing around some scuz who was into cooking garbage and

balling apemen. Sex wasn't everything. We were adults. I'd just get her to wear sweatpants to bed and everything would be cool.

On the way uptown I bought her flowers. I had never bought flowers for a girl in my life. I couldn't smell them because my nose was stuffed up from running around without a hat, but they were nice — orange, red and pale blue. Maybe I would bring flowers home as a matter of course. The new me.

Out in the hallway I couldn't smell her, but my nose was so stuffed I wouldn't have been able to smell a corpse in a phone booth.

The apartment was dark. Without turning on any lights I tiptoed down the foyer. The bedroom door was open. No lights on in there either. I soft-stepped to the bed and sat on the edge. "La Di?" I reached out and touched sheets. No La Donna. I hit the light on the night table. The bed was unmade. I tossed the flowers on the crumpled blankets. There was a note pinned to my pillow and my insides hit a bump: "I CAN'T BELIEVE I LET YOU WALK OUT ON ME." First line and I felt a flush of love.

"I SHOULD HAVE KICKED YOU OUT. NOBODY EVER HUMILIATED ME LIKE THAT IN MY LIFE. I AM JUST AS ANGRY AT MYSELF FOR SITTING THERE AND TAKING IT AS I AM AT YOU FOR BEING YOUR USUAL SELF CENTERED SELF. GOODBYE."

My first reaction was to get an "oh my God" disaster rush like I had received a telegram that I had cancer. It passed. Then I felt scared, as if she were hiding somewhere in the dark apartment waiting to pounce on me.

"LA DONNA!" I barked, like, if you're out there don't fuck with me. I hit the overhead light switch in the bedroom. That gave me enough illumination and courage to dart into the living room and hit the switch in there. I screamed. What I thought was another person was my image in the living room closet full-length mirror. I'd forgotten about that mirror be-

cause it was on the inside of the door and I never used that
closet. It was La Donna's, and it was pretty empty. As a
matter of fact, the only things she'd left behind were her Frye
boots and about six pounds of song sheets and music books.
I didn't know if that was supposed to be symbolic of something but I just closed the door. Then I chained the front
door. I took off my coat, draped it across one of the dinette
table chairs, retrieved the flowers, put them in water and
started to change the bed sheets. The vibrator still lay where
I had murdered it. I got another rush of dread but I picked
it up with a dish towel and dropped it out the bathroom window, plugging my fingers in my ears so I wouldn't hear the
crash. It worked. I threw her letter in the garbage, fished it
out and sent it for a one-shot flying lesson via the same window. I finished changing the sheets and checked the *Post* for
the TV listings. *Death Wish* was on *Tuesday Night at the
Movies* at nine. *The Honeymooners* at eleven and *Bring Me
the Head of Alfredo Garcia* was the cable TV homebox movie
at eleven-thirty. Out of sight. The super had the heat coming
up the pipes for a change. It was going to be a heavy TV
night. But first, a little nappy.

I woke up sweating like I'd just broken a fever. I whipped
my head right and left searching for who knows what in the
darkness, then flopped back and let out a cranky moan. There
was no one in the world but me, and the world was my dark
apartment. The digital read 10:40. I hit the light on its
lowest wattage, made it to my feet and squinted around the
room for something to bring me back to earth. I turned on
the TV. Two guys were bouncing up and down in the cab of a
truck eating sandwiches and talking with their mouths full. I
hadn't had any dinner. And I hadn't done my sit-ups. First
things first. I fumbled around the bed for my sneakers, got
my barbell from under the night table and dragged my jockey-
shorted ass into the living room. I did my hundred and fifty

in the dark and went into the kitchen. I stared into the refrigerator spaced out, nothing really registering, absently
fingering the muscles and ravines of my cast-iron, flab-free
gut. The only thing with any potential was an unopened
round cardboard of Swiss Knight cheese wedges, which I carried into the bedroom. It was eleven o'clock. *The Honeymooners!* I hit the remote control on the cable box and
breathed easy. I knew every one of *The Honeymooners* by
heart. There was something comforting about that show,
something safe. Just having them on was like taking a ten-
milligram hit of Valium. I sat there wolfing down cheese
slices while Jackie Gleason rolled those eyes in that hippo
puss for the ten millionth time since I was five. Talk about
anchors.

At twenty after eleven I started nodding out. I figured I
could use a good night's sleep for a change so I turned off the
TV and the light.

I sat up like a jack-in-the-box. It was 4:03.

I had had a dream that my father apologized for fucking
me over when I was an infant. I asked, "What happened?"
He explained that he used to bring me down to the playground
on a walker so he could pick up young mothers. When he
scored he parked me in the woman's living room while he did
his business in the bedroom. One time when he left me in a
lady's living room her cat scratched the hell out of my legs.
The reason he was bringing the whole subject up was that he
had just received a check from the lady to pay for the damages
to my legs from twenty-seven and a half years ago. While he
was telling me this my mother stood, arms folded, nodding
solemnly by his side. The main sensation I woke up with was
feeling sorry for my father because he was hanging out with
ladies in the middle of the day when he should have been
working or hanging out with men. It was just a dream, but
sometimes when I sacked out those things came at me with
everything but screen credits.

I couldn't get back to sleep. The whole package of cheese

slices was lying in my gut like wet cement. Work in four
hours. Suck-ass work. I started thinking about La Donna.
I kept seeing her stretch out her arms to me and it started
ripping me up. I touched my stomach — it still felt flat. Stop
it. She was gone. Maybe she'd be back and maybe she
wouldn't. The more I analyzed it, the more I realized the
vibrator incident was no accident. That little Tuesday afternoon flip of mine was called "Kenny Makes a Move." A few
times in my life I made moves — always with the grace and
finesse of a butcher hacking up a mastodon, but they were
moves nonetheless. I wasn't saying that little scene was
planned, but if I looked back at the big ones, the big moves,
they all had the same MO. They seemed thoughtless and
stupid or dangerous, but they always got me out of check-
mate. I could remember at least three incidents where I had
pulled some heavy number and changed my life. After high
school I was still living at home. All my friends had split but
I couldn't get it together to leave. College was depressing, an
extension of high school, a subway commute. I was dying, but
I was afraid to leave. Then one night my junior year I fucked
this girl in my parents' bed when they were out. After we
finished I couldn't find the condom. I had tossed it somewhere
and couldn't find it. When I came home from school the next
day, the house turned into Guadalcanal. My old lady had
found the condom that morning. It was in her slipper. By
nightfall I had moved in with three guys from school living in
Manhattan.

Kenny makes a move.

A year after that I was engaged to a girl I didn't love. She
had a screechy laugh and hated sex. Her father ran a chain
of stationery stores. The deal was I marry his daughter and
I would start out at the top. Two weeks after our engagement
was announced I was feeling cocky. I figured I had it made
so I quit school. Her old man went berserk over my disrespect
for education and broke off the engagement.

Kenny makes a move.

Three years after that, I'm involved with a chick up in Woodstock who lived in a cabin, ran with a heavy psychopathic drug crowd, thought Charles Manson was misunderstood, pushed coke for a living, had six cats and wanted me to drop everything and run off to Canada with her to open a health food store. I started pushing a little coke myself to make up for all the stuff I was snorting. All we did was snort and screw, snort and screw. And then I'd wheeze all night from the cats, drive the next morning to Saugerties General Hospital for allergy shots, drive to the city to work, drive to Woodstock at night, and so on and so on. In those few months I had done so much coke the insides of my nostrils had calluses, my eyes were bugging out of my head from fatigue and I was so paranoid about getting busted I had a permanent terror knot in my belly. When I tried to leave her she wound up in the hospital after throwing herself in the path of a car.

Then one fine day after we'd been running together for three months I left the house to go into town. She was with friends in the city at the time. I was in town an hour when I heard a tremendous explosion in the distance. Fire engines, sirens, etc. I had left the gas on and blew up the cabin. Killed all six of the cats and destroyed ten thousand dollars' worth of cocaine.

Kenny makes a move.

Something else all those moves had in common: they always ended in throwing the baby out with the bath water. I didn't talk to my parents for two years, I never finished college, and I could have killed somebody in Woodstock. And now La Donna was gone and something in me still ached for her. Ached for when it was good with us.

I could even remember the exact day everything started going downhill. It was a Tuesday in October. She had told me over breakfast that she had been taking singing lessons since August, was running into a financial snag, and asked if I could help her out.

I gave her a lot of grief about expenses and even got into some hoopla about the energy crisis and we had an enormous riff. Then a strange thing happened; about halfway through the fight we did a complete turnabout, from her asking for a few bucks and me withholding, to me demanding all future bills and she not wanting a dime. I persisted and wound up paying for the whole shot. I have no idea why I did that, but I'm sure it had nothing to do with me having a heart of gold under a gruff exterior. As a matter of fact, the money was the least of it as far as the fight went. I was pissed because she had been taking lessons for two months without telling me. I felt cheated on. I felt like she only bothered to tell me because she was in a financial hole. That night for the first time since we met I didn't want to screw. I didn't even want to hug. She cried herself to sleep, but I wouldn't even turn my face to her. Halfway through the night I woke up feeling lonely and out of it. I wanted to forgive her, to cuddle, but she wouldn't even let me touch her. And it had been a little like that ever since.

And that was one major difference between La Donna and the others. I was used to women chasing my ass. A lot of times a big problem was having to face their sexual desire, which felt totally unreal given the crap that would be going on between us. With La Donna I was *getting* the straight arm, not giving it. And it made me horny beyond endurance.

I started feeling myself up, hugging myself, stroking my thighs and balls. I even popped a finger up my ass and passed it under my nose. I started pulling my dick thinking of La Donna. Me banging her wasn't doing the trick. Suddenly I flashed on something that sent a baby-sized roller coaster from my brain to my fingers. Nineteen seventy. Army reserve boot camp. Three guys out on maneuvers. Pitching a tent near a stream. Me, Jerry Wexler and Willy somebody. Staying up talking about pussy, busting cherries and oral finesse. Waking up in the middle of the night. A hand pumping my cock. I pretended I was asleep and squinted my eyes without moving my head. A spot of silver, cold, going up and down on my cock. That silver moving fast like a blip on a radar screen leaving a trail of its own image. Up and down. A ring. A silver ring. That memory got me so shook I popped like Vesuvius. I never found out which guy gave me that hand job.

I cleaned myself off with the cardboard from a laundered shirt sticking out of the garbage can. Four-twenty-nine. All I had to do was look for that silver ring. All I had to do was remember the next day instead of seven years later.

I turned on my lamp, twisting my head away from the light. I touched my gut again. It was still flat. I lay there staring at the spots of buckling paint on the ceiling. Stop it. I hit the buttons on the cable box, gave the dials a quick spin, scored for twenty minutes' worth of *The Three Stooges* dubbed in Spanish, then switched to some organic-looking bozo in rimless glasses and plaid shirt sitting behind a telephone switchboard. He had long, stringy hair, a hairline that receded to his sideburns and a forehead you could have landed a 747 on. He smiled out at me like he didn't realize he was on the air. It must have been a local cable TV station. The black and white reception had that cheap shakiness like the roving eye cameras in a supermarket. A telephone number zipped in under his chest and he came to life:

"Well, it's five A.M. and I'm Rod Ramada, so Ramada's in and it's time for *Rod Ramada's Swapline*."

"Rod Ramada," I repeated out loud. His voice was soft but not rich, like a college DJ.

"Our number here at the Swapline is on your screen below me. Please limit yourself to three items you want to sell or swap — no mattresses, stocks, bonds or real estate — and give your phone number a little slower and louder than you usually would in a normal conversation, okay, people?"

The phone on his switchboard started ringing. "Here we go. First call of the night. Hello, Swapline, you're on the air."

"Hello? Am I on the air?" The voice sounded like a middle-aged lady; it was crackly and riddled with static like from a crystal radio. "Yes, Rod, I have a child's rocking horse and a GI Joe doll with removable clothes and weapons. I'm asking ten dollars for the horse and three dollars for the doll. The horse is very sturdy, both Kenny and Larry played with it when they were younger. My name is Mrs. Moskowitz and I can be reached at TU two, nine-four-one-six." Rod Ramada kept the phone pressed to his temple, his head down as though he was hearing heartbreaking news. "You know, Rod, the little one, Kenny, just entered the Bronx High School of Science, so there's really no need to keep their toys around." She made a laughing noise and Ramada chuckled weakly. "Okay then." He hung up on her as she was about to say something else.

No good. No good. You don't hang up on people like that. A little compassion and manners go a long way, and he could have talked to the old broad a little longer. He wasn't network prime time. Things like that got people on my shit list fast.

"Hello, Swapline, you're on the air."

"How are you, Rod? I have six early issues of *Crypt of Terror* in mint condition that I would like very much to trade one for one for any *Supermans* from before nineteen forty-five or two for one for any *Star-Spangled War* comics from the Korean War. Also, Rod, if you or your listeners are interested I would like to start an old comic collecting club. My name is Aaron Gold and I can be reached at five-one-six, three-three-two, four-one-four-zero. That's in Lake Success, Rod. I'm sorry to inconvenience any of your New York City–proper listeners, but I can't accept any collect calls."

"Okay then."

The kid's voice had that perfect, nervous nasal diction of a highly intelligent, totally fucked up mama's boy. Sad case. But I was a freak for comics in my day, too. I even had some *Crypt of Terrors* myself. To be honest, I felt like being in a comic book club with that creep would have been cozy in a rainy-day sort of way. Out of habit I poked my gut and it felt like Silly Putty. I shoved La Donna's pillow under mine to prop up my head more. It was nice having a queen-size to yourself.

"Hello, Swapline, you're on the air."

"Good morning, Rod, my name is Mr. Rosenbusch, and I got a wife about fifty years old with a big mouth. I would like to swap her for a young broad with a nice body."

That had me sitting up. The guy sounded like my grand-father. I wanted to laugh, but it felt eerie laughing with no one around. Ramada was chuckling, his shoulders jiggling up and down. What a gentle phony son of a bitch.

"Ha, ha, no seriously, Rod, I love my wife very much. We've been married thirty-one years and she's asleep now."

"Have you got anything to swap?"

"Hah? Ah, no, Rod, but I wanted to ask you, that last caller, Aaron Gold with the joke books? Didn't that guy sound a little too old to be playing with joke books?"

"Well, you know, different strokes for different folks." Rod adjusted his glasses.

Stroke this.

"Yeah? Okay, goodnight, Rod."

"Thank you. Hello, Swapline, you're on the air."

I turned myself around, cleared away the pillows, stuck my feet between the mattress and the headboard and did sit-ups.

"Hello, Swapline, you're on the air . . . Is anybody there?"

All that could be heard was a tentative breathing, a shud-dering, as if someone was either very cold or about to cry.

"Hello, is anybody there?" he repeated, ducking as if to look under the screen.

"So hang up, schmuck!" Oh good. I was yelling at the TV now.

"Rod? Hey . . . Hey . . ." It sounded like a kid, a girl, six-teen maybe. "I'm sorry" — she started to cry — "I'm s-so depressed, I don't . . . I don't . . ."

Later for sit-ups.

"I'm s-sorry." There was nothing after that other than some very disturbing snuffling and *huh-huh* breathing. Ramada straightened up and frowned for real.

"Hey, what's your name?"

"Nno-nno, I'm sorry." Suddenly she belted out a moan like she was going through natural childbirth. "Oh God!" she gasped. "I'm gonna kill myself! Oh, yeah I am!"

"Hey! Hey! Don't hang up! Hey!"

"No! I'm gonna! I'm gonna!"

I was on my feet. I felt as if I'd been goosed with an icicle.

"Hey look, whoever that was, don't *do* anything. Call back! *Please!* Please call back!" Ramada pinched his temples. "Oh, Jesus." The phone rang. "Yes!"

"Listen!" The voice was young male PR. "Listen, ah would like to talk to that chick that just called you, man? The one who wants to kill herself? Hey, listen, baby, don't . . . do it! Ah wanna tell you, man, mah life was more bad than anybody's, you know? Ah was on drugs? Ah got off it. Ah was in *jail?* Ah did mah time and now I'm free. Listen, sister, you don't get no breaks in life, you gotta fight for everything, but you gotta *fight,* you gotta *want* to, you know? 'Cause sometimes I think that people are their own worse enemies, but they can be their own best friend too. And life can be beautiful, baby! See what I mean? Now, you feelin' blue? You feelin' lonely? Thas okay, we all been there. You feel like doin' deep six? We all been there too. Okay, now, you need someone to talk to? Sit down have a, have coffee with? I was gonna say smoke but ah cut out cigarettes and reefer 'cause that shit'll *kill* you, man. Ah tell you what I'll do. I'll give out mah number on the air. I ain't afraid and ah believe in people. Mah name is Little Flower and mah number is two-two-two, nine-six-two-six. *Any* a you people feelin' that way you call Little Flower and I'll rap to you 'cause life . . . can . . . be . . . beautiful! And Rod?" Rod had been punctuating Little Flower's rap the whole time with sage head nods. "Rod? I think you are a beautiful cat, man."

"Thank you," he humble-ass mumbled.

"So you call me, baby, any a you people, you call me, Little Flower, two-two-two, nine-six-two-six."

I wrote down the number on the corner of the *TV Guide* cover. I couldn't help it; he made me feel positive. Maybe me, him and Aaron Gold could start a psycho comics club.

"Hey, please, whoever that girl was, if you're still listening please call back, please! People *care,* the number's right on the screen." Rod looked sincere. He was okay. I was always quick to jump down people's throats.

"Hello, Swapline."

"Hello, Rod." Some lady with a Bronx accent so thick I could have probably guessed not only what part of the Bronx but what building she was from. "If I can I would like to say something to that young lady."

"Please do."

"I just want to say, that, ah, I had a daughter who would be about your age now from your voice. We lost her two years ago, she had Lou Gehrig's disease. It was a terrible blow. I don't think my husband will ever be the same. But right up to the end, she was so full of life, full of love. She knew she was dying but you wouldn't know it from her mood, her spirits. You would have thought she was in the hospital for a cold." I sat back on the bed. "She would say, 'Ma? I don't want to see you cry.' " The lady started choking up. " 'Ma? You . . . You . . .' " She hung up. That one had me under the blankets. I hadn't called my mother in a month. I wrote down "Pistachio V-day" next to Little Flower's number. Every Valentine's Day when I was a kid I would buy the old lady a heart-shaped candy box, dump out the candy and load it up with red Zenobía pistachios. I was going to do it again this year and blow her out of her socks.

"Swapline."

"Hey, Rod, knock-knock."

"This isn't Dial-a-Joke."

"No, please . . . This is good. Just quick, knock-knock."

Unbelievable.

Ramada sighed, "Who's there?"

"Allen Freed." A chortle.

"Allen Freed who?"

"Allen freed *my* people but Lincoln freed *yours!*"

A high-pitched giggle and a click. I kicked off the blankets.

Ramada muttered something like "Idiot" and apologized to
all offended listeners. This show was the best. I ran into the
john, pissed fast and scooted back in. The heat was off and
my goosebumps gave my skin the texture of quilted Baggies.

". . . obviously on drugs, Rod, obviously just wants our attention, and I think people should *stop* calling trying to talk to
her because she's nothing but a goddamn spoiled brat and if
her parents knew how to raise children to begin with she'd be
home in bed fast asleep and everything else anybody has to
say on the subject is crap. Goodnight."

"Says fuckin' *you!*" I jumped up and shot out my jaw like
motherfuckin' Mussolini. I fucking hated scumbag people like
that. They should have their fucking lungs boiled in oil. I
punched the palm of my hand. And they rule the world, those
people. I took a long walk around the room. Ramada
shrugged. "Swapline."

"I'm a mother and I think what that lady who just called
said was cruel and stupid. Honey, if you're out there, don't
listen to that. We all wish you well and we all love you. And
Rod? I think you're doing a wonderful job and God bless you
and *she's* crap!"

"Goddamn right!" I punched my palm again and got a
terrific spasm at the base of my neck that fanned out in the
shape of an inkblot down my spine and across my shoulders.
I pretended my hands were someone else's — not La Donna's
though. Then I felt this rush, this elation, this strength like

something good was about to happen. I felt like something was rising in my mind. I was going to help that girl. The pain lifted from my neck like it had sprouted wings.

"Swapline."

"Hey . . ." It was the girl.

"All right!" I was totally wired, ready to help. I was hunched over like a shortstop after the crack of the bat. Ramada sat up straight in his chair. Me and him. "Look, I'm okay now." She sounded beat. "I'm okay now. I freaked but I'm okay now."

Still hunched over, my head cocked up, I listened to her carefully. Checked out the mood of her voice.

Rod looked flushed and exhausted with relief like a cop who just delivered a baby in the back of a cab. "You sure?" He took the words right out of my mouth.

"Yeah, yeah. I'm okay now. It's over . . ." She hung up.

Rod collapsed backward in his chair, slid his fingers under his glasses and rubbed his face. The phone rang but he ignored it. I felt like a tire with a slow leak. I collapsed on my bed. I was depressed, not high like I expected to be. The fingers of pain crawled back into my neck. Maybe the next suicide call was going to be from me. But I wouldn't be bullshitting.

"Swapline."

"Well, I'll be goddamned." Another middle-aged broad. "How's *that* for gratitude? She didn't even thank us for helping. Thank us for calling in, for worrying about her. I'm sick, just disgusted. Goodnight."

Ramada stared at his receiver in disbelief. I inflated to my feet. "You stupid . . ." My eyes were almost shut in hate, my chest felt sixty inches across. "Die!" I whispered.

"Swapline."

It was the girl again. She was sobbing. "I'm sorry! I'm sorry! I didn't mean anything! I didn't . . ."

"Hey, hey, it's okay! It's okay!"

"No no, oh God, I didn't want to . . . I didn't."

"Hey, don't hang up! Don't . . ." Click. Buzz of dial tone.

"We had her!" I shook my fists at the TV, slapped my forehead. The noise that came from my throat was not of this planet. I was fucking out there. I sat on the floor in my underwear in front of the TV and dialed the number on the screen.

Busy busy busy busy . . .

"Please call back," Ramada was pleading into the cameras. "You had one grouch; think of all the people who *care*."

I kept getting busies. I punched the phone, smacked the receiver against the wall and kept dialing.

"Swapline."

A husky male voice. "Stop sucking up to her. She's laughing at us all."

"Swapline."

"I got a pair of Nordica ski boots I want to swap or sell for cross-country skis. My name is Larry and I'm at KI seven, five-six-nine-nine."

"Swapline."

I jerked back. Ramada was talking in my ear. My heart felt like a bee in a bottle. "Hullo?" My voice came at me from the TV along with a barrage of sonic squawks and flutters.

"Move back from your set." Ramada was looking at me through the screen. I nodded okay to him and hopped backward into bed. "Hullo?" Still the interference.

"Move back more."

"Sorry." I dropped to my knees on the other side of the bed and knelt, elbows on the mattress. I felt like a radio advance man in a foxhole. "Hello, Rod?" I couldn't get used to hearing my voice come at me from the television. Ramada wasn't looking at me. All my anger drained out in my confusion. "Hey, you know people have been calling and saying she's bad news, a junkie and such. Rod, could you look at me?" Ramada slowly looked up. "That's not right, because maybe she isn't gonna kill herself but she's lonely, you know? I mean lonely enough to call up a TV swap show in the middle of the night and ask for help. It doesn't mean dick if she's *actually* gonna kill herself, okay? You know what I mean?"

"That's true," Ramada in my ear. I could hear my breathing over the TV.

"Yeah. That's all." Click. Yow. I was sweating. My hand was glued to the receiver. I gripped my chin with my thumb and forefinger. How did all those clowns sound so coherent? I started playing back every word I said.

"Swapline."

"Yeah, Rod, you know that guy that just called?" My heart stopped. "It's assholes like him that make people kill themselves. I have a right to my opinion and no moron is gonna tell me not to."

"That's true."

I went into a numb stun. I gawked at the screen, my jaw on the floor. I felt betrayed, knifed. Then I shook the shit out of my head, grabbed the phone and dialed. Three busies, then:

"Swapline."

"You tell that bitch *she's* the goddamn moron and asshole, not me. She don't give a flying fuck if that kid lives or dies. *She* probably hates *her* kids, you know what I mean?" My voice yelled at me from the box. I started butting my head into the air. "Whatever happened to human decency hah?" I slammed the phone down. My kneecaps were chattering with tension. I yawned nervously and my whole body shivered like a loose window in a windstorm.

"Swapline."

"You tell that prick to go fuck himself!"

"Swapline."

"Fuck *you*, you cancer cunt! Fuck *you!*"

That was that. The end. I vaulted over the bed and tried to turn off the TV, forgetting the remote control box on the night table. My fingers were too sweaty and I wound up pulling the plug by stomping on the wire. I walked around bumping into furniture, then I walked nose first into the edge of the bedroom door. I staggered back, whining in rage, grabbed a hammer over the bookcase and bashed the door like I was fucking Thor. My floor was littered with paint chips like confetti. I staggered into the living room. It was getting light out. "Goddam fuckin' dammit! You! You! How can . . ." I realized I was snarling and screaming at the swag lamp over the dinette table. It was six in the morning. I hadn't slept, wasn't even tired, just withered and blown away. When I went back into the bedroom, there was Little Flower's number scribbled on the *TV Guide*. The phone receiver was still sweaty. My nose hurt like a bitch. What the hell. I dialed the number. It was busy.

WEDNESDAY

The alarm went off and I jerked upright. Seven-thirty. I had snagged ninety minutes' sleep, but I didn't even remember getting into bed. I wasn't tired. La Donna's absence made the bed feel as springy as a diving board. I dropped my shorts and stretched. It was a nice, sunny blue day. I did a few toe touches, then my hundred and fifty, all the time fantasizing that La Donna was in bed watching with frustrated desire that rock-hard bitch of a washboard that some people might have confused for my stomach. No doubt about it, I felt energized, but I was pretty sure it was that speedy energy you get from being wired and sleepless. You could move like sixteen French acrobats but the minute you accidentally put your head on an even surface you would be gone for eight hours. I threw an Al Green jam on the stereo and pretended that that was me singing in some get-down club, shoulders hunched, face pinched, hittin' high whining notes and La Donna would be sitting there with some big momo from Duluth front row center. Whenever I broke up with a woman, she turned into a phantom, admiring audience for all my fantasies about myself. It could go on for years. At this

point I had an entire peanut gallery watching me. I jumped
in the shower after turning up the volume, came out, dressed
to kill, a chocolate gabardine three-piece suit over an egg-
shell shirt, a cocoa and tan silk tie, and I looked most bad,
most bad. I had a bowl of Country Morning granola, a hit of
coffee, grabbed my case and headed out the door. I left my
keys in the bedroom and when I went back in for them I noticed Little Flower's number. I felt like that was from two
light-years ago, and I couldn't even remember the headset I
wore when I saw fit to jot that down. It was a beautiful day,
and if I twisted my body out the window I could catch a
glimpse of the Hudson. It was a new day. I got one of my
mystical rushes of elation like a gigantic GOOD NEWS! headline
on a *Watchtower* flyer. Something was most definitely in the
air.

When I arrived at the diner, it was still early. Only Fat Al
sat in back, smoking a cigarette and filling out his order sheet.
Charlene sat at the counter reading the *News* and drinking
coffee. I snagged the stool next to her.

"How you doin', kid?"

"Hey, Kenny." She didn't look up as she clucked her tongue
and shook her head grimly. "Isn't that awful? Six kids."

I peeked over her shoulder. A school had burned down in
Montana.

"Mr. Cheeseburger." I motioned to George for a coffee.

"How come you not sit in back? You no like boys no
more?"

"Hey, George, you know the Greek national anthem?"

"Never leave you buddies' behind." He winked.

"Charlene, I didn't embarrass you in front of those girls
yesterday, did I?"

"Whata you mean?" She scanned the paper.

"You know, when I said that thing."

"What thing?" She licked her thumb and flipped the page.

"You know, that thing you know, 'scuse me, girls . . ."

"Oh, no no no." She stuck out her bottom lip, pouted and checked out "Moon Mullins."

"Good, because I was a little worried, because I like you and you know I didn't want, I don't want . . ." Two soda truck drivers took a booth. Charlene got up and pulled out her order pad in one motion like a gunslinger.

" 'Scuse me, Kenny."

What the hell was I doing? She was pushing fifty, probably had sixty kids and a steamfitter husband. I felt embarrassed and stupid. La Donna was out twelve hours and already I was looking for a replacement. Always, always, when in doubt, whip it out. Think, Kenny, think. I carried my coffee to our table.

"How you doing, Big Time?" I slid across from Al and slipped my case under the table.

"Hey, Kenny." He didn't look up. I peeked a look at his totals. He had down $650 in orders for the last week. I pulled in four and a half and I was scaling the heights. He must have been giving head with every order of five dollars or more. He finished up, stacked and tapped his sheets even, slipped them into his sample case and gave me a smile like "Now, where were we?"

"You're here early." He made a sweeping motion with his arms as if he were getting ready to conduct an orchestra and pressed the button on his red-tinted digital wristwatch.

"That's a nice watch, Al. How many zorts that set you back?"

"This is a two-hundred-dollar watch. Look." He twisted the face to me and tapped the light button to illuminate the dial. "Digital second hand, and digital date."

"Big fucking deal, my watch tells me about the tides so I can go clamming." I made to spit in his coffee, then grabbed his wrist. "Hey, wait, lemme see that again." I hit the button on the dial.

Al glowed. "Nice, right?"

"Today's the fourteenth?"

"If that's what it says, that's what it is."

"Cock . . . sucker." I collapsed back into the booth. "It's Valentine's Day then, right?"

"All day."

How very depressing. I could at least mail my mother those pistachios, but that one got instantly vetoed. It would only make things worse. Make me more glum. I haven't not had a girlfriend on Valentine's Day since I was thirteen.

"You forget to buy your girlfriend a present?"

"Nah." I held my head between my hands and pointed my nose at my coffee.

"Whatsamatter, Kenny?"

There was something about that question, the way he said my name, that made me want to cry, to gush out the whole thing. I'd worked with Al for three years and I didn't even know how many kids he had, what his wife looked like, what he did after work. Sales. Everything was sales.

"I dunno. I broke up with my girlfriend."

"Huh." Al frowned. "Was it serious?"

"We were living together."

"Christ." He compressed his lips and shook his head like Charlene had over the six kids in Montana.

"It was no good, man, no good." I hunched over, rested my elbows on the table and gestured with my hands held out facing each other as if to cup something. "You know what was no good? What else — the sex. The oldest story in the world. In the beginning we were like every other goddamn couple; we thought we invented it. Then, it went the way of all flesh."

Once I started talking I had a terrific yet miserable feeling of letting go, of confessing, as though the only way to alleviate the craziness, the up-and-down mixed lunacy, was to dispense it orally, like a Sabin vaccine. Sixteen years after ninth grade I was finally hip to the compulsion of the Ancient Mariner.

"You see, I, I am a very sexual person. I need, I need . . ."

I tapped his watch case absently with my fingernail. He sat there motionless as if his shirtsleeves were filled with sawdust. "I *need* to have sex, just to make me feel like I'm loved, vishtay? I need to feel like I'm being *loved*, like I'm *needed* . . ."

Al squinted and grimaced politely like I was going to ask questions later to see if he was listening.

"See, she used to have nightmares all the time. Not run-of-the-mill nightmares, but nightmares that were so bad she would jump out of bed crying, still in her sleep, mind you, and try to run away from whatever monster she had made up for herself. You follow?"

Al frowned harder and fingered his chin.

"And when that happened, I would run around to the foot of the bed and *catch* her, see? You know, like a Chinese fire drill. She'd still be dead asleep and shaking in my arms." I shook for emphasis. "But in a few minutes, she'd nod out peacefully. Then I'd carry her back into bed and she'd curl up into me for the rest of the night."

"Huh." He scratched the side of his mouth. The flab of his neck lapped over his starched collar.

"Those times were the most intense physical experiences for me. I would tell her in the morning about it, but she'd never remember. She used to say she had never had a nightmare in her life." I shrugged. "One time when I caught her she kept saying 'Morto, Morto' over and over again. I figured what the hell was that? It sounded like a Japanese monster movie, or maybe it was like *muerto,* which is Spanish for death, you know? Who knows? When I mentioned it to her in the morning she told me her grandmother's name was Marta. That's German. But she didn't remember having a nightmare. So we were back to square one."

"Huh." Al twisted his neck as if his collar were too tight, bared his teeth and moved his jaw back and forth as though he were recovering from a sock on the chin.

"But! Now comes the sick part. In the last two months, I

have been feeling so hard up, so needy around this bitch, that
I've been trying to bring on her nightmares!" I leaned forward,
lowering my voice. "I've been trying to induce her nightmares
so I could hold her when she jumped out of bed! Is that
sickness or what?" Al rested his hand on his wrist. "I would
lean over her when she was sleeping and go 'Wwwooo!
Wwwooo!'" I made a soft ghost-haunting noise. As I did,
Al slightly moved his left hand and tapped the button on his
wristwatch. His eyes dropped for an instant to check the time,
then he quickly looked up again, a nervous grin on his face,
like a bank teller sneaking a push on the silent alarm button
while staring at the hold-up man. I stopped dead. I was
furious. I was making an asshole of myself again. He didn't
give a shit. Wooo. Wooo. Who the hell was I talking to?
Fat fucking bastard. Jerry and Maurice came in then and for
the next twenty minutes I clammed up. Al sneaked nervous
glances at me every now and then but he wasn't saying dick.

"Gentlemen, today we have a little change of pace." He
poured the contents of two cardboard boxes onto the table, a
cascade of small pale green plastic vegetable brushes.

Suddenly it dawned on me why Al couldn't hear any of the
stuff I had been saying. Why he kept sneaking those nervous
glances at me. It was as clear as the nose on his face. Al
didn't fuck. The guy was seriously overweight, he was pushing
middle age, he was married — must be close to fifteen years
from what I heard. He was the first in the diner in the morning, the last to leave at night, he never talked about anything
but the business. He was a super salesman. Of course. He
never fucked anymore. And to sit there and listen to me talk
like a normal man with a healthy sexual drive must have
driven him batshit. And once the other two donkeys sat down
he shot me those glances because he knew I knew. It was right
in his eyes.

As we filed out of the diner, Al slapped me lightly on the
back.

"Don't worry about it, Kenny."

"You neither, Al."

"What's this now?" The sixtyish guy stood barechested in his doorway, grumbling to himself, holding a vegetable brush at arm's length, jerking his head back and squinting at it as if it were a newspaper.

"A vegetable brush, hah? Well, young man, I couldn't buy it, because vegetables give me the shits." He had a sharp-nosed narrow face, a gray brushlike crew cut coming down in a V between his eyes, and a heavy, well-groomed gray mustache.

"You don't have to buy it, it's free, Pop."

His thin sagging arms and chest were covered with tattoos. Down his left arm was a list of girls' names followed by dates — all from the 1930s. Over his left nipple was SWEET, over the right SOUR. A big anchor tattoo covered the inside of his right forearm.

"I've got some other things you might be interested in."

"You wouldn't have a banana brush, would you? I like bananas."

"I might. Can I come in?" I lifted my case off the floor and he stepped back.

It was a one-room studio on West Twelfth Street, almost by the piers. The place was immaculate, and even though he had plenty of furniture, its cleanliness made it seem almost barren. The yellow walls were thrown into deep shadow by drawn manila shades. There was a drab floral print convertible couch, a desk, a small coffee table topped with a dish of wrapped rock candy and the dried remains of a Rice Krispies breakfast. A black velvet wall hanging of a bullfighter in action was centered over the couch. A huge black and white television squatted in a corner, and a forties' vintage refrigerator topped with a generator stood in a kitchen alcove. The television was on without sound. The picture was rolling. A bunch of spotted bananas nested in the crotch of the antenna. I sat on his couch and peeled off my coat. The apartment was hissing with heat. I took out my hand cream, put it back, stared at my room sprays, mop head samples. I didn't know what to show him.

"Young man? I noticed you couldn't help staring at my tattoos." He sat stiffly at one end of the couch and peered at me. "My name is Harry Bloom. Is anything unusual about that?"

"Whata you mean?"

"What does the name Harry Bloom tell you about me?" He smiled and placed his extended palms, elbows rigid, on his kneecaps. I didn't know what the fuck he was talking about.

"I dunno, you're Jewish?"

He dipped his chin to his left shoulder. "That is absolutely right. So, is there anything unusual about me?"

Besides the fact that he was totally fucking insane I couldn't think of anything.

"I dunno, Pop, you got two dorks or something?"

"No." He dipped his chin again. "Use your eyes."

"You sure got a lot of tattoos."

"And?" His voice lilted, like there was more to it. He had me stumped.

"I am the only Jew you will ever see with tattoos; it's against the religion!"

"No kiddin'." Maybe he was a renegade rabbi or something.

"In nineteen twenty, when I was sixteen years old, I enlisted in the merchant marines." He spoke like he was reading his lines, telling the story for the two hundredth time. "When I was younger I lived with my holy mother on the corner of Stanton and Eldridge streets on the Lower East Side. I was trouble — in and out of jail, drove my mother insane — so when I was sixteen I up and joined the merchant marines, lied about my age. Wound up on the *Black Patsy* bound for Barcelona and Algeciras. I was the youngest A.B. on board and the only Jew. I was a galley aid. Helped serve the meals. I

took a lot of razzing about being a Jew. Got into a lot of
fights too. I was a tough son of a bitch then." He unwrapped
a rock candy and chewed it like a pretzel nugget. The muffled
crunches inside his mouth sounded as though maybe he was
eating his dentures.

"One day in May of nineteen twenty I was serving dinner
and the first mate, Blassingame, called me over for a cup of
coffee. He said, 'Hey sheeny, more coffee.' Well sir, I decided
to ignore him, but he kept it up: 'Hey Jewboy, hey sheeny!' "
he shouted across the apartment. "Well, finally I couldn't
take it anymore so I dumped the pot of coffee on his head.
Got thrown overboard for it." He chuckled. "Lucky I wasn't
keelhauled. The next week we came into Algeciras, everybody
was treating me white, we got to a whorehouse. They paid for
me, we go to another whorehouse, out drinking. Next thing
I know I'm back in my bunk. It's Sunday morning, my
head's exploding and my arm is feeling sore. I look down."
He looked at me, his eyes popping with astonishment. "There
was a big blue crucifix tattooed there! They got me drunk and
took me to a tattoo parlor." He hoisted himself back farther
on the couch. "Well, I'll tell you, I took off from my bunk like
a bat out of hell. Went right back into town, found the tattoo
parlor, woke up the artist and told him to change it into this
here anchor. At first he wouldn't do it, told me I would get
gangrene, but goddamn, I said, I would rather die from
gangrene than come home to my mother with a crucifix
tattooed on my arm. So he did it, and I was sick for damn near
three weeks with blood poisoning, but here it is. Once I got
that one I figured I would be just as damned for one tattoo
as a hundred so . . ."

"My father was in the navy." As if that would make us
relatives, or at least sea buddies.

"Navy's the most anti-Semitic a the lot." He nodded. He
looked down at his breakfast plate, got up and whisked it away
to the sink.

I started fantasizing about living in a house with the guy — father and son off Gloucester. Both of us in stocking caps and cable knits, hauling up full fishnets, sea chanties in the background, hot buttered rum, glass fishing balls, fishermen's bars, gray skies, bar wenches soft and big-eyed. Yo ho! Yo ho!

"How long you out of the merchant marine?"

"Since nineteen thirty-eight. Drove a truck for the next thirty years. Now I get a nice triple pension, Seafarers, Teamsters and Social Security." He washed his dish and returned to the center of the room wiping his hands. "Whata you got to show me?"

"I dunno, Pop, whata you need?"

He shrugged. "Not much. I could use a new deck of cards."

"I'm the wrong guy for that."

"I could use a new TV." He grimaced at the rolling picture. "Can't you fix that?"

"Knob busted off in the back. I can't get at the vertical hold."

"Shit, I'll fix it. You got pliers?"

He opened a drawer in the desk and foraged around. "Got a screwdriver."

"Give it here."

I sat lotus position behind the TV and checked out the problem. Like he said, the knob on the vertical hold was gone and the metal rod that controlled it was recessed inside the back panel out of finger reach. I stuck in the screwdriver, poked around, and a silent jolt of electricity shot up my arm.

"Ah shit!" I dropped the screwdriver and shook my hand. I felt like a jerk.

"Ah, no matter." He opened a closet and pulled out a heavy chambray shirt. "I'm goin' over to the club today anyhow."

I was pissed he wasn't concerned. I could have fried.

"I belong to the Poseidon Club, ever hear of it? I don't know why you would have, just a bunch of senile ex-sailors playin' cards. Boys got some interesting tattoos though. We got a nice library there too. You ever read Joseph Conrad? We get a concert now and then, truly can't complain. You ever hear of Oscar Brand? Serve meals there too. I almost ate myself into the hospital last Christmas. Good bunch of boys."

I got up and put my jacket on. He slipped on an old Chesterfield and opened the door.

"Who runs this club?"

"Seafarers."

"I mean they actually *plan* stuff for you? They hang around there?"

"Oh no, no. They hire people, social directors, recreation workers, librarians, good bunch a boys."

"Do they have to be sailors?"

"Oh, hell no." We walked outside together and headed downtown at a slow clip. "You know, the boys I play cards with, we added up last week, we got two hundred and forty-two years at sea among us. I'm the baby." He laughed. "Also, I'm the only Jew still, but they're good boys now."

I walked him down to his club on Varick Street. It was a white brownstone, POSEIDON CLUB etched in a bronze plaque over the cornerstone.

"Pop, whata you play?"

"Pinochle." He started climbing the steps.

"You need an extra hand?"

"G'wan." He laughed and headed inside. I went across the street to a phone booth and got the number of the club.

"Hello?"

"Yeah, hello, my name is Kenneth Becker. I'm majoring in social work and I was wondering if you have any job openings at the Poseidon Club. I've spent three years in the navy and your organization intrigues me." Intrigues me. Bad word. Wrong word.

"Aw gee, that's nice, Mr. Becker, not many people ever heard of us, but ah, see, we're a permanent staff of three here.

We do take an MSW intern every now and then from Columbia. What school you go to?"

"University of Texas. I'm just visiting."

"I see. Yeah, well, I can't really help you much, but ah, thank you for your interest and good luck to you."

"Right." Just a thought.

What happened to me next was so incredible I still don't believe it. I decided to do lofts on Spring Street for a change of pace and I wound up walking in on a sculptor who ordered fifteen wax applicator heads for a conceptual piece. Then he called up some friends who came over and went through my catalogue, raving about what a gold mine it was. One chick wanted two hundred of my free sample vegetable brushes. I felt like a right-wing capitalist sitting there in my suit. These people were my age, but they all seemed like college kids. Like we were from two different planets. I left with over two hundred dollars' worth of orders for things I had no idea how to spiel about because I had no idea what they were going to be used for. I was afraid if I pitched I would be laughed at. I asked for and got a fifty percent deposit on all the orders. I felt like a pig, or one of the over-thirty establishment slobs, because customarily I never ask for more than a twenty-five percent deposit, but their orders were so big and all those dudes were wearing ripped T-shirts and shit — I just needed the security that I wasn't going to be taken off when I delivered that coming Friday. The whole thing embarrassed me, because I wasn't a redneck, but we were just from different worlds and I had to be sure.

I think in reality it wasn't even them. I felt like everybody was from a different solar system than I. To tell the truth, I even envied their togetherness despite their slob front. They all seemed to like each other. I had a setup like that when I lived with those guys after I left home, but I couldn't hack it, I couldn't live like that. I never could hack living in a group, even when I was a kid. At Boy Scout camp I cried myself to sleep every night. Other kids were homesick, too, but I never noticed anybody as bad as me. In elementary school, whenever the teacher made us stay late for being bad, the class could count on me to cry so the teacher would freak and send us home.

Come to think of it, outside of my high school hangout days, there was only one really good time I can remember having when I wasn't either by myself or with a girlfriend — Hell Week. I was eighteen years old, a freshman at Baruch and I was invited to join a fraternity. I heard they gave good parties so I figured why not. The fraternity was in a brownstone in Chelsea. The razzing was nothing serious — except for the last week of the pledge period, the initiation week, Hell Week. Those motherfuckers ran us through the wringer like we were supposed to come out of it brain-damaged. We had to walk around campus wearing our underwear outside our pants; they made us eat every dinner at the house without silverware, usually mashed potatoes and/or spaghetti, we could talk only in duck quacks like that guy at Fantasia; every night after dinner we had to "bathe," which consisted of stripping down, marching into the communal shower room and being bombed with molasses-and-water-filled balloons — the typical juvenile hazing garbage. One night we rebelled. We staged a pledge raid. About four in the morning all twenty of us attacked the house, barraging the windows with eggs, grenading smoke bombs and stink bombs down the dorm corridors, lobbing plastic bags of flour at every brother we saw. I was one of the leaders. We all got "captured" and had to spend the rest of the night cleaning up but nobody seemed to mind — not even the brothers; as it worked out, the pledge raid was tradition.

The last night of Hell Week they told us to show up in dungarees and clothes we didn't care about. It was supposed to be the coup de grâce and we were all a little nervous, like virgins who wanted it — also most of us were stoned. Just

as the evening's festivities were about to begin a brother came
bursting in, agitated, whispering frantically to the other
brothers, and suddenly all the pledges were hustled into the
library without a clue as to what had happened. They kept us
there for an hour. We all started freaking out because we
didn't know what went down. Then one by one they called
us out at intervals of about twenty minutes. I was in there
five hours in dim light before they called my name. I was
brought down into the dining room. Under glaring lights sat
the entire brotherhood, all sixty of the boys, in a horseshoe
of tables, looking angry. I couldn't see too well as my eyes
hadn't adjusted yet to the bright light. Whatever was going
on, it didn't look good for me. The president of the house
told me that the brothers hadn't liked my attitude during Hell
Week and had decided to revoke their invitation to me to
become a brother.

"Pledge Becker, do you have anything to say in your de-
fense? Is there any reason why you think you deserve to be a
brother?"

I turned to the horseshoe of hanging judge–kissers and collected myself.

"Look, guys, this fraternity means a lot to me." I mopped
my forehead. "I don't think under any fraternity roof on any
campus in New York would I ever find" — I looked around
and smiled — "a sweeter collection of cute little asses." Dead
silence, dropping jaws. "But I'll tell you fellas" — I dropped
my pants — "nobody's got a sweeter one than mine." I bent
down, whirled around and shot everybody a fast 360-degree
moon.

That brought down the house.

I found out the next day that I was the only pledge to pin
that phony tribunal — which amazes me to this day. I heard
half my fellow pledges broke down and cried when it was their
turn in the dining room; two of them even fainted.

To this day they still talk about me and that night. In
Gamma Phi, Kenny Becker is legend.

The next day they gave the new brothers a banquet. We all had literally come through a psychological and physical hell, but we were the happiest, highest bunch of guys in the world. I never felt so tight, so close to a bunch of guys.

I totally understood why no pledge ever walked out, went berserk, threw a punch — we were comrades, we did it together; we ate shit, but we ate shit together. Of course, three months later I lost interest and dropped out of the fraternity, but that's just me, Cut-and-Run Becker.

After a two-hundred-dollar sale, door-to-door can feel a little anticlimactic, so I walked uptown to Eighth Street for an early lunch. The diner food was getting me sick. It was a bad place to hang out, very depressing.

I was standing in front of a Jap restaurant window display of raw fish platters when a short guy in a beige Cuffney cap tapped me on the arm.

" 'Scuse me, is it true Bluecastle House men suck cock?"

An unusual question. My first reaction was to wonder how he knew I was a Bluecastle House man. I stepped back more frightened than angry, not sure whether to say fuck off or what. He stood there in a full-length tweed coat, one hand in his pocket, the other shading his eyes. The collar of his coat was turned up over the nape of his neck and the top half of his face was lost in shadow under his hand and the bill of his cap. He looked like a 1920s gangster. When I jerked back, he jerked back in imitation. He was smiling and the teeth looked familiar.

"Do they, or what?" he asked.

"Donny?" I ducked down trying to see his eyes. His grin widened. "Fuckin' Donny?"

He arched back and held out his arms.

"Donny O!" I screamed, and we bear-hugged right in the middle of Eighth Street.

"Jesus Christ Almighty." I gawked at him. "How you doin', man?" I smiled for the first time in weeks.

"Good, good." Still grinning he gave me the up and down. "Yourself?"

"Fine, man, fine. Jesus, how long?"

"Twelve years, Kenny, twelve years."

"Twelve years." We bobbed our heads, checking each other out. Donny Obert and me were tight from elementary school right through high school.

"Wow, that was when?"

"Graduation, man."

"Right, right. Hey, you were supposed to call me." He pointed a finger.

"No, no, *you* were supposed to call *me*." I pointed back.

"Who gives a fuck?" He shrugged, then pinched my arm. "Hey, I heard you're doin' good."

News to me. "Okay, how 'bout you?"

"Can't complain." He shrugged, shoving his hands into his coat pockets.

"What are you doin'?" I was starting to get cold and shuffled my feet.

"I'm a, I'm a building inspector for the city."

"No shit." I didn't know if that was good or bad, but at least it didn't make me feel shitty. He pushed his cap farther up his forehead. He hadn't aged at all. Same heavy Yid toucan nose, same bad skin. He looked great — *that* was threatening.

"You married, Donny?"

"Sure. You?"

"I'm, I'm living with some chick. I dunno what's what."

"Fuckin' Kenny, I thought you'd be in Vegas now."

"For what?"

"Comedian, for what," he said, as if I'd asked him if it got cold in the winter.

"Me?" I touched my chest. "You! You were the one."

"You were the fastest man." He shook his head. "You had the baddest riffs."

That was very true. "You're lookin' great, Donny."

He nodded his head again but didn't return the compliment. I panicked. Did that mean I got older-looking? I wanted to find an excuse to show him my stomach muscles.

"Kenny, whata you doin' now?"

"Now? I was gonna do lunch; you wanna do lunch?"

"C'mere." He slipped his arm through mine and started walking me down the street. "I wanna blow your mind."

We headed down Eighth Street toward Fifth Avenue.

"So, Kenny, how's your parents?"

"They're okay. My old man retired last year. They moved upstate. You remember that house I used to go to in Shrub Oak?"

"Yeah."

"They're living there year round now. They put in central heating. My old man's gonna build a patio there in the summer. I was thinking of going up and helping him if I take off a few weeks in July. How's your old man doin'?"

Donny shrugged. "He's still with the city. He could of retired five years ago but I think he's afraid of being bored. He got me my job."

"Is he still living in the projects?"

"Nah. He moved out ten years ago. He remarried, you know that?"

"No, when?"

"About eight years ago. She died, too, two years ago. Guy's got a lot of bad luck." Donny ushered me into an Earth Shoe store.

"Just stand here and shut up." He planted me by the cash register and leaned over the counter to a young girl in a dungaree jacket and turtleneck. He took off his hat and smoothed back his hair.

"This man" — he pointed back at me — "came in here last week, bought a sixty-dollar pair of kicks. He took 'em home, they were both left shoes. He wants his money back."

The girl raised her eyebrows, then leaned around the cash register. "Do you have the shoes?"

Before I could answer Donny butted in.

"Nah, he's gonna keep the shoes because he dances like he got two left feet anyhow. He just wants the money back, okay?"

Both me and the girl cross-fired Donny with frowns.

"Look, lemme talk to the manager, okay?"

"He's having lunch now. I can't . . ."

"You tell that fat slob he don't need lunch. He should come out here and take care of business." He smiled pleasantly.

She backed away and skipped to the rear of the store.

"Whata you doin', Donny?" I thought he was going to crack the register and beat it.

"What's the problem here?" A huge man mountain lumbered from behind a curtain and my first impulse was to run like hell. "Who's the joker?"

I took a second look and almost fell on my ass. "Candy!"

He squinted at me, then his eyes opened like somebody had goosed him from behind.

"Kenny? Holy God, Kenny?" I held out my two palms for a double slap and Candy grabbed my wrists, laughing in my face. His puss was so flabby his chin looked like a dimple. I was glad he'd gotten fatter.

Donny was grinning, leaning his elbow on the counter. When Candy noticed him, he shook his head in mock reproach.

"I shoulda known it was you." He let go of my wrists and slapped palms with Donny.

"Fuckin' Kenny." Candy ran his fingertips along the inside of my suit lapel. "Whata you now, a bank tycoon? You look like a million dollars!"

I shrugged modestly. "Salesman. This your place?"

"Yeah, I got a franchise. C'mon in back." He slapped a hand on each of our shoulders and guided us to the storeroom. He was too big to stand between us, so he trailed slightly behind. The top of my head came up to his chin and I had a good four inches on Donny.

"When you grow that?" I nodded up at his mustache. He had the same baby face I remembered and his black Zapata 'stache looked phony, as if it were glued on.

"Aw, Christ, I had this so long I don't even know it's there anymore."

We entered a ten-by-ten room, the walls lined with hundreds of pale green shoe boxes. There was a dinky overhead light which reflected the sickly green and made me feel like I was under water. Candy seemed to balloon even larger in contrast to the small area. In one corner was a small desk covered with ledger books and half a cream cheese and white bread sandwich was lying on a crumpled sheet of wax paper next to a sky blue coffee container decorated with Greek columns. Candy sat in an old desk chair by his lunch. The chair had a ball-bearing pivot, and when he leaned back in it clasping his fingers behind his head, I was afraid he might tip and we'd smother in Earth Shoes. There were no other chairs in the room. Donny leaned against a ten-foot-high ladder and I leaned against a shoe-lined wall. It was like lounging with two people in a phone booth. Candy beamed at us, then suddenly realizing we had no place to sit, he jerked forward like he was doing a sloppy sit-up.

"It's cool, Candy." Donny put out a placating arm.

"Nah, I'll bring chairs!"

"Fuck it, Candy."

"You sure?"

"It's cool."

"You want half a sandwich?" He offered his lunch to me. I declined.

"Donny?" Donny declined.

Twelve years had passed. I felt the same, but as I glanced at Candy I knew the road downhill was only a matter of time.

"How's it hangin', Candyman." I winked. He must have gained at least a hundred pounds since I last saw him. He looked like he had a pillow stuffed in his shirt.

"Kenny, it's a good life," he said soberly. "I truly have nothing to complain about, right, Donny?"

Donny raised his hands in submission and skimmed the shoe boxes to his right with his fingernail. "Candy's doin' good." He nodded. There was a touch of resentment in Donny's tone.

"You married, Candy?"

"Oh yeah! You know who I married? Remember Estelle Spatz?" I flashed on a skinny, plain, bright girl in ninth-grade Spanish.

"No shit, Candyman."

"No shit, Kenny, I got three kids." He held up three eggroll-sized fingers. "Just had one six months ago, the ugliest thing you ever seen." He gave his patented high-pitched Candyman laugh, and it was 1965 all over again. I felt the impulse to crack them up, put them on the floor, but the impulse was so strong it jammed my brain and nothing flowed.

"Kids." I shook my head in shock. "Marron. I can't even handle a dog." It stunned me. I was supposed to have kids now.

"Yeah? You did okay with Lisa Fuchs." He hit his laugh button again and this time Donny joined in. I figured what the hell and pitched in a few chuckles myself, even though she wasn't that bad.

"You don't have kids, do you, Donny?" Somehow it had never entered my mind that he would.

Donny drew his chin into his neck, recoiling like "Who me?"

"You married, Kenny?" Candy was still smiling. He wiped his eyes with his middle finger and took a sip of coffee.

"Me? Nah.' I thought of La Donna's voice and drooped against the shoe boxes on the wall.

"Fuckin' projects, Christ." Candy stared off into space, still smiling, biting his lip.

"Where you live now, Candy?"

"The Island. Bought a house in Cedarhurst. You know the Five Towns area?"

"Five Towns, huh? That's pretty ritzy." I was impressed. I wished he would gain about fifty more pounds and die. Candy shrugged with affected modesty.

"How 'bout you, Donny? Where you live?"

"Take a guess." Donny clasped his hands behind his back and bounced absently against the ladder.

"Queens?"

"Queens! Get fucked! I live right here in the Village, man! I been livin' there since nineteen sixty-nine. You remember, I went to NYU. I dropped out after six months but I stayed in the area. Queens!" He turned his head away in disgust.

"Where you live, Kenny?" Candy wolfed down the rest of his sandwich.

"He lives in fuckin' Queens." Donny spat.

"I gotta crib on the Upper West Side. Nice."

We were all silent for a moment. I wondered about Candy's heart, if he was having trouble with it. At least he wasn't smoking.

"So, Donny, you really live in the Village?"

"Shit, yeah."

"That's my territory. Where you live?"

"You know Carmine Street?"

"What number?"

"Two forty-three."

"Red brick, modern, fucked-up front door buzzer," I rattled off.

"You got it." He ducked his head in acknowledgment.

"Huh! You know, in a way I'm not surprised you live in the Village, Donny, you know?"

"Whata you mean?"

"You were always into that fuckin', ah, ah, I dunno, coun-
terculture shit, remember? Hootenannies, schvugs. You used
to read the *Voice* back then too. You and your main man
there, Maynard."

Donny smiled gently, nodding his head.

"Maynard." Candy laughed low. "Remember fuckin' Maynard? Maynard G. Krebs. Beatnick Maynard." Maynard had
been Donny's best friend. His real name was Larry Epstein
but everybody called him Maynard after the character on
Dobie Gillis because he wore a beret, grew a goatee and
smoked reefer.

"Fuckin' Maynard," Candy repeated. "Hey-y Mis-ter Tam-
bo-reene Man," Candy sang and played the bongos on the
insides of his pillow-sized thighs. I noticed he was wearing
Hush Puppies, not Earth Shoes. Five Towns.

"What ever happened to him?" I asked Donny.

Donny shrugged. "Last I heard he went to North Africa."

"Aw, he's been back for years." Candy waved in dismissal.
"You know what he's doin' now? Maynard's a fuckin' travel
agent. He set up his own business with his brother in the
Bronx, this joint called On the Road up on Two hundred
thirty-third Street. You know that plane that crashed last
month going to Vegas? He booked the entire plane. That
was a charter junket coming out of some lodge or other in
the Bronx." Candy exploded with giggles. I started to join
in but I noticed Donny wasn't even smiling. He was staring
down at the floor.

"Hey, what happened to the other guys?" I wanted to
change the subject.

"Fuck the other guys. What happened to you?" Candy
asked. "Where *you* been since high school?"

"Me? I went to Baruch for business. I got fucked up the
ass. My senior year I got engaged to this girl there. Her
father owned Meyer Brother stationers. You know that chain?
The guy was gonna break me in at the top. He loved my ass

'cause I told him I lived on a kibbutz for a year. Anyway, I got cocky 'cause I thought I had it in the bag so I dropped out of school with six months to go. He hears this, gets pissed at my disrespect for education and makes his daughter break it off." I shrugged. "Fuck it. I didn't really love her anyway. I was a kid, you know? But I never went back to school. After that I did some income tax work with my uncle. Then I did a gig in the reserves and, ah, the last two, three years, I've been working for Bluecastle Housewares, which I'll tell you the truth is ideal for me because" — I counted on my fingers — "I got no boss, I make my own hours and I meet people. My income is directly proportionate to my, my, ah, ability to communicate." I tried to come off as sober and mature as possible. What a steaming pile of horseshit, though. I felt ashamed of myself. I even cut in half the number of years I had been doing door-to-door.

"What about you, Candy? You went to Bronx, right?"

"Yeah, Bronx Community. I quit. I got drafted, I was in Nam for a year behind a desk. I got caught selling government office supplies." He laughed and his chins jiggled. "Christ, did I get into a jam."

"You look like you're into a little more than *jam*, my friend." Donny smirked.

"Hey, fuck you, I'm on a diet." Candy sucked in his gut. Donny imitated Candy inhaling and cracked up.

"Yeah? I'll still run *your* ass into the ground."

"You can probably *squash* it into the ground," I blurted.

Donny jerked with laughter. "Fuckin' Candyman." Donny snorted. "Fuckin' Candyman, he, he was any bigger he'd have his own Zip Code." We both cracked up and staggered toward each other for a double palm slap.

"Oh no! Oh no!" Candy smiled, waving his finger between me and Donny. "I ain't gettin' caught in no crossfire between *you* two jokers!"

When Candy said that I started twitching like an electrified frog. "Hey Candy, Donny! Donny! Yesterday Candy went down to Port Authority; two families with suitcases asked him what time's he leaving for Saratoga!" Donny and I collapsed in each other's arms. I couldn't breathe. I felt like I was drowning in riff, smothering in riff. They were starting to come so fast and furious I couldn't see straight. But it felt right, comfortable, like a car that rattled until the speedometer hit 80, then it purred like a Caddy. It felt like *me*. And it felt like Donny. We were joker soul brothers. Always had been.

I was laughing so hard I was drooling. After a moment I went to turn away, but Donny put his arm around my shoulder and squeezed me hard. He turned me toward Candy, slapped his arm around my neck and pinched my cheek.

"He was the fuckin' funniest, wasn't he, Candy?" Candy sat there, his fingers clasped across his gut, smiling like a benevolent Sidney Greenstreet.

"Kenny the Riffer," Candy glowed.

I hugged Donny back. No wonder I was so goddamn lonely. Friends, man. I didn't have any fucking friends. And friends were the bottom line.

"No kiddin', Candy, you should watch it with fats and shit." I stood arm in arm with Donny like Tweedledum and Tweedledee. I felt better, less jealous. I wished he would shed three tons just on my good vibes alone.

"Hey, no, I am! I am! Vitamins, Tab and yogurt! Vitamins, Tab and yogurt! That's all I eat all fuckin' day. I lost six pounds this month!"

"Oh, yeah?" Every few seconds a ripple of laughter would lightly spasm my gut and pass through my lips in a weak bleat. "What . . . what was that cream cheese sandwich there?" I nodded toward the now empty wax paper and wiped my eyes.

"What, that?" Candy waved. "That wasn't shit."

"Hey." Donny detached himself from our embrace. "Speakin' a food, anybody up for some lunch?"

"Lunch is on me." Candy got to his feet.

"Anybody like Japanese food?" I asked.

Donny and Candy both made to puke.

"God, remember when we all used to go to Lucky's for lunch?" Donny mused.

"You wanna go there now?"

"How we gonna get up there?"

"I got wheels." Candy tucked in his shirt. "You guys got time?"

"I do." Donny shrugged.

I was going to pass but then remembered I had already scored two yards that day. "Me too."

"Well, then, let's go!" Candy held out both palms. And Donny and I slapped simultaneously.

Friends, man. Fucking friends.

Candy split to get his car while Donny and I hung out in front of the store waiting for him.

One of the last times anything felt consistently right for me was with these guys almost half a lifetime ago. Except for a few brief periods I felt as though I had been in a bad mood since high school graduation, but these were the guys and that's when it was happening for me . . . Maybe the answer was them. The boys. Even the old merchant marine was hip to that, to the power and need for the boys.

"Damn Candyman, he better watch his heart, huh?" I turned up my collar.

"I think he got turned down for life insurance, or they charged him something outrageous."

"You been seeing him around, Donny?" I felt slightly jealous.

Donny shrugged. "Now and then, you know, I drop in sometimes when I'm in the neighborhood, nothin', ah, nothin' to speak of."

Candy pulled up to the curb in a long battleship gray Continental, honking the horn and waving us forward.

"That's *his*?" I moved toward the car hunched over and

frowning in awe. I tossed my case in the rear and sat in the death seat. Donny climbed in the back. The door closed with a heavily cushioned thud.

"Mr. Candy, awright!" I extended my palm. The seats were charcoal gray velveteen. Candy wore deep green racing sunglasses.

"What you picture me for, a VW?" Candy laughed, twisted his head to traffic and pulled out onto Eighth Street. He punched in an FM station and the car turned into Carnegie Hall. He had more speakers than stations.

"Hey, this is nice, Candy. What year?" He turned the volume down.

"Seventy-five?" He drove slowly, with his wrist on top of the wheel, his banana fingers dangling almost to the steering column. "I got a deal on it from my father-in-law, Estelle's old man. He's a mechanic for the Police Department. This car was impounded three years ago. The guy who owned it was pushing smack. Some Central Park West Jew. Estelle's old man had to take it apart looking for dope, you know, like in *The French Connection*."

"Did he find anything?"

"Well, I'll tell you, *my* theory is he did but he didn't tell the cops. I think he sold the dope himself because two months later they moved out to Forest Hills, but what the hell do I know, right?" Candy grinned into his rearview mirror to catch Donny's eye. The car hummed as we headed up Sixth Avenue.

"There's a bar in the back."

"A what?" I turned around, knees on the seat, and hung over the backrest. Sure enough, there were two gray padded velveteen cabinet doors built into the back of the front seat. Inside were two glasses, a small copper ice bucket, but no booze. I looked up at Donny. He was leaning back, legs crossed, arms flung out along the rear window ledge. He gave me raised eyebrows but didn't say anything. I couldn't tell if he was pulling out on us. Sometimes Donny would do that, be into things with the guys then all of sudden go off on his own planet, and as they say, when you get older you don't change, you intensify.

"So that's funny about Maynard, huh?" Candy turned onto the West Side Highway.

"What happened to everybody else?" My brain filled with more faces than a yearbook.

"You remember Brazil? He lives near me out near Malverne. He's got a big liquor store in a shopping center around Green Acres. Doing very well. He married an Irish girl, got a daughter now, and Bobby Bizarro? You know, Bobby Gallo? He's drivin' a cab, living out in Queens; *he's* married, got two kids, boys. And Terry Fischer? Oh, this'll blow you away. Terry Fischer runs an aquarium store on Staten Island. And! And! He married a yom."

"Terry did?" It wasn't that big a deal to me. "He was dark anyway."

Candy turned to me, slightly disappointed at my lack of amazement. Donny was staring out the window, chewing his thumb. I leaned my head back and cast my eyes in his approximate direction. "Everything okay back there, Mr. Donny?"

"I'm good, I'm good," he said without gusto.

"Oh, and Andy Cady? Andy and Frankie Fahey are somewhere down in Florida now. They got some business going with trailers, boats, I don't know. Neither of them are married or got kids last I heard. Oh, and Richie Perry? Richie married Jeanette Pella; he's teaching English in Yonkers; they got a boy and a girl. As a matter of fact, Kenny" — Candy was beginning to sound a little matronly to me — "I'm pretty sure Jeanette's an *Avon* lady now that I think of it." He smiled at me and if there had been enough headroom in the car I would have stood up and kicked his teeth in.

"Oh yeah?" I said flatly. My brains were cooking. He just made me feel like a pile of shit. I felt like saying "Oh yeah?

As a matter of fact, Candy, I know some nigger who sells stolen Earth Shoes from the back of his station wagon." Avon lady. We drove in silence for about ten minutes. Candy made me feel like I was doing everything wrong. Kids, Continentals — I didn't have shit. Donny wasn't saying dick either. I bet he had less than me.

"How do you know all this shit, Candy? Kids and jobs and all."

Candy seemed oblivious to the vibes. He made a face and shrugged. "My mother knows. She keeps tabs. I been to all the christenings and the circumcisions. Kids, man." He smacked his lips like he wanted some for lunch. "Kids is what's happening."

When we hit the Bronx, I got excited and wanted to start a memory lane riff, but I was also still sulking from listening to the Queen Bee. I shot another glance at Donny. He had left the planet three days ago.

"Hey! Mosholu Parkway!" Candy extended his palm for a slap and I halfheartedly complied. The car purred on at Candy's leisurely pace past De Witt Clinton High School, well-kept lawns and thirties-style blond brick apartment buildings.

"You know, this place still looks good?" Candy nodded, then turned to me and clapped a bear paw on my knee. "So how you doin', Kenny, you doin' okay? Financially?"

"Oh yeah, oh yeah, and you?"

Candy raised an eyebrow and bit his lip as if trying to remember a date, his hand still on my knee. "Well, I would, at this point in my life, describe myself as, slight-ly higher than middle middle class."

"Me too." Fuck you.

"You know, I just bought into a parking lot out in River-head out in Suffolk. I don't have the pension security of a city job like *this* cocksucker back here." Candy laughed and tossed a few chins back to Donny, then threw his arm over the seat to slap Donny's knee. Donny brought his knees together to avoid Candy's swipe but ignored Candy otherwise.

Maybe Candy was getting back at us for goofing on his fatness in that goldfish bowl on Eighth Street.

"Hey, Candy." I winked at Donny. "Maynard got any kids?"

"Not that I know of, but his brother Elliot? He got twins." Donny and I cracked up and I held out my palm over the seat for a slap. Candy smiled slightly but couldn't take his eyes off the road. "What's so funny?" He laughed uneasily. "It's true, man, he got twins."

I started howling, clasping my hands between my knees, jerking my head back and forth.

Donny was laughing so hard he bumped his head on the window. I leaned over the seat, opened Candy's bar, panto-mimed pouring booze into one of the glasses and splashing it over Donny. Donny exploded, pointed to the bar tears rolling down his cheeks and jumped back in his seat like his neck had been yanked. I collapsed flat over the back of my seat like wet wash. I was so tired from laughing I could only moan. Every time I moaned, Donny erupted into high-pitched, staccato giggles.

"Nice fuck, fuckin' c-car, Candy." Donny held his stomach, and I started howling all over, nodding yes! yes! yes! and pounding his palm with a million slaps. Joker soul brothers. We could have torn Candy to shreds with our fingernails. Our rage.

"Aw, you guys are nuts." Candy raised the volume on the radio.

"Hey, Lucky! Remember us?" Candy beamed down at the little German Jew luncheonette owner in T-shirt and apron who had been dishing out lime rickeys since the year one. He looked up at us, squinting behind his Dr. Cyclops glasses.

"Yeah, yeah, I remember you," he said defensively like we were bill collectors. The place was deserted. It looked identi-cal to when we were there as kids — high ceiling, gloomy, messy, greasy — and I was hit with a great feeling of "so what." As a matter of fact, I didn't even want to eat there because the place was such a pit. I didn't want to ruin my stomach for the sake of a sentimental journey. Donny thumbed through the *Post,* by the cash register. He looked like he couldn't have cared less either. Only Candy was excited, twisting his head this way and that, his mouth gaping in delight. Actually, maybe it was just the idea that we were going to eat soon that was turning him on.

We sat on stools across from the grill, under aging fallacious paintings of juicy burgers and chilled Cokes. In one picture, against a faded lime green background, two blond kiddies, the boy crew cut, the girl in short yellow curls, avidly licked their chops for an orange Creamsicle as Mom and Dad in pearls and pipe benignly smiled on. "It's nutritious too!" was scripted underneath.

"Remember that picture?" Candy chuckled.

"They should take out the Creamsicle and put in a prick," said Donny.

Lucky stood before us wiping his hands on a towel. His almost bald noggin was topped with a wispy gray fuzz, and his mouth was locked open a good two inches, had been since the fifties.

"Lucky, can I get a spinach salad?" I asked, scanning the food paintings.

"A *what?*" Lucky scowled.

"A spinach salad!" Donny turned to Candy hand to mouth then across the counter to me.

"Hey, Kenny, where do you think you are, Soho?" He slapped palms with Candy and I was afraid the alliances were going to shift.

"Okay, gimme some lettuce and tomatoes."

"Guy eats like Bugs Bunny," Candy snorted. No comment.

"I'll have a ham sandwich, Lucky." Candy pressed his palms together.

"Yeah, make sure you give it to him on Melba toast." I grabbed a fistful of love rungs.

"And a Coke," Candy barked, trying to disengage my claw with his elbow while twisting his hip away from me.

"Make it a Tab!" I corrected, letting go.

"Coke for me," said Donny.

Lucky brought me a lettuce and tomato on white bread and Candy got a ham on white toast.

After eating we ambled over to the cash register. Candy whipped out a five to pay for everybody and neither Donny nor I protested.

"Hey!" Candy spied a box of rubber balls. "And *now!*" He bounced. "You skinny dudes think you're so bad? C'mon." Candy marched us across the street into the housing projects playground. As we hit the sidewalk, an el train overhead drowned the street with its grinding roar. For eighteen years that sound was as unnoticeable to me as my heartbeat. It was unseasonably warm for February, almost fifty degrees, and the basketball and handball courts were lightly sprinkled with people.

"Whew." Donny gazed around him, hands on hips. "This was the place, remember?" We stood in the middle of four basketball courts separated from four handball courts by a high link fence. Beyond another high link fence were a sandbox, benches, a seesaw, a sliding pond, monkey bars, a wading pool, and a tiny parks department supply cottage, all fenced in, all metal and concrete, all surrounded by red brick city housing. The basketball court boundaries, key and foul lines had been freshly painted over in bright yellow on the gray-black macadam.

"C'mon." Candy violently bounced his rubber ball. "I'll take on both of you." He headed for the handball courts, and we trailed behind, slightly blown out like soldiers returning home from a three-day gig at Gettysburg.

Three of the four handball courts were occupied, and Candy started throwing the ball against the wall of the empty court. All four walls were tattooed with massive explosions of spray-painted graffiti. A thick jungle of purples, reds and blacks, numbers and names. Every time Candy threw the pink ball it seemed to get swallowed up in the artwork and bounced back like it was being spit out by the color scheme.

"Look what those bastards did." Candy grimaced, nodding toward the walls. Donny kept walking in circles as if he were stunned.

"Listen, Candy, I'm gonna pass on the game. Why don't you play Donny solo," I said apologetically.

"Aw, c'mon," Candy pleaded like a ten-year-old.

"Nah, really, Candy." I raised my hands in submission. "I rip this suit, I go to work in a barrel, no kiddin'."

"Yeah, me too," Donny said.

"No, Donny, play him, play him." I motioned Donny toward the court. "I'll keep score."

"C'mon, Donny, let's go, eleven points." Candy tossed the ball against the wall. Donny took off his coat and hung it on a piece of wire protruding from the fence. He effortlessly touched his toes, then did back stretch exercises. He was as thin and wiry as he had been at fifteen. And the bastard probably never did a sit-up in his life. I walked over to a low foot-high concrete ledge against the fence by the first court and sat my ass down. The handball court walls were backed by the rear wall of a factory and I recalled the hundreds of balls I'd lost over that factory roof. On the court nearest to me a young black mother played paddleball by herself. She had an enormous dungareed butt, an expression on her face like a stoned cow as she lethargically swished her paddle in the air, missing the hard black ball nine times out of ten, walking after it each time, her head jiggling on her shoulders. Her baby half-stood, half-dangled, suspended by his crotch in a walker parked about five feet away from me on the sidelines. The kid was listlessly chewing on the saliva-soaked cookie in his tiny hands. He kept twisting his head to me, but I had nothing to say. Maybe I should have adopted him and invited Candy to the circumcision.

On the farthest court from me, three Puerto Rican teen-agers played paddleball — two, short twitchy butted girls in hip-high pea-coats against a skinny kid in a brimmed porkpie hat and a premature mustache. The kid was showing off, hitting the ball behind his back, between his legs, smacking one girl on the ass with his paddle, adjusting, readjusting his hat. The girls were laughing, stiff-arming their swings, in-nuendoing to each other with their eyes. He had a hard-on. Anytime the girls scored a point he groaned or slapped his forehead or said, "Ah must be gettin' old!" Once in a while he slammed a killer just so they would know he was a layback but active volcano.

Candy moved his weight well. They both had good coordi-nation, but it had been a long time, and they played like shit.

By the basketball courts, on *our* bench, three identically dressed Puerto Rican guys sat on the top slat, backs against the fence, hands in coat pockets, feet on the seat slats. Against the far mesh wall a kid also in a porkpie leaned into his girl-friend, whose back was curved into the fence. His hands were in his pockets and he supported himself by resting his long thigh in her crotch.

That was us. All of it. All of it. Me and Sandy Talla against the fence. Me and Suzie and Dawn and Ronnie play-ing handball. Me and Donny and Brazil shooting hoops. Me and the boys bullshitting on the bench listening to WMCA, WABC, WINS.

I felt a rush of panic. For a second I thought I had lost my sample case. Then I remembered it was in Candy's car. Out-side the playground two sixteen-year-old blond Irish girls walked by in pea coats and I got hit with a sweetness, a sweet horniness, and I remembered what it was like to thrill to a tongue in my mouth, a tit in my hand, perfume in my nose. The delicious gut-wrenching agony of the time in my life when titty was king and I never even knew girls *had* cunts. Another el train roared overhead, bringing back the millions of el trains that had roared past my window and I started crying.

Nothing heavy. Just misty sadness. It was over. It had been the best and now it was over and nothing had ever felt as good. We had peaked back then, and all we'd been doing since was dying.

I heard Candy groan as though he just got skewered with a sword. I glanced up in time to see the pink ball soar over the factory roof. End of the game. They slowly staggered over to me, breathing heavily. Donny looked miserable. Candy's chest was heaving like a bellows and perspiration dripped steadily off his nose. I wasn't sure if it showed that I had been crying. If any of us had had anything *real* going on in our lives we never would have come back.

"Gentlemen? We are very lost people."

Donny caught my eye for a second, then looked away. Candy stared at me, still wheezing. Raising his hand above his head, he wiped the sweat off his face with his shoulder. "Speak for yourself, Kenny."

"Yeah, Candy? Whata *you* got?"

"Kids. I got kids, Kenny, and they're the best." He lightly slapped Donny on the chest with the back of his hand while looking at me. "C'mon, I'll blow you guys to Tabs."

After the drinks Candy wanted to tool around the Bronx, go over to the high school, the park and maybe even drop in on Maynard at On the Road, but me and Donny just wanted to go home so he drove back to Manhattan.

It was only two-thirty but I couldn't psych myself for any more selling that day, so I talked Candy into dropping me off at the Seventy-ninth Street exit on the West Side Highway. As I was getting out of the car the three of us made big promises to get together, exchanging phone numbers and addresses, but all I could think about doing was getting the hell away from Candy. His car smelled like baby shit.

*

The *Post* was rolled between the doorknob and the jamb and my first thought was that La Donna was out. Then I remembered how "out" she really was and I felt slammed again by that strange mixture of pain and relief.

I hung up my suit, slipped on dungarees and did my hundred and fifty. Then I took the *Post* into the bedroom, turned on afternoon cartoons and lay down. It was three o'clock. Automatically I skipped from the movie section to comics to sports. I only liked two or three comic strips and had the most passing of passing interests in sports — mainly if the team was from New York it was nice if it won — but movies were my meat. I checked the four or five local movies on the Upper West Side. Nothing registered and I wound up watching old Popeye and Mighty Mouse cartoons. Every time La Donna popped into my mind I raised the volume on the cartoons a little higher.

Three books were stacked on my night table: *Tropic of Capricorn*, *Franny and Zooey* and *Prize American Short Stories*. I read a page in each. They all sucked, all were boring. Books were boring. I'd make some goddamn teacher. Maybe I could get a schedule that would let me teach only when I was in a good mood.

Wait up. Hang in there, Kenny. You're just out of shape. The thought struck me that now that she was gone I could get back into reading. Now that she was gone. It sounded to me like, "Now that I'm unemployed." It might take some time to learn how to relax again, that's all.

At four o'clock I fell out. When I woke up it was five twenty-three on the digital. My mouth felt dehydrated. I was having a nightmare about two Japanese lovers. A Japanese lady took her lover down to a spot on a beach in Japan where years before her husband, a sea captain, had gone down with his ship. The two Japs fuck and then fall asleep in the sand. A skeleton rises from the sea, floats up the beach, sticks out his tailbone over the sleepers and pantomimes spreading his asscheeks. They start strangling in some disgusting odor emanating from his nonexistent asshole. The skeleton is grinning like a bitch.

I jumped out of bed in a panic. I realized I'd left my sample case in Candy's car. Relax. Big deal. I'll get it tomorrow. I slumped down on the side of the bed. And what if I never saw that case again? What would I do? I got up and rifled through the Yellow Pages in the living room.

There must be fifty colleges listed in New York City. I started writing down some of the names when suddenly I felt I had to get out of the house fast. I was itchy and antsy.

The phone rang, cutting off my escape.

"Hello."

"Hello, does Kenny Becker still live at this number?"

A big down. I didn't need this. "Hi, Pop."

"Kenny? Is that you? Jeez, I forgot what your voice sounded like."

"Funny."

"How come you don't call, yah big stiff?"

"I called you last month!"

"Last month! What are we, third cousins?"

"C'mon, don't break my back." I wanted to say, "What do you want?" but I was afraid to be that short with him.

"Listen buddy, can, uh, can you do me a favor?" Call your mother.

"What kind of favor?"

"Your old lady hasn't heard from you in a while, and, ah, she's kind of hurt. She's in the other room. She don't know I'm on the phone. Lemme hang up, and you give her a call now."

"I'll call her later, okay?" Like next February.

"Call her now." That came out slightly like a no-nonsense order and my gut jerked.

"I'll call her later, Pop."

A defeated, disgusted hiss.

"Thanks a lot."

"C'mon, Pop, I'll call her later."

"Thank you very much." He hung up.

I knew there was no way I could call her later. I felt that whatever time existed between my old man's directive and the phone call was limbo death time.

I held out for ten minutes before I dialed. The line was busy. Ten minutes later, still busy. A half-hour later, still busy. I became obsessed. I couldn't concentrate on anything but getting through. I tried reading again. I tried TV. After an hour I wigged and called the operator, checked with verification. They were talking. Another half-hour and I had the operator break in with a life-and-death interruption.

"Ma!"

"Kenny, are you okay?"

"Jesus Christ! You tell me to call, then the goddamn phone's busy for an hour and a half!" I was sweating.

"Kenny, what are you talking about, who told you to call? *I* didn't tell you to call."

"Christ." I felt like an asshole — a child.

"So how are you?"

"Fine," I muttered.

Silence. "And happy Valentine's Day to you, too, my son."

Twenty minutes later I managed to get off the phone feeling like I had just been handed the receipt for the Brooklyn Bridge.

I turned on some old Motown albums to wash my face by and lost myself in heavy fantasies about being a dancing, tuxedoed Temptation. Once again La Donna was front row center chewing her fingernails down to the wrist with frustration and regret.

I went out food shopping on Broadway. Juice, Swiss cheese, chicken, chuck steak, eggs, vegetables. No candy, no cookies, no potatoes, no Pringles, no crap. In line I checked everybody else's shopping carts with a feeling of superiority. It was amazing how ignorant and lazy women were about what poi-

sons they shoved down their families' throats. Their goddamn
shopping carts should be rammed down their gullets. I caught
myself grinding my teeth. When I got home it was almost six
and I was starving. I threw the chuck steak on the broiler,
boiled canned spinach, made a nice lettuce, tomato and cucumber salad, poured a big, frosty Tab, put the whole thing on
a stack table and carried it into the bedroom. I loved to
watch TV while I ate. The only thing on other than the news,
which I never watched, was *I Dream of Jeannie*. I'd forgotten
the silverware and the salt and brought them in. I forgot a
napkin and I had to pee. It was okay; the longer I delayed
eating, the better the food would taste when I finally got it
down.

Halfway through the steak I felt full but I kept eating.
Jeannie's gushy diction made me nauseated. The show, like
everything else on TV, was geared for mental defectives. At
one point near the end of the show, Jeannie grabbed Tony's
arm and said, "Oh, master, I'm *so* glad you liked it!" and
started crying with joy. That gave me a lump in my throat and
my eyes teared as if I were ready to cry along with her. My
reaction felt totally out of my control and it alarmed me as
much as if I had peed in bed.

I turned off the set. Later for that. Screw TV. And screw
me. I was thirty years old, and I might be dying, but I was
still mobile. The playground didn't do it anymore, but there
had to be other things, other passions — the death I was feeling that afternoon was reversible and optional. Romance
wasn't the answer and television wasn't the answer and talking to myself wasn't the answer. I needed new scenes and new
people. Not new girlfriends, just new friends. I thought of
that dynamite feeling I'd had at the shoe store. Friends to
bring me out. Help me out. Try with a little help from my
friends. Go back to college and make new friends.

I had to make me a new world. A new life. Call somebody
up. Find a new friend. Who did I know? Maurice? Fat
Al? Candy? Donny? The old merchant marine? No, new

meat for the new me. Who . . . Jackie di Paris. No. Yes. No. Yes, and why not?

Information had no Jackie di Paris. Then I recalled that that wasn't his real name. John di Something. Di Maris. Marco. John di Marco.

"John?"

"Who's this?"

This is your new goddamn friend. "This is Kenny Becker. I was in line with you at Fantasia Monday. The Bluecastle Housewares guy."

"Oh yeah, yeah, yeah, the guy from Burke Avenue."

"Right."

"What can I do for you?"

"Nothing, I was just wondering how that turned out there."

"You didn't see it?"

"Nah, I was in the bar area the whole time."

"It went good, it went good. I made the finals, but ah, I ah, I don't think I'm gonna go back. I didn't like the house. How'd you get my number?"

"Information. Listen, ah, my old lady went home to see her people for a few days and I was thinking about going to a movie or something. I dunno, you feel, you doing anything? I'm talking to the fucking walls here." That was real hard.

"Whata you mean?" He sounded suspicious.

"I don't mean nothin'. I mean you feel like hangin' out."

"A movie?"

No, I wanna suck your cock, you paranoid asshole. "Yeah, you know."

"Ah, I got something goin' here about midnight."

"Well, you know, something about eight, nine, something fast."

"Yeah, I guess so, awright." No enthusiasm whatsoever. I could almost sense him shrugging over the phone.

"You wanna meet at eight o'clock? Forty-second and Broadway? There's about a million movies down there."

"I gotta be back by midnight."

"No problem. Eight o'clock?"

"Yeah."

The minute I hung up I felt like a jerk. He was the craziest angriest bastard I ever met. I could sure pick 'em. Movies seemed a good idea, but not with him.

I washed my dishes and scanned the *Post*. The Carnegie Cinema had *Beach Red* and *The Loves of Isadora*. I remembered *Beach Red* from college. It was a bitch of a war movie, and it was playing at eight-forty. If he didn't want to see it, fuck him.

I grabbed a cab in front of my house at a quarter to eight. As we rocketed down West End Avenue, a guy stood in the middle of the street straddling the double yellow line. He was hesitating, contemplating dashing out before the cab and beating it to the other side. I hated his guts. "Stay fucking there!" I hissed.

The cab dropped me off at five to eight. I stood waiting in the cold until the electronic time monitor on the Allied Chemical building registered eight-o-eight. I wasn't going to goddamn freeze all night, so I split, walking uptown on Broadway.

The night wasn't much colder than the day and the streets were hopping. I hadn't been to Times Square in a while and the place looked like a nighttime Mardi Gras in a Caribbean city. Mainly spades and Puerto Ricans. A lot of couples. Street magicians. I had never seen street magicians before. Guys hawked bright lime green phosphorescent chokers, dozens of them glowing up their arms. Every ten feet or so stood wasted-looking dudes, both young and old, handing out flyers and discount cards for massage parlors. Lots of traffic — mainly taxis — and everything was illuminated by that lunatic neon, riffing and bubbling like a heart right before cardiac arrest. There were crowds in front of most of the movie houses bunched around TV-sized preview screens.

I passed a porno shop with a neon sign that caught my eye: LIVE NUDE GIRLS · 25¢. As a rule I never went into porno

stores because that shit would do nothing for you except tease
you about what you didn't have — if you *did* have, you
wouldn't be in there to begin with, but that sign was intriguing
and in I went.

The store was big and bright, and the smell that hit my nose
the second I entered was a combination of come and Lysol. I
walked through a magazine section to a long well-lit corridor
lined with what looked like tall toilet stalls. About twenty guys
cruised and strolled up and down the lane, examining the color
photos framed on the side of each movie booth. There were
red light bulbs over the stalls and the stalls that were locked
had lit bulbs. When the bulb would go out, either the door
would swing open and some eyes-down slob would emerge or
the clink of a coin would be heard and the light would go on
again. A middle-aged PR in a stocking cap and floral shirt
swabbed the corridor with a mop and bucket. When he came
to an empty stall, he swiped a few times at come on the floor.

I walked up two steps to a change booth. In front of me was a
darkened area that had more booths arranged in a long U shape.
From somewhere in the middle of the booths I heard a girl's
voice over a microphone: "Oh dat feel so goooot, dodd-dy," followed by a lot of droning moaning. I gave the guy at the change
stall two singles. He tapped the bottom of what looked like a
microscope and four quarters dropped into his palm. He
tapped it again and handed me eight quarters. I slipped into a
booth and locked it behind me. I felt around in the darkness
for a coin slot and dropped in my two bits. I put the rest of
the quarters in my mouth. For five seconds nothing happened
and I figured I was supposed to beat off in the dark. Then I
heard a whining hum and a glass window a foot wide revealed
itself, as a metal plate slid open in front of my face. At first
all I could see was a red glow, but as my eyes adjusted my dick
almost burst through the wall. The window looked onto a
red-carpeted, red-tinted, small, U-shaped room. In the middle,
about five feet from my nose, a totally nude girl lay spread-

eagled on her back on a slowly rotating pedestal. With one hand she was diddling her clit and with the other she held a microphone to her mouth. Her head hung backward off the edge of the platform; the look on her face, glassy disinterest, as if she was on downers. Her eyes traveled around the room as she slowly revolved, staring upside-down into the faces in the booths surrounding her. Every few seconds without changing her expression she moaned into the mike. My prick was in my hand. Like faces in the car of a commuter train, there were fifteen heads in my line of vision around the U. Fifteen guys in booths like mine with facial expressions ranging from "Marry me" to "Oh God, I'm coming" to "Hey, I'm just waiting for a friend." Some guys were obviously jerking off. Either that or they were so cold they were shaking. Others smoked cigarettes. Some waved at her like they were movie fans at a celebrity première and she was one of the stars.

My booth hummed again, the metal plate slid shut and a bright light came on. I freaked, stood motionless waiting for the cops to kick in the door of my stall, the pop and flash of photographers only doing their job. Nothing. I spit a quarter into my hand, dropped it into the slot and the booth darkened again. I welcomed the darkness. It felt as comforting as ten minutes' extra sleep. The glass grew as the metal receded and I proceeded to jerk off. The keys in my coat pocket jangled loudly with every motion of my arm. I put them on the floor and continued in silence. A second chick entered the room. She was Latin and naked except for an Indian headdress. "Fellas, welcome White Sparrow!" a male voice announced over a PA system, and abruptly disco music was piped into the place. The girl on the pedestal sat up, then rolled off her stage. White Sparrow climbed on top of the pedestal and started dancing. Watching all this, I was totally absorbed and spaced at the same time. As White Sparrow danced, the other chick unwound about twenty feet of wire and moved from booth to booth with the mike, talking to the guys like Art

Linkletter cruising his audience on *House Party*. She stood on tiptoes and peered down inside. "C'mon, Daddy, lemme see wha' choo got. Yeah, aw, aw das tiny." The next booth. "C'mon. C'mon, ooo, das a nice one. There there, ah ah. Ah, there you go. Oh my God, all over! Yeah! C'mon, dat all you gonna show me?" She moved on down the line coaxing guys into jerking off over the mike. I started jacking off in earnest while staring at her ass and White Sparrow's muff. I wanted to finish fast and slip it back inside before she stopped at my booth.

"You don' wanna show me?" She hassled an old guy with rimless glasses. "You don' wanna show me, huh?" The guy smiled, embarrassed, and mouthed something through the glass. The metal plate began covering his screen, and she ducked her head inside his shrinking view. "Put another quarter in! Put another quarter in!"

The metal plate immediately reversed itself. "Now, don' you wanna suck my pussy? You don' wanna suck my pussy?"

The old guy laughed, looking away.

"Ah ast you, you don' wanna suck mah pussy?"

He put his hand in front of his mouth and jerked his head forward as if he were going to puke, then pulled out his dentures, holding them to the glass as they clacked in his hand. His mouth caved in without them, and the chick with the microphone looked up to White Sparrow and they laughed.

My booth lit up and I quickly slipped in another quarter to recover the darkness.

"Who wants to fuck me in the ass?" She whirled around with the mike. "Who wants to fuck me in the ass?"

"Ah do!" I heard some big dumb spade in the adjoining booth shout through the partition. He must have caught her eye because she bopped saucily toward my neighborhood.

"You wanna fuck me in the ass?"

She stood in front of my booth staring at me and my gut turned to iced slush. I leaned forward, my chest pressing against the bottom of the glass so she couldn't see my cock. I wouldn't meet her face. I was on fire with shame.

"What you hidin', huh?" Her voice sounded heavy and everywhere.

Go away. Go afuckin'way. I was dying. I stared blankly past her arm until she lost interest and moved to the next booth. As soon as she was gone I started pumping my meat again. I wanted her to watch. To come back and see me come. My knees were quivering and my hand raced at the speed of light. After getting nowhere with the guy next door, she came back my way. I stepped back, widening my eyes to catch her glance. She looked down into my booth again.

"Ow! That's a giant! A giant, yeah! Let her go! In my ass! In my ass!" I stood spread-legged like I was playing a sax, shaking like a bastard, pulling frantically on my cock.

"C'mon c'mon c'mon c'mon. Yeah! Yeah!" she hissed.

I shot all over the coin slot and almost fell to my knees with nervous exhaustion.

"Aw yeah, yeah." She trailed off and moved down the line.

I couldn't control my hands. They fluttered to my legs and to my face like they'd never heard of gravity. When the light came on I struggled putting in another quarter to buy back the darkness. I just stood there breathing heavily, staring at nothing. I staggered from the booth. The chicks were still visible because the time hadn't run out on my quarter. A blond kid in a ski jacket slipped inside and bolted the door. I walked past the change booth out into the street. I felt stoned, like I lost all sense of time and place. And it hit me; I didn't feel anything anymore. I didn't feel anything. Nothing got to me anymore. I had to do *that* for anything to get to me. I was dying.

I still had a half-hour to catch the movie. I was in desperate need of some clean beauty. Across the street from the Carnegie was a big Bookmasters. It had the same harsh lighting as Come-a-Rama but it had books. On a long table were stacks of picture books, remainders. I made a major production of not looking at the ones that featured studies of nudes, pin-ups or the history of burlesque and thumbed through a thirty-pound edition of the history of the Olympics.

The Carnegie Cinema was a nice little movie house built into the ass end of Carnegie Hall. It had the most unique food concession lounge in the world. It was more or less an art theater and the crowds they got there were more intellectually hip on the whole than, say, Times Square joints and I guess they figured if the subject was movies then anything French was right on, so they set up the entire lobby to make you feel like you were in a French sidewalk café. You walked down a long flight of stairs from the street level into a room where an entire wall was painted up as a row of French stores, boulangeries, patisseries, etc., etc., with little painted breads in the little painted windows. There was a blue sky over the storetops too. Along the back wall there was an espresso bar where you could get cappuccino, orzata, tamarind, croissants and assorted pastries from a girl in a striped blouse and a beret. You could sit at little café tables, your ass squatting on delicate heart-shaped wire-framed chairs and groove on the make-believe French street. Actually it was very nice and I was sure for a lot of people slurping their espresso there it stirred up either heavy memories or heavy fantasies. I sat there at one of the little tables drinking cappuccino. The more I sat there, the more I grooved on it. Paris. I remembered a photo-essay autobiography of Henry Miller's I once read. Paris in the thirties. Kenny in *his* thirties. Down, down, down. Then up! I could go to Europe! Start over. Leap the maze, don't go through it. I could, I would! I was young and healthy, the world could be my oyster. I could bust the rut!

I strode to a phone booth by the candy machine. New York! New York! What a wonderful town! Call La Donna, tell the news! Spread the word! I figured she was staying at her sister's. She didn't know anyone else. I hated talking to her sister, but this was big doings.

Halfway through dialing I hung up. I was sure her sister knew about the vibrator thing by then. I didn't want to talk to her, listen to her smirk at me over the phone. Tell me La Donna wasn't there when La Donna was four feet away pantomiming "I'm not here." Stupid bitch. Bitches. I'll go to Europe without her. Send her a post card from the Eiffel Tower. At that moment, wherever they were, I was sure the two of them were laughing at me. I felt a deep shame. I was flushing with humiliation. Why couldn't they just leave me alone?

Beach Red was horrifying. I never could understand why I went to war movies. They never failed to terrify me. It was two hours of soldiers confronting their fears of death. Many of them resolved the fear by dying. My going to a movie about dying was like my bringing my own bread to a bakery. As each guy snuffed it on the screen I could almost feel myself slipping into his new infinite blackness. Even for the young healthy guys who survived — I figured that movie was World War II, over thirty-some-odd years ago — that meant most of them were dead now. Somewhere I knew it was just a mid-sixties movie with actors but I started tripping out on the arithmetic of mortality and by halfway through the flick I felt like jumping up and doing sit-ups in the aisle.

There was a girl sitting behind me. She was Chinese, with a puffy nose and pushed-in face, but she was young; long hair and dungarees. Even though we were in the movies and she sitting directly in back of me, I could tell she was the silent type. I slid down slightly and leaned back, resting my head so that my hair came over the top of my seat. I wanted her to slide a hand through my hair, brush my cheek and come to rest on my forehead. Up front, half the screen actors' guild was being blown to Jell-O. I closed my eyes and waited.

La Donna and I met in a movie theater. It was similar to

the Carnegie too. An art theater in Los Angeles. I was in Los Angeles on vacation. I had never been to the West Coast. La Donna was there visiting some aunt. It was a rainy, shitty afternoon, the movies the only place to go. I saw her in the lobby, gave her the eye, but couldn't get it together to go over and say anything. I sat in the same row about ten seats over; the theater was pretty deserted. For two hours I alternated staring at her and staring at the screen. When I stared at the screen the message I was trying to convey was "Who needs you?" She never looked at me once. The movie was called *A Page of Madness*, a silent Japanese film about a nuthouse. When the audience filed out of the theater I followed her down two blocks into a big old bookstore. As she dawdled and traipsed through the aisles, me always one aisle over, I was wigging to the point of urinating on myself. I couldn't bring myself to say anything to her. I could never do that. If a girl gives me any kind of high sign I'll take it from there, but I could never make a move without some kind of sign. I knew she knew I was there, *why* I was there, but I couldn't, I couldn't . . . I was blindly thumbing through *Robert's Rules of Order* when she started strolling down my aisle. She said "Excuse me" and smiled as she slid past me. Thank you. I got it from there. Within thirty seconds of conversation we discovered we were both from New York and the connection we made was like Stanley bumping into Livingston. To make a long story short, I took her to dinner that night. To make it even shorter, we went back to my motel and I would like to say sex was ecstatic, etc., but the fact of the matter was I don't think I was ever so paranoid in bed with anybody in my whole life, before or since. I wanted her so bad I couldn't enjoy myself. I know what I'm doing when I rack, but that night I was so hungry, so needy, I felt like a high school senior. I came right away and then I kept balling because I was embarrassed to shoot so soon. I balled in a panic for thirty minutes after I came. She didn't come. She was quiet. When

I finally came up for air, rolling over to her side, she was still quiet. She started hugging and kissing me. I'm not a kisser, but I got into kissing like it was a new freak drug.

Her silence was driving me crazy. She kept them long-lashed baby grays downcast and the few times she did look up at me she had the most subtle smirk on her face. Then she would hug me more and kiss me more, rest her head on my chest, her face toward my feet. I went nuts. I started apologizing for coming so soon, I started telling her how nervous I was, how she turned me on. I apologized for everything but the rain and every time I apologized I flinched. It was so stupid, it made things worse, but I couldn't stop. I wanted to show her how human I was and I felt like I was making a jerk out of myself. I was in a panic. That shy smirk was driving me berserk. What was it, contempt? Contentment? Modesty? Self-consciousness? Those silent hugs and kisses. The notion that she would be thinking I was a lousy lay had me climbing the walls, drove me to more false chuckling, panicking confessions and apologies. Finally, I felt like I had to ball again, to set the record straight. As I tried to move her on her back she pushed into me on her side, hugging me powerfully, her nose in my chest — she didn't want to ball. Fuck, *that's* what the hugging was all about — to keep me from hopping on her again. But the hugs were so deep, so burrowing — they were wonderful.

She couldn't stay — she told her aunt she'd be back at ten-thirty to see her cousin or someone. I turned away as she dressed. Fuck love, infatuation, crushes and all related emotions. I jumped out of bed, slipped on my dungarees to be less vulnerable, more in control.

"Maybe I'll call you later tonight?" she mumbled, giving me that smirk.

My first thought was, why? It was a strange thing to do. Then I figured, yeah, I'll take anything. I resisted one more apology, she kissed my chest, gave me a last over-the-shoulder smirk and was gone.

I lay on the bed for two hours, sniffing my fingers and trying to remember the license plate of the truck that hit me.
Every time I flashed on how lousy a lay I was and how I tried
to apologize I twitched in embarrassment and agony. Finally,
I couldn't stay in that room any longer. It was twelve-thirty.
She wasn't going to call and why would she want to anyhow?
I left to drive around the Sunset Strip, but I asked the receptionist to take any phone messages for me. The guy said he
would only be on duty another hour but if I wasn't back by
then he would pin anything he got for me on my door. I drove
around, had coffee in three different places, got lost in the
hills somewhere and started driving back to the motel. The
closer I got the more I knew there was going to be a message
for me — I felt it. I even wished I had asked the receptionist
what color his message paper was so I could have a clearer
mental image of what my door would look like with a note
pinned on.

Two A.M. The desk was closed. I walked slowly down the
corridor. My room was around the bend. The wallpaper was
orange with a raised, pebble-grained texture. My room was
out of my vision, ten feet around the bend. I turned the
corner and yes! Blue, robin's-egg-blue paper push-pinned into
my door. I turned the corner and yes! A million times since
that moment I turned the corner and yes! Pebble-grained
orange and then yes! Robin's-egg blue. Yes! Da ba du dat dat
yes! Yes! Doo ba do blue yes! Do ba do orange yes!

An explosion on the screen sending palm fronds and body
parts flying snapped me back. I slunk down low in my seat,
not sure if I had been jerking my head in tune to my trium-
phant memories. I thought of the girl behind me, and mom-
mies, I was very blue.

After the movie I went back into the café section and had
another cappuccino.

I didn't want to see *The Loves of Isadora*. I didn't feel like
sitting there through all her dance triumphs, waiting for that
scarf to get snagged in a propeller and make a figure eight

out of her neck. Besides, that movie would have been something La Donna would have dragged me to. As a matter of fact, half the solo girls sitting around me in the Café Carnegie reminded me of La Donna. Minor dancers living in body stockings, hair in a bun, shy, always giving and getting something ceramic and Chinese for presents.

I started fantasizing about picking somebody up. Taking them home and blowing them away with tenderness and warmth. At first they would be distrustful. They had always been wary of men — their fathers were cold New England patriarchs; once they became twelve they weren't even allowed to kiss him goodnight anymore; sex had always been a jump, jerk and squirt affair. All they lived for now was dance, they rarely spoke, they could only come if they masturbated, they got six-page letters from Mother which read like scripts from *Medical Center*. They kept Hesse novels and ballet photo books in a small brick and plank bookcase, had a cat named Gabriel or Damien. I would softly raise their chin to me and — bullshit I would. I would not. No more. No more La Donnas. No more laying low. No more hiding out with pretty, isolated, depressed loneliness moll.

Get it together, Kenny.

She never told me what she was smirking about or what her thoughts were that night. Just as well. If I could be cold and analytical about it I would say that the main intensity I felt with her in Los Angeles was a mixture of loneliness and specialness — mainly because we were both lonely and we were both three thousand miles away from home — which made meeting somewhat special. But when we got back to New York and started dating among familiar faces and backgrounds that feeling of lonely specialness lingered. And we called it love. And as I sat there by myself drinking my cappuccino, still buzzing from Times Square brain-rape and two hours of Technicolor death, all the force of that special loneliness soaked through my bones and I hurt. I hurt bad because I still loved her. Or maybe what I *really* loved was that special loneliness. Now *that* was a thought.

Suddenly I felt as though my surroundings were mocking me, my travel plans — but it was a different type of embarrassment than the phone call shame — it was a sobering embarrassment. This was what Europe would be for me — Kenny the loner, slurping cappuccino, going to movies and debating whether to try to score or not. Europe. Wherever I could go, I would take my head with me. I felt like I was sitting there sipping my cappuccino under false pretenses, like I was on the lam, laying low from reality in that two-bit Parisian Disneyland. Like if the two pussies from the circle jerk place were reality cops and they were stalking Broadway and Seventh Avenue looking for me, I could have hid right where I was with all the other cinema fans.

On the lam. On the *double* lam. If I ever ran into Jackie di Paris again I would be so much hamburger. The guy gets a call, gets dragged down to Times Square and then gets stood up. If that was me I'd turn headhunter. On the lam. My whole *life* was lived on the lam. All I ever did was grab a chick and hide out, lay low. What the hell was I afraid of? Even when I wasn't living with a chick, when I was living with those guys, all I ever did was try to figure out how not to be there. All I ever did was maneuver for an opening, a space away from them all. That was the reason I started working income tax with my uncle — so I could be in an earning position strong enough to move out, to live alone — to go into hiding. "I need my space, my privacy." I had it in spades, my space. And I did right by calling up Jackie di Paris. I fucked it up for sure, but I was on the right track. I needed people. I didn't even have senile pinochle partners to buddy with. Something told me it was going to be a bitch of a struggle because laying low sounded like a real fine idea most times, but there was more to be had, there was more to be had. And I wasn't the only one. I looked around the room — at least

half the people there looked like rejects from *The Fugitive*.
All the old ladies, the Lincoln Center dancers, bassoon players,
Columbia University instructors, professional Communists,
used-book-store owners. We were *all* on the fucking lam.
Everybody there might not be hiding from a nude twat with
a microphone or an enraged postal clerk, but whatever they
were hiding from, if those reality cops were going to pull up
front to raid that joint they had better bring with them some
king-sized paddy wagons.

I took a cab home. When I got to my door I couldn't find
my keys. Then I remembered putting them on the floor of
the stroke booth so they wouldn't jangle when I jerked off.
After kicking the door for twenty minutes like an enraged
baboon I called a locksmith. I could have gone back down
to Times Square and found them, but I was afraid if I walked
into that booth again I would never come out.

THURSDAY

The locksmith was a young dude about my age but he had shoulder-length hair and tiny round glasses that reminded me of one of the artists I sold the stuff to on Spring Street. He had my door open in three minutes, changed the cylinder in another five and gave me new keys. Set me back thirty-five bills. I invited him in for a cup of coffee but he declined. After he left, I got the first solid night's sleep in a week.

Thursday morning came on like the weatherman remembered it was February. The wind was a sidearm bitch and as I made coffee my windows were moaning like kazoos. When I got downstairs the bus stop and parking regulation poles were jerking back and forth like they were in a tug of war. Loose trash and newspapers skipped down the street faster than taxis.

I took a bus down to the diner and did some oatmeal with the boys. Al lent me an extra case for the day. I laid on them the story of my two-hundred-dollar sale in the loft and I got back the expected barrage of *Daily News*–mentality comments on long hair and artists. At first I got into my

attitude about being the wise owl among the birdbrains and
feeling sorry for myself, but then, I figured, I knew how they
were going to respond *before* I brought the whole thing up,
and then when they did I wound up down on them and sorry
for myself. So, question — why did I bring it up to begin
with? What was I trying to prove? These guys were clods,
artists were from Saturn, and in the middle was me, a man
without a country. Poor me.

The free sample of the day was a small, round, rubber-
spiked scalp massager that fit into the palm of your hand.

Due to the wind-chill factor I decided it would be a good
day to find an enormous building that would take from nine
to five to go through and picked a twenty-story affair on Charles
Street. I had worked it before; it was decent enough. The
only problem was that it was a doorman building. Technically
doormen weren't allowed to let solicitors inside but some you
could slip two, three dollars to and they would go for coffee in
their minds. Once I swung a bribe with a doorman I never
forgot his name. When I came back six months later I could
greet him like a long-lost friend, kibitz, laugh, slip him his
money and get down to work. Heavy warmth always blew
people away and if you came on friendly to most people, they
would walk your dog through a minefield for you.

The doorman at Charles Street was an Irish dude named
Phillip. The last time I was there he showed me the Silver
Star he'd won at Okinawa, told me about his family, half here,
half in Ireland, and after we bullshat for a while hipped me to
which tenants were more likely prospects than others. He
even hipped me to which tenant would probably give me a
blowjob if I played my cards right. What he failed to tell me
about that tenant was that he was a guy. I had gone through
the building savoring and saving 10J for last and when I
knocked on the door some dude who looked like my
barber.

After breakfast, I took a ride with Jerry, and he dropped

me off on his way to the Lower East Side. Before heading for the building I slipped into a luncheonette on the corner and bought a coffee to go.

"Hey, Phillip!" I grabbed his hand while he was still trying to place my face. "Remember me?"

Phillip was thin, fiftyish, wore a dark blue uniform and tortoise-shell glasses.

"Oh! Yer the Bluecastle House fellah!" He gripped my hand harder. "Yes the guy ay sent up to Ten-J." He laughed. His voice had a high lilting leprechaun inflection like a voice-over on a TV ad for Irish tourism.

"Yeah, yah bastad." I lightly punched his arm. "But I'll tell you, you were right on target." I winked and for a second a saints-preserve-us look crossed his face. "Hey! I'm kiddin'!" We both laughed. Me in reassurance, him in relief.

I handed over the coffee. He took it like a gift for Father's Day. "Here you go, it's cold outside."

"That's kind of you." He smiled, bobbing his head in thanks as he placed it on his small lobby desk next to a miniature TV.

"Okay, Mr. Phil, I'm gonna get to work." I clasped his hand again with both of mine, slipping a five into his palm, and walked toward the elevator.

"Oh!" I backtracked and took out a scalp massager from my pocket. "Here." On the back was a plastic loop to slip around your middle finger for a better grip. "You see, you slip in your sazeech like this" — I put my pinky in the loop, then flipped over the massager to the rubber-spiked side — "so when you're schtupping with the old lady she'll come like summer rain." I left him examining it in his hands.

It was another good day. I averaged a sale a floor for the top ten floors and by noon I'd totaled sixty dollars.

I did some lunch in an egg restaurant, then took a cab the four blocks to a high-rise on Fourteenth Street and by four o'clock I'd collected another fifty dollars' worth of orders.

When I got home, the *Post* was curled up in its spot on the doorknob like a daily reminder of "Whatcha gonna do *tonight*, Kenny?" The apartment was dark even though it was twenty minutes shy of five o'clock. I hung up my suit, put on dungarees and a sweatshirt, flopped on the bed with the paper and turned on the cartoons.

Beach Red was still playing at the Little Carnegie, but *The Loves of Isadora* was gone. Instead the second feature was *Anzio*. Now that made sense at least. I laid on my stomach and watched cartoons with one eye. I buried one side of my face in my pillow. My arms were straight down my sides and I felt a trickle of drool slip over one corner of my mouth and spot my pillow. Sit-ups. Go do your sit-ups. *You* go do your sit-ups. The phone rang and I almost slammed my head through the wall. La Donna. Parents.

"Kenny?" A familiar male voice but I couldn't place it.

"Yeah?"

"Hey, it's Donny."

"Donny!" I jumped up and clicked off the TV. "How you doin', man?"

"Pretty good, pretty good. Whacha up to?"

"Not a thing," I blurted.

"Listen, Kenny, they painted my crib this morning an' these fuckin' fumes are makin' me nauseous. I can't open the windows cause a the cold an' the fuckin' heat's on like full blast."

"Hey, you wanna come up?" I would have begged him to come up.

"Well, I was thinkin' maybe you could invite me up for dinner if you were a real nice guy and not a fuckin' prick, or even if you *were* a fuckin' prick maybe we could at least eat out someplace."

"Hey, Donny, come on up." I was grinning and my skull was pounding with joy. "You know where I live?"

"You sure it's cool? You think you better check with your old lady?"

"She ain't here, it's no problem. You got the address?"

"Yeah. Listen, I'll pay for the food."

"Get fucked. You know how to get here?"

"What, the uptown local?"

"Seventy-ninth Street, walk down to Seventy-seventh, I'm three buildings up from the deli on Broadway. Two ten West, apartment ten B."

"What, in about two hours?"

I squinted at the digital. "It's ten after five. Figure seven, okay?"

"You got it."

"I'll make nice . . . You like chicken?"

"Hey, do beavers piss on flat rocks?"

"Maybe after we'll go downtown, do a movie, get laid." I winked to the phone.

"Sounds good, my man."

"Awright! At seven, Donny."

"Hang in there, kid."

I hung up, snapped my fingers. "WAAO!" I yelled and started dancing with my shoulders. I felt like a million big ones. I ran into the kitchen. I had plenty of vegetables but the chicken was frozen. I would have to run down to the supermarket. I turned on some lights. I couldn't help dancing. I ran down the foyer in my stockinged feet and slid into the front door, did an about face and slid into the living room. Isaac Hayes on the machine. I held my fist in front of my mouth and did the whole midnight show. Then I straightened up the living room. My joint was always neat so in fifteen minutes I was heading out the door. I felt so goddamn good I didn't even feel the cold. It was like the first few weeks with La Donna. I picked up chicken thighs, a can of bread crumbs. Next door at the liquor store I got a bottle of Bolla Valpoli-cella. I hated wine but it seemed like an adult purchase for a dinner. I wasn't sure I had a corkscrew so I bought one at a hardware store on Broadway. By six I was whacking up a salad in the kitchen and double-dipping the chicken thighs in bread crumbs and eggs. By six-thirty the salad was covered and in the refrigerator, the breaded chicken was laid out in a baking pan in the unlit oven, the salad dressing was sedimenting in an old fashioned glass on the counter and the dining table was set like a window display for tableware in Bloomingdale's. I put a package of frozen broccoli in the sink, washed up and slipped into some leisure threads which would show off the fantastic shape I kept myself in. I put John Coltrane on the changer. Even though I only had a slight interest in jazz, it seemed to me, like the wine, the thing to do.

At ten of seven the downstairs buzzer rang. I buzzed Donny in and hit the change button on the record player. "A Love Supreme" soundtracked the apartment.

"Hey, ya fuck!" We slapped palms in greeting at the door. Donny's face was death white blotched red from the cold.

"Here you go." He handed me a bottle of Mateus, my sample case and draped his ski jacket on the doorknob of the foyer closet.

"You couldn't forget this?" The case slid from my middle finger to the floor. "Lemme get a hanger."

"Nah, nah, c'mon, c'mon." He pushed me down the foyer into the living room.

"I don't have brandy. You want a Scotch?"

"Anything, man." He rubbed his hands and shivered while checking out my living room. "Nice, nice, very nice. Whata you pay here, three?"

"Two seventy-five." I poured a Chivas. "Water?"

"A little. Last week I had to check out this guy's apartment, over one block on seventy-sixth? He had the corner roof apartment, nice view. His ceiling caved in during a rainstorm and he got a concussion from falling plaster. Also, the guy had a five-thousand-dollar stamp collection ruined. Very nice." He admired the kitchen.

I showed him the bedroom, and he immediately noticed the paint blisters on the ceiling.

"When you get painted last?"

"Six months ago."

"Cocksuckers. You can get another paint job. They used a shit grade of paint. What they give you, one coat or two?"

"Hey, Donny, I'm not a building inspector. Relax, hah? Drink your drink."

"And I hate that fucking job, too, Kenny, that's the funny thing about it."

"C'mon, let's just sit down for a while."

We sat at the dinner table and sipped our Scotches. "Kenny, Kenny, Kenny," he droned.

"Donny, Donny, Donny."

"Bullshit, bullshit, bullshit," he responded, and we clinked glasses.

"Lemme put on the chicken." I turned on the oven, ripped open the broccoli package and slipped the frozen rectangle of greens into a wide pot.

"Fuckin' Candyman, huh?" I shook my head.

"Candy's Candy." Donny drained his drink.

"He made me feel like shit yesterday."

"Ah, he does that to me all the time." He refilled his glass two fingers.

"So why do you run with him?"

Donny shrugged. "I don't run with him that much. Sometimes I stop in, that's all." He looked embarrassed.

"Lemme ask you something, Donny." I squinted to signify a bottom-line question coming up. "You think he's right about the kids an' all?"

Donny hunched his shoulders and winced. "I swear, I don't know, Kenny, I don't know anything anymore."

"Well, different strokes, right?" C'mon, Donny, help me out here.

"I guess." He rubbed his mouth distractedly. He was a big goddamn support.

"So where's *your* old lady, Kenny?"

My gut sank. "She's visiting some people." I wanted to crack to him, but it felt too painful right then.

"She nice? You got any pictures?"

"You know something, I don't think I do."

Coltrane clicked off. Donny got up. "You mind if I find something?" He motioned to the records in my wall unit.

"Be my guest." I started slipping into a trip around La Donna. La Donna seemed like such a beautiful and unique name.

"Play this!" Donny sat cross-legged on the floor facing the wall unit. He held up my *Murray the K's Boss Golden Gassers — 1962*. I joined him on the floor. The Scotch gave my nose a little glow like a two-watt bulb. " 'Soldier Boy'! Whew! Do you fuckin' remember that?"

"I haven't heard this album since high school."

"It'll probably destroy your system. Whata you got here?" He twisted around, searching my walls for speakers.

"JBL decades, a Sansui seven seventy-one and a Garrard box."

"What that run you, six?"

"Eight." I scanned the songs on the album. "Hey!" I pointed to a title.

" 'Sixteen Candles.' " He frowned, then lit up. "Oh ho!"

"Remember that?" I raised my chin and winked.

"Barbara Abbadabba."

"Barbara Abbadando," I corrected with significance.

"She fuckin' *took* 'Sixteen Candles,' remember?"

"Well, she took two candles that are sittin' here right now!" We slapped palms again.

"Bad Barbara." I put the golden oldies album on, but it was so scratched I took it right off.

Legend had it that this chick in the projects, Barbara Abbadando, would fuck anybody in high school if they got her alone in a room and played "Sixteen Candles" for her. I know *I* never fucked her and I doubted that Donny did either.

"No offense, Kenny, but I hate jazz."

"I know what *you* like." I got to my feet and opened La
Donna's closet. While trying not to notice her boots and sheet
music, I grabbed two record boxes from the hat shelf, then
kicked the door closed. "Into the vault!"

Donny opened both boxes, glowing with reverence like a
kid being handed a complete set of baseball cards.

He gingerly extracted a half-dozen old 45s, looping his
finger through the holes. "You saved yours, hah?" His voice
was a hush.

"Every one." It was one of the proudest moments of my
life.

"Aw shit! 'Wooly Bully'! You remember fuckin' 'Wooly
Bully'!" He laughed.

"First time I heard 'Wooly Bully,' Donny, I almost ruined
my father's car. You remember my old man's Fairlane Five
hundred? I had Diane Fishman in the front seat and we were
parked over the Safeway on that hill by Burke Avenue. I was
on top of her, grinding. I had the motor off but I left the
radio on for atmosphere. When 'Wooly Bully' came on I went
batshit. I almost humped her to death. Ten minutes later I
go to start the car, it won't start." I shrugged. "Plus! It stinks
like gasoline. You know what happened? When I was humping her I had my foot on the accelerator for leverage, you
know, and every time" — I rocked back and forth on my ass,
grinding my hips — "every time like that, I flooded the en-
gine."

"Oh ho! 'My Girl'! Whata fuckin' song! You got a disc,
Kenny?"

We put it on, singing along and I felt the years slip by my
closed eyes, as if I could lose my present life in the sweetest of
sweet amnesias.

"Nice, right?" I smiled.

"You know who used to go berserk over 'My Girl'?
Maynard."

"Maynard? I thought he only dug like Bob Dylan and Pete Seeger and Library of Congress Chain Gang recordings."

"Nah." Donny chuckled. "That was an act. Maynard knew everybody expected him to be like that, protest and shit, but he dug the same stuff you did. He just did it privately because he didn't want to blow his image. Maynard was a complicated dude. Hey!" Donny brightened, holding a record to my face. " 'Walk Like a Man' — who's that?" he quizzed me.

"Oh." I snapped my fingers in frustration. "I got the face, I got the face."

"Mikey," he hinted.

"Mikey Feeny!" I blurted. One summer night about thirty guys hanging out in the park rechristened themselves with the title of a rock 'n' roll song they particularly identified with. If the title was too long the guy just did a variation of the first word. Michael Feeny chose "Walk Like a Man," so he was dubbed Walker. In most cases those names stuck only until school started again.

"You remember your name, Donny?"

"Shit yeah, Gypsy. 'The Gypsy Cried.' You were Speedoo, right?"

"You got it. Remember Candy's?"

"Fuckin' *Duke*, right?" He laughed. " 'Duke of Earl.' "

"Duke of Shit."

We sat in silence, nodding and chuckling. On the one hand I could have just kept riffing and dredging up names and memories all night. On the other hand I started feeling tired. Not sleep tired, more like slack-jawed. That part of me couldn't riff anymore, refused to do the stroll down memory lane.

"Hmph," Donny snickered, staring at my shoes, "Duke of Shit."

I could sense him knotting up with the silence. His eyes were all over the place but never more than three feet off the ground. I could have helped him out, said something funny, but I was absorbed in watching his desperation, my desperation. His brain was cooking for a riff. The fact that I wasn't doing the same almost made me feel as though I had floated out of my body and was watching both of us. Ever since I was a kid I always felt the need to explode into a ball of entertainment whenever I was with a group of people. When I was ten I remember being over at Donny's house watching TV with his parents and seeing him erupt into compulsive joke after joke. Even though I couldn't put it into words I knew exactly what was going on in his head even then. If we were at my house I would have done the same.

"Hey, did you know Mikey's brother Ernest?" he blurted, cocking his head at me.

"Nah, I never ran with Mikey." I felt sorry for both of us.

"Oh, so you don't know Ernest, his sister Linda, none a them?"

"Nope."

"So you never heard about that game between Our Lady of Sorrows and Sacred Cross?"

"What game?"

"I'm surprised you never heard of it." He handed me "Shout" and "Pretty Little Angel Eyes." "See, Ernest, Mikey's brother, no wait, lemme backtrack. Mikey had a sister, Linda. She used to blow the goddamn phonebook, both the white pages *and* the yellow pages. I mean, if you went up to the roof of her building *now* there's probably *still* two permanent kneecap depressions in the gravel. So, anyways, the thing was, every time Ernest heard about his sister blowin' some guy he went berserk, tracked the guy down and beat the poor guy to shit. You *sure* you didn't know Ernest Feeny?" He became more relaxed.

"Hey, man, I hardly remember Mikey."

"Well, you remember how tough Mikey was, right? Well, fuckin' Ernest used to destroy Mikey, just as a workout before breakfast. That's why Mikey was so mean. Anyway, so Linda

would give head then Ernest would break head. In the spring
of nineteen sixty, we were in junior high, you and I, Linda
starts running with Freddy Victor, who played ball for Sacred
Cross. This guy was hip to Ernest but he figures if he stays in
his neighborhood he's safe. So Linda always went over to *his*
house because she didn't want her brother beating on him."

"Where'd he live?"

"All the way over in Marble Hill, and Ernest knew what
was going down, but he knew if he started something in Marble
Hill it would be like GI Joe stepping into a Vietcong strong-
hold and saying, 'Who's bad here!' Okay? So he was very
frustrated. Anyway, like I said, Freddy was on the baseball
team at Sacred Cross and that year Sacred Cross won their
division. Now, Ernest, he pitched for Our Lady of Sorrows,
in a different division. I mean when he wasn't stomping on
Linda's blowjobees. That year, Our Lady of Sorrows won
their division title, okay? Of course there had to be a playoff
between the two divisions to see who represented the Bronx
and played whoever the Catholic school champs were gonna
be in *Manhattan*, right? Big game in Yankee Stadium. Bronx
versus Manhattan, dinner with the mayor, the whole thing."

"Ernie is pitching. Freddy is scared because he has got to
stand up there against Ernest. And fucking Ernest had a fast
ball; his catcher, Frank Mazza, had to soak his hand in brine
and tape sponges to his palm. I mean Ernest had a smoker.
You used to get up there to bat, next thing you knew somebody had to hand you a school newspaper so you could read
that you were struck out. So Freddy's fucking scared, and he
is a good hitter too, but he didn't know what was going on in
crazy Ernie's brain, and he felt very vulnerable. The first two
times he gets up Ernie is not only *not* using his fast ball, but
he's feeding them over the plate so nicely that the ball was
coming in, it should have had a knife and fork on either side
of it. Freddy hits a double, then a triple. Ernie's smoking
out everybody else though, and by the bottom of the ninth, the
score is one up. Ernie walks two guys, strikes out a guy, gives

up a single, strikes out another guy. Now that is what you call your classic baseball drama situation. Score's one up, bottom of the ninth, two out, bases loaded. And who do you think comes up to bat? Freddy Victor. Freddy is having illusions of Bobby Thomson. He's got the golden bat that day and he's not too worried about Ernie anymore. As a matter of fact, he's thinking maybe Ernie is a little worried about *him*, you know? So . . . he's up there. Ernie runs him to a three-and-two count. Okay, you got the tension mounting, the drum roll in the background. Ernie takes off his cap, just stands there, not winding up. Just glaring at Freddy for a long time, and then suddenly he *rockets* this smoking fireball down the lane. *Boom* it hits Freddy right in the fucking chest! Freddy gets blown back right into the umpire and collapses. He's dead. The ball smashed a rib, the rib punctured the heart. But dig! Here's the irony. Sacred Cross, Freddy's team, wins the game! Because even though he was killed, he was hit by a pitch, so he *automatically* advanced to first, the bases were loaded, so a run came in. Sacred Cross wins, two to one."

We stared at each other for a whole minute. A scratchy 45 was stuck on "Kick mah heels up an'," "Kick mah heels up an'," "Kick mah heels up an'."

"What a huge steaming pile of bullshit," I said softly, shaking my head in amazement.

"I know, but it's a great story, ain't it? I love tellin' stories about the neighborhood." Donny reached over and removed the needle from the record.

I wanted to tell Donny he didn't have to entertain me, but I thought, who the hell am I to tell anybody to lighten up on riffing? I didn't know how to tell him without incriminating myself and getting into a whole heavy thing about our heads, and frankly I would have rather riffed.

"Lemme check the chicken." I got up. The chicken wasn't ready yet.

"Did Mikey really have a brother and sister?" I squatted

back down. I bet the old merchant marine sat around the Poseidon Club telling bullshit sea stories with the boys just like us. The only difference was he was pushing seventy-five and Donny and me were thirty.

Donny shrugged and pulled a Brasil Danneman cigar tin from his breast pocket. He flipped it open with his thumb and extended it to me. "Before-dinner mint?"

There were six joints rolled in banana-colored paper. "Awright, Mr. Donny!" I extracted one and put it between my lips. "Okay, I gotta watch this now, 'cause I'm prone to the horrors when I'm high," I cautioned.

"Oh, you know from the horrors?"

"Huh." I half-laughed. "I know the horrors like a nigger knows the blues.".

"Shit. Me too." He shook his head.

"Sometimes, man, I'm by myself. It's nine o'clock at night, but I got a full refrigerator, there's sixteen Bogart movies on the box. I figure shit, I'll blow this little jay and . . . wail! Raid the box, hole up with the Bogey, you know? I do the joint, next thing I know I'm curled up in a fuckin' ball on my bed, TV's off, lights off. I'm wiggin', like what's it all mean. Whew!"

"Fuckin' Kenny. Maybe we should pass on the grass?"

"Nah, it's cool. That shit only happens when I'm alone."

"Yeah." I leaned toward him and he lit me.

"This is very strong." I snorted in raw throat pain.

"Uh-huh."

I put on an album so we wouldn't have to keep changing the record every ten seconds and we did the whole joint listening to an old Nina Simone record.

After about ten minutes of nonblink space cadet paralysis I rapped Donny on the knee. "So, Donny, what's the story? What's it all about, huh?" We stared at each other, half-smiling. "What's your old lady like, Donny?"

"My old lady!" He stretched, his clasped knuckles cracking

in an arch over his head. "I don't got an old lady. I ain't married, I'm divorced. I was married to some girl I met at NYU like twelve years ago. I'm divorced." He yawned, clasping his hands behind his neck.

"You told me you were married." I knew he did, and it freaked me out.

"Nah, I said that? I'm divorced."

"You seein' anybody?" I ditched the roach, squashing it with my thumb.

"This one and that one. How about you?"

"I told you, man, I'm living with someone." I felt angry that he had lied to me.

"Oh, right, right. Sorry."

The dope had us both whipped to shit. I started getting hungry and brought in the salad bowl so we could nosh. The minute I sat down I realized I'd forgotten about the chicken so I got up again and went back to the kitchen. The chicken had about twenty minutes to go, but I was afraid of a fire so I turned off the oven. Donny began nibbling salad, bringing diced vegetables blindly to his face, his jaws working on automatic pilot, his eyes never dropping to his food.

I snagged a diced cucumber. I wanted Donny to tell me I looked good. I looked good. "You're looking good, Donny."

Slowly he turned to me and nodded a drowsy thank-you. I speared another cucumber wedge, then realized I hadn't done my sit-ups yet that day. I slid across the polished wood floor to the couch, jammed my feet under the bottom, took off my shirt and started doing sit-ups. After about fifteen, Donny watched me go to thirty.

"Kenny, what are you doing?" He laughed.

"Sit-ups, man. I do fuckin' sit-ups every day." I grunted. "I been doing this shit for years. I got a stomach harder than boilerplate." Fifty.

"Huh." Donny watched me with an amused grin frozen on his face, then turned away.

After seventy-five, I couldn't do any more. I lay flat on my back, my feet still under the couch, my hands still clasped behind my neck. And I had even forgotten the barbell.

I stared at Donny's hunched back for a while, then my eyes zeroed in on the ceiling.

La Donna grew up in Trumansburg, New York. I'd never been there, but every time I thought of Trumansburg, it broke my heart. *Anytime* I fell in love with a girl and I would think of her town, or her block or her state if it was out of town, it would tear me up. When I was a kid and a girl I loved lived on a certain street in the Bronx, anytime I heard the name of that street I would get a melancholy pang.

I was lying there staring at my ceiling thinking of little baby La Donna growing up in Trumansburg, New York. La Donna was the baby of the family — *that* tore me up. The baby. I had this picture of her at two years old frowning in a highchair. Her gigantic head. She *still* had a gigantic head. She would crack up anytime I made a joke about it. Her sweetest baby-faced head. Baby face. When La Donna cried, her forehead wrinkled up and two little red storm clouds formed over her eyebrows right before the downpour.

Donny had asked to see a picture of La Donna, and I had forgotten about the highchair picture when he asked me. It was somewhere in the bedroom. I struggled to my feet. Donny was squatting cross-legged like a Buddha surrounded by a fan of old 45s, glassily eyeing the lit dials on my amplifier. In the dark bedroom I forgot what I'd come in for and wound up lying down to take a fast nap.

La Donna's baby face floated like a balloon around my head. Rushes of angles of her expressions, her sadness, her fear, her eyes. I pretended I was hugging her, pretended we were naked and hugging. Kissing. Hugging and hiding under covers. Everything was okay.

I was a very lonely man. A lonely man. I never thought of myself as a man but as a kid or a guy. I wasn't a kid anymore. I was a man. A lonely man.

"It's the horrors, Kenny." I could make out Donny's silhouette in the doorway. "Don't let it get away with you, it's only the horrors."

"I'm good. I'm good." I hooded my eyes with my hand although it was totally dark.

"Snap out of it, kid. C'mon, we gonna eat, go downtown, do a fuckin' movie, nice, nice."

"I'll be out in two minutes, Donny."

"It's just the horrors, man."

"Two minutes."

Donny walked back into the living room.

Donny. Donny was A-OK.

It was freezing. Get up, asshole. I didn't have a shirt on. I took a T-shirt from the dresser and shaking my head to rattle out the crap I went into the bathroom to wash up. I didn't feel stoned anymore. As I was washing, I thought about the lonely man riff. Yeah, I was lonely, but I *chose* to be lonely. Nobody was telling me to be lonely. And if I could choose to be lonely, I could also unchoose to be lonely. I was just promising myself how I would turn a new leaf and make friends, millions of friends. There was an old, good friend right in my living room and I was crying like a goddamn mope about loneliness. Now, what kind of bullshit was *that?* I felt a strong rush of optimism, of manifest destiny. The bullshit was *over!* We were going to party, and we were going to party *hearty!*

"Okay, Mr. Donny! Here we go!" I danced back into the living room. Donny was on the floor, his back to me, his head resting on his extended arm, like the Statue of Liberty lying on its side. He didn't move. The record player was off. I took a seat at the dining table and watched him lying curled up in his own private cross on my floor. It was eight-thirty. My buoyancy and optimism hitched a ride out of town.

Donny. Who the fuck was Donny? He was a memory. A character from some novel I'd read years before.

An hour later, I heard a deep, long nasal inhale, a groan, and Donny slowly dragged himself to a leaning position, propping himself up with his arms. I was still sitting at the table, my head against the wall. Donny rubbed his face, then squinted at me as if the light killed his eyes.

"Whew!" He shook his head and looked around him. "I'm sorry, man," he croaked. "Mmph, nine-thirty." He held his wristwatch to his nose, then struggled to his feet. He wobbled into the foyer, put on his coat and wobbled back into the living room.

"Listen, Kenny," he whispered hoarsely as though he had a sore throat, "I should go, man, okay?"

"It's cool." I'd hardly moved since he woke up, my knee running, my thumb knuckle in my mouth. "It's cool."

"Yeah."

I held out my hand for a slap. His half-swipe at my palm ended in a brief clasp, then he split.

After Donny left I put away the records, not looking at the labels. I just wanted them packed and out of sight. "Oh What a Night" by the Dells. Son of a bitch. I hadn't heard that in a decade. What a dynamite jam. I slipped it on the box. Just one record.

> Oh what a night, to ho-old you, dear
> Oh what a night, to ki-is you, dear

It was scratched horribly. Almost inaudible, like playing a radio station too far out of its signal range. It was almost as if that *time* was crackly and losing its power, its clarity, and all that could get through from those days of my life was some weak hazy echoes. Blast from the past my ass. It was fading, going. How sad, how very goddamn sad.

I didn't dare put on another 45. I piled them in their beat-up boxes and put them in the closet. I saw La Donna's stack of sheet music. The top one was "Raindrops Keep Falling on My Head." I tried to envision her singing that song.

If I had had it in me to laugh I would have bust a gut. Despite myself, I sat down on the closet threshold and thumbed through her music — "Feelings," "I Who Have Nothing," "I'll Never Fall in Love Again," "Blue Moon," "My Way," "I Am Music." She was another one. Me, Donny, her. We were all hurting so bad we were beyond pain.

I moved to the phone, my heart going like a tom-tom. My grip was sweaty on the receiver. I could slide my palm back and forth over the plastic as if it were lubricated. I had to shit my brains out.

"Hi, is La Donna there?" I sounded as though I'd just run up a flight of stairs.

"Who's calling?" Her sister knew my voice. Bitch.

"It's Kenny." I rubbed my chin on my shoulder for three hours.

"Hi." It came out angry and short.

"Howya doin', kid?" I started calming down.

"I'm okay. What do you want?"

She was putting it on. I could tell.

"I just called to say I'm sorry. It was stupid what I did. It was an emotional thing of the moment."

"I don't want to talk about it."

I didn't know what to say next. I didn't even feel like asking her to come back. I just wanted to talk to her, explain something to her.

"Are you okay there?" I asked.

"I'm fine. I really have to go."

"La Donna?" The panic returned.

She waited on the other end. Are you coming back? You're lonely. I'm lonely. We're cut from the same fabric. We could help each other. I was looking at your sheet music. If I can't love you, I can't love myself. "Are you sure everything's okay?"

"Yeah . . . I'm fine." She said that with a hesitating mutter of disappointment. She was waiting for me to say "Baby, come back," and I didn't. She needed me. She wanted me.

"Baby, come back," I said, breathy with hungry joy.

"No," she responded too fast, as if she'd been waiting for the line. It was okay; she was just saving face. She was mine.

"Come back." I winked at the phone.

"Lay off, Kenny." Flat.

"I'm coming over, Mommy."

"No you're not." Clenched teeth.

"I'm coming over."

"I'm not gonna *be* here!" she almost shouted. Maybe she wasn't playing after all.

"I'm coming over." Neither was I.

"Kenny, I'm not kidding. I'm leaving!"

"Good."

I grabbed my coat and cabbed it over to her sister's brownstone on Eighty-eighth Street. I sat back in the taxi wobble-jawed, heart thumping. Like I was taking a cab to a fistfight. The cabby was a young curly-haired Porto. He popped in a cassette of some disco Mau Mau noise, checked me out from the corner of his eye, decided I was a young groover too and slid back the partition so I could dig his taste in jams. Sixteen thousand soul sisters backed up by every violin in New York chanted dance, dance, dance, dance, into every opening in my head and face. I wasn't going to leave without her. I rubber-fingered a dollar-fifty through the bulletproof partition and leaped from the car like a G-man getting ready to take off a speakeasy. The hushed street consisted of thirty brownstones and twice as many nude trees.

She was standing outside at the top of the stairs like a street patrol sentry. I strode halfway up, stopped six steps below her and extended my hand upward.

"Let's go home."

"No!" she barked. I moved up one step. She shifted to the left. It looked like we were dueling in a swashbuckler.

"La Di, I'm for real. Come home." I stretched out my

hand again and looked away like time was tight and stop wasting it.

"Kenny? Leave!" She fanned out her hands in front of her in a short sharp motion as if to make me vanish.

"I need you, La Di. I can't make it there." I shrugged.

"Kenny . . ."

"You need me, too, La Di. I know you do, I know you do." I was still staring away, swinging my head like a metronome. I moved up another step. "Come on." I almost touched her.

"I *need* you?" An outraged hiss, furious amazement.

"Yeah." I inched closer.

With a sidearm swipe she slapped my hand away. I gasped and staggered down two steps.

"I need you?" Her eyes were blades. "You arrogant son of a bitch! I need you like I need a *heel* in my throat! I'm so goddamn sick of you, your contempt! Your . . . your anger!"

I couldn't hear her words, just the sound like the steam rising from water poured on sauna rocks. I ran my eyes up and down the quiet brownstone row. A movement caught my eye overhead — her sister standing in a window. My armpits were soaked.

"Ssh, keep it down." I couldn't think.

"Keep it down? You bastard, you . . ."

"Me! Me!" I hit my chest, lurching my head forward in amazement. "*Fuck* me!" I didn't even know what the hell I was saying. If I had been driving right then, we both would have died. "I stayed home for you! I . . ."

"Who the hell asked you to?"

Someone walked down the street, slow and elderly, and we both looked away.

She paced the top step like a lion. I stared at a plaster-smeared crevice by my shoe. I couldn't collect my brains. What was happening?

"Who the hell asked you to?" A hot whisper. She crouched forward as though she were going to leap on me. "I didn't need you stomping around, sulking about my snatch. You don't give a *damn* about my singing, about me! Anything I do that takes me out of your bed you hate! You think I'm helpless! You think I can't sing!"

"Naw." My underwear was damp. I moved up a step, then down a step.

"Well, I *can* sing, but it's *hard,* Kenny! It's hard. But you make it worse. You're breathing down my neck, thinking I suck, you *smother* me, Kenny!"

"Naw." Again, a bleat.

"I know what happened Monday. It was a *clown* show, and Sunday's showcase is gonna be *another* clown show. Maybe I got a hundred clown shows after that. But I was *good* Monday night! And Sunday I'll be *better!* And I'll be better and better and soon those assholes are gonna *stop* laughing!"

"I know," I said weakly.

"I don't ever want you to see me sing again, 'cause you don't *want* me to make it! You don't *believe* in me, you don't *care* about me, you don't *love* me."

"I do." A squeak. I felt myself starting to cry, not sad tears but the panicky stop-stop-please-stop tears that my rageball mother used to reduce me to when I was six. I began squirming.

"All you care about is my cunt! And you can't figure out *why* I don't wanna fuck with you anymore? Well, then *you're* the helpless one! *You're* the stupid one. *You're* the goddamn *Blue*castle *House* man!" She started bawling, doubling over in a half-crouch as if she had stomach cramps. "I'm gonna make it! I'm gonna make it!"

My face melted down like a Greek tragedy mask. I stood six steps below her in my own weeps.

"I'm gonna make it too," I said halfheartedly. Nightmare of sadness. I slowly backed down a step, hoping I would slip and smash the back of my head. "I think you're a good singer," I whispered weakly, lamely.

She turned, went inside and slammed the door.

"I'm gonna make it too, La Donna."

I stood there like Dondi. At some point I turned and started walking down Eighty-eighth Street lost in thought, dragging my feet like I had had a stroke. Behind me came a sharp wooden whack. I ducked. La Donna shouted "Kenny!" When I wheeled around she was flying down the street to me.

"Yay!" I shouted. The brownstone door was swinging back and forth on its hinges. Before I could raise my arms she grabbed me around the chest and bearhugged, her chin drilling into my collarbone.

"Oh, Kenny, I'm sorry. I'm sorry. That was horrible to say to you what I said. I'm *so* sorry, baby. I'm so crazy. Everything's got me *so* scared."

"It's okay, baby. It's okay." I laughed with joy. I didn't want to waste time hugging her. I wanted to break free, snag a cab and take her home. I saw a Checker and tried to hail it, but La Donna wouldn't let go.

"No, Kenny, no." Like we were in bed.

"What?"

"No, not yet, Kenny."

"It's cold, baby." I laughed uneasily.

"I'm not going back yet, Kenny. Please, the other stuff I said is real. I need time, Kenny. I need some time. I really do, I really do . . ." Her chin was still nailed to my chest, her eyes angled upward at me, wet and desperate. She started talking fast and crazy as if I was an executioner who could sometimes be bribed.

"I want this so bad. I can't with us . . . We're not . . . We're like . . . We're not *happening*, we're fighting, and I can't do both. I need to concentrate. We're not *helping* each other. You need time, too, Kenny. You got to figure things out, too."

What time. What. No good. No goddamn good. "What . . . How much time?" Twisting my face, blurting the question like a six-year-old's "AmIgonnagettaneedle?" Three empty cabs and two buses floated downtown past us.

"I don't know!" She released me and her hands fluttered

and swooped like trapped birds in front of my chest. I grabbed
them. Her palms were spongy with sweat. She wasn't wearing
a coat. It was freezing.

"Oh please, Kenny. I know you love me. You just don't
. . . I love you too, I do, but can't you *see*, we're not, can't you
see. Every day is like — look, I'm not doing us justice now.
I need this space. I'll come back. I *swear* it, Kenny. Please?
Please?" Begging. She made me feel as if I was doing something horrible to her. I backed away as if to deny responsi-
bility. I'm no monster. Don't make me into a monster.

"Sure, sure." I shrugged, backpedaling. "I understand.
Sure."

She calmed down and caught her breath. Rubbed her arms
across her chest. "Kenny, I just need to be selfish now. I
don't have enough in me for you and what I want to do. Let
me just get something going. Then we can . . ."

"Just tell me how long." Splotchy islands of perspiration
sprouted on my stomach and chest. I felt like barking and
scratching myself behind my ear with my foot. "A day, a
week, three months, what . . . ? Gimme something to hang it
on, okay? Gimme some motherfucking perspective, okay?
Because . . ."

"I don't know! I don't know! I don't know!" she whisper-
whined, crouching and jumping up and down like a little girl
having to pee.

"Okay. Okay. Okay." I moved forward, then backward,
hand up. "Relax, sweetie, it's okay." My mind was going a
mile a minute. I didn't want her to leave. I didn't want to go
home alone. "Can I just tell you something?"

"What?" She didn't hear me. Her eyes were all over the
place. She started walking back and forth, her face slashed
with her imprisonment to my presence.

"Can I just tell you something?" I repeated halfheartedly.

"What!" She danced in place. She wouldn't have heard a
word I said. Shit. Shit shit shit. "Never mind. It's okay."
Defeated, I extended my arms for a paternal bon voyage hug.

She grabbed me again, her chin finding the same spot, squeezed until she trembled. I could smell sweat. "I love you, Kenny. Thank you, my love." She sprang away from me and trotted back to the brownstone.

I stared at my shoes as they chewed up the pavement, one after the other. Thank you, my love. Thank you, my love. When I finally looked up I had hoofed it to Seventy-ninth and Broadway. What the hell did I ever do that was so goddamn bad she had to do *Prisoner of Zenda* takes on me? You want to fly? Take off. Don't lay it on me. Damn, I'm more lay back than death. Don't lay it on me.

It's just as well I didn't tell her what I wanted to. I wanted to share a memory with her. It would have been inappropriate. If it clicked with her it would have been dirty pool, and if she didn't respond I would have folded like a chaise longue right on the street corner. I wanted to remind her of the first time we said "I love you" to each other. It was our first night back in New York after LA. She was staying over at my place. We were in bed, heavy and cozy after a slow-motion ball. I was lying on my back. She was on her side curled into me, her nose nuzzling and burrowing into my armpit to find a comfortable spot for sleep. The covers were up to her neck and my chest. I had never felt so safe and capable of protecting someone. I said, "I love you." She said, "I love you." And there it was, as natural and as un-self-conscious as baby breath. It was so simple, the timing so perfect, neither of us remembered saying it for days afterward.

Her "I love you, Kenny. Thank you, my love" was a pile of bullshit. She could have squeezed me till my ribs cracked, stuck her tongue down my throat until she tasted my dinner. It was bullshit — it was a hug of relief; she was getting away from me. "Thank you, my love." She never said "My love" like that, like a ham actress.

Okay. So I'm Kenny Solo for a while again. I can handle it. Until she gets straight. Until *she* gets straight. Dig *me*.

FRIDAY

And who the hell did she think *she* was? I'm gonna make it, I'm gonna make it. *You're* the goddamn Bluecastle House man. Fuck *you*, bitch. If it wasn't for me, if I wasn't *paying* for Bossanova, if, what un*grate*ful . . . She didn't have to worry about me wanting her to fail — that attitude of hers would bomb her out soon enough. I hoped she made it. G'head, make it, bitch. I'll die of vitamin deficiency sitting front row center your opening night at the Winter Garden with a big goddamn sign on my chest. "I would've eaten but I had to pay for singing lessons." No goddamn joke. Don't yell at me. You want to talk to me then you talk, but don't goddamn yell at me like everything's black and white. Screwy bitch, that's not right. Maybe I did think she shouldn't go on with her singing but that was for her own goddamn good.

It was my delivery day, which meant I had to go out to Long Island City to the warehouse to pick up the orders I took that week and spend all day backtracking my sales, delivering goods and collecting money. I rented a neighbor's car every Friday for ten bucks, the only time I needed my own wheels. Otherwise I was a staunch believer in what my old man used to say: "If you can't get there with five dollars' worth of cab, then it ain't worth goin'."

I hated Long Island City. It was the ugliest place north of hell — factories, warehouses, grit, shit and cars. I usually went there early because if I showed up at eight-thirty like most of the salesmen I would never get out before ten o'clock. Besides, the less of my fellow Bluecastle House men I ran into the better the day would be.

But as much as I hated Long Island City, I loved getting there. Since I so rarely drove a car, I always got a rush revving up my neighbor's Mustang, pulling out into early morning Manhattan and cruising as bad as I could be over the Queensboro Bridge. That Friday I could have just kept going, done a wheelie on the bridge like Roy Rogers goosing Trigger, whipped around and headed west. I could've hooked up with some roadside diner waitress in New Mexico, lived with her for two weeks, then moved on, hooking up with some young museum tour guide in Tucson. After her two weeks were up I would drive north to Seattle and do two weeks with a young antique store owner. And then I would just keep going, two week affairs, two a month, twenty-four a year. Yessireebob. Just like some big fucking gerbil.

All the way to Long Island City I daydreamed about my roadside diner waitress in New Mexico. Had to be a divorcée, too.

I sat in the diner with the boys. The Mustang was triple-locked up the ass, double-parked in front, so I could watch it from the booth. It had $500 worth of merchandise piled in the trunk and the back seat.

I stayed put as Maurice, Jerry and Al filed out the door.

"You want some more coffee, Kenny?"

"Please."

Charlene poured me a cup, then sat across from me yawning into her hand. "Oh God, I didn't sleep at all last night." Her gypsy hoops gleamed in the sunlight. She could have been anywhere from forty to sixty. "One a my kids got the flu. I was up all night." She massaged her neck.

"How old?"

"Huh?" Her chin was touching her chest.

"How old's the kid?"

"It's the little one, he's eleven."

"What's your husband do, Charlene?"

"Packy? Packy was a mover. He worked for a moving van company."

"What do you mean 'was,' you mean he retired?" Be cool.

"Packy? Oh no. I mean 'was' meaning we're divorced." Tilt.

"Huh." I sipped my coffee while she thumbed through the breakfast orders on her pad.

"You live in the Village?"

"Oh ho." She laughed, not looking up. "Don't I wish it. I live with the poor people out in Queens."

"Whereabouts?"

"You know Whitestone?"

"That's quite a schlep, huh?"

She raised an eyebrow and shrugged, still looking down at her orders.

"You know, ah, I've got a car today. If you want, I can drive you home."

"Oh, thank you, dear, I get a ride with George." Still not looking up.

I glanced over at the grill. Cheeseburger George leaned over the counter reading the *News*, hairy forearms and light-reflecting bald dome. He sang something Greek into his hand as he flipped the pages. The diner was relatively deserted.

"Charlene, you wanna go out, have a drink some evening?" Evening sounded less dirty than night, as if there was still some Daylight Savings Time in it. I was braced for the big no.

"Kenny, I told you." She looked up and not unkindly. "I get a ride with George."

Charlene got up to take an order. I rubbed my face in my palms. I remembered one time when La Donna was deliriously sick — she had 105 degrees, sweating, freezing, a heavy-duty flu was going around — I crawled into bed with her and held her. She fell asleep in my arms and I lay there furious because she didn't acknowledge my sacrifice, the comforting strength of my goddamn presence. I had wanted her to say "Thank you" or "I don't know what I'd do without you" or "Oh, Kenny" or something, but she just slept, and I was sulking while she was crackling with fever next to me. I starting thinking she didn't need me, she didn't need me, you don't need me, bitch? I'll show *you!* So I got up, noisy enough to wake her up, and she freaked and said, "Kenny, don't leave me." Just what the doctor ordered — for me. So I got back into bed and held her for hours.

I felt like taking a goddamn fork and jabbing it in my face. A real nowhere man.

She wasn't asking for anything that unreasonable. Time, that's all. We all need time. Time to think, time to grow, time to work, time to die on the vine. My mind kept doing uncontrollable flip-flops — within minutes I'd go through a rainbow of changes: don't leave me, who needs you, I understand, you're killing me. All very exhausting.

I went to the old German lady's house to deliver her Car-Vac and assorted goods. She invited me in for coffee. We sat and talked and I tried to ignore the cats, which seemed more dense than roaches on a 3:00 A.M. kitchen floor.

"How can you *valk* out dere?" She shivered in her chair and clutched the neck of her dress like a shawl.

"Ah, it's not so bad today. It was colder yesterday."

"Oh," she said, as if I'd just broken down the Rosetta Stone for her.

I pretended this lady was my grandmother. I loved my

grandmother. On Saturdays she would take me to the roller
derby, to monster movies and to wrestling matches. In the
evenings we used to watch more monster movies on her old
Stromberg-Carlson. She hated spics, niggers, other Jews, Ger-
mans, my mother's in-laws, other old people, the neighborhood, her arthritis, her gross heaviness, and any kind of
animal. She was a Hatpin Mary at the wrestling matches, a
rage queen par excellence. But she loved me ferociously, and
it was me and her against the world.

This old German broad didn't even remotely remind me of
my grandmother, except that she was old; that and the fact
that I was sure if we had been related she would have loved me.

"This is good coffee." I winked.

"Ah!" She waved me away. "Why don't you get indoor job!
You get pneumonia!"

"Well, I don't do this all the time." I set my cup on the rug
and three cats drank the rest. "I go to school. I only do this
part time." I was raising my voice as if talking to a deaf
person.

"You go to school!" She nodded in approval. I guess I still
had that need in me from childhood to glow and perform in
front of older people, adults.

"Yeah, I go to college! I'm gonna be a teacher!" I was
almost shouting. Why not medical school, schmuck? Go the
whole route.

"That's good. To teach people." She nodded. I felt insane.

"Yeah, people need teaching. I got a year left, then I graduate." I waved in dismissal at her order in a shopping bag at
her feet. "I'm quitting this soon, this is only to pay for tuition."

"You a smart boy." She squinted in appreciation of my
craftiness.

"Yeah, I'm almost finished."

When I left she was beaming as if she was proud of me. I
walked out, dizzy and totally out of touch with my body. I felt
high but more a high of anarchy than of pleasure.

I almost never lied like that.

Ever since I woke up I had been walking around as if La Donna was some goddamn star, as if she had already made the big time and I was a nobody. It wasn't something conscious; it felt more like a physical pain, a crick in the neck.

I passed Gordon's apartment house. I felt like I wanted to lay off a load something fierce. But not with her. Not there.

"Bluecastle Housewares, Mrs. Macready."

I stood in the doorway of one of my coffee klatchers holding her order in a bag next to my heart, my elbow sticking out at a stiff angle like a Victorian suitor with a box of candy.

Macready opened the door. She was a short juicy chunk of a lady in tan slacks and brown rayon pullover which showed off the concentric stitching of her bra. She was about forty with Prince Valiant bangs and a sharp nose.

"Well, it's the Bluecastle House man!" She had guffawed the loudest of the four when I was riffing with them on Tuesday. She was the most hopeful prospect.

I extended her goods. She stuck her nose in the bag. "What's the damages?"

"Eight-o-nine. Let's call it eight even." I paused significantly. "Plus a cup of coffee."

She read my eyes and I was in like Flynn. She stopped smiling. "Come on in."

I sat at a round Formica table in her kitchen under a six-bulb fake brass chandelier. As she made coffee she sneaked glances at me as if she were going to slip me a Mickey Finn.

"It's cold out." I rubbed my hands. The kitchen dinette was wallpapered with black and white flowers on a mustard gold background.

"I was out earlier," she said.

"Oh yeah?"

She tightrope-walked back to the table, a brimming cup in each hand.

"How do you like it?"

"Black's good." I slipped my hand over hers.

She looked at me as though she wanted me dead, as though she was already nude hugging a pillow on her bed as I remade my Windsor knot in the mirror, hemming and hawing about not being able to make a definite time to meet again because the next five weeks were going to be so crazy for me. But she didn't slip her hand away.

It would be a most unhappy and rageful screw, a grudge hump. But I could have given two shits. Without dropping my stare I nodded toward some vague bedroom over my left shoulder as if to say "Let's get it over with."

She drummed her fingers under my hand. I heard footsteps approaching the dinette. The walk was an unsteady shuffle. I fought down a cooling shudder. A kid appeared in the doorway. He was mongoloid with small, glassy, unfocused pig eyes and a saliva-slick tongue protruding slightly from a small gold-fish mouth. He raised his eyebrows in surprise and cocked his head at me, his mother, then back at me.

She stared at me and withdrew her hand, like he was *my* fucking fault.

"Herbert, what do you want?"

He stared at me, raising and lowering his eyebrows. "Who a you?" in a loud singsong croaking splutter.

"Herbert, what do you want?" Flat and icy.

"Who a you?"

"Hi, Herbert!" I sounded weak and self-conscious like a game-show contestant unexpectedly forced to sing on television.

"Who a you?"

"Excuse me." She shepherded him back down the foyer.

"Who was him?" In that same brassy dingdong singsong. I heard a door quietly close.

"I'm sorry." She stood in the entrance.

"For what?" I shrugged like I ate with mongoloids three times a day. "How old is he?" I tried to make light conversation. "Fourteen?"

"He's twenty-six. I think you'd better leave."

She paid me and as I left I kissed her on the cheek like a jerk.

I stood out in the hallway and for a second I felt as if I could have been anywhere. I didn't even know what part of Manhattan I was in. That anarchy rush got stronger. I could have either killed or gone to sleep with equal gusto. I found a cream sachet foil in my coat pocket, walked down the corridor and knocked on a door.

"Yeah?" A male voice answered.

"Free gift from Bluecastle."

"Slip it under the door."

"You got it." I placed the foil halfway under the door and stomped on my end. I was walking to the elevator when the door swung open; the guy popped out into the hallway in T-shirt and pajama bottoms. He was about my size. His hair was wild and his face was turning colors.

"Whata you, a *smart* son of a bitch?"

He was in a slight crouch. I turned slowly. I was up for it.

"You ruined my fucking rug!"

"Oh yeah?" I felt sleepy. "That's too bad."

"That's . . ." he sputtered.

"Larry! Come inside!" a lady yelled.

"I'll kick your fucking ass!" He moved toward me. I took off my jacket and extended my arms, palms up like a saint.

"Anytime." I nodded serenely.

He stopped, enraged and flustered.

"Larry!"

"Listen, you bastard! I know karate!"

"Anytime." He wasn't going to karate shit.

"I know your fucking boss!" He pointed a finger at me.

"That's too bad." I smiled.

"Larry!"

"It's gonna be too bad for you!" He stormed back into his apartment and slammed the door.

"Anytime." I continued to stand there like a plaster saint

as the two of them screamed at each other behind the door.

I didn't make the rest of my deliveries, just headed home in-stead. I felt bushed.

There was a funny smell in the kitchen. The broccoli floated in the pot in a puddle of melted ice. The salad dress-ing had been out all night and there was a two-inch layer of sediment in the old fashioned glass. I opened the oven door; the half-baked chicken thighs looked nasty and withered. Sur-prisingly, I didn't see any roaches. They must have eaten themselves to death overnight.

After trashing the food, I did two hundred and twenty-five sit-ups; my usual hundred and fifty and the seventy-five I couldn't do the previous night because of the dope.

My phone rang.

"Yeah?"

"Kenny, what the hell happened?" It was Fat Al.

"What?" I felt sleepy again.

"You fucking know what."

"The guy got pissed." I shrugged.

"He got . . . We're getting *sued*, Kenny."

"That's too bad." I ran the edge of my pinky around the square corners of the Touch Tone digits. There was silence on both ends.

" 'That's too bad.' " Al read back my quote. "Whata you goin' mental on me, Kenny?"

"Nope." I wiped the accumulated dust off my finger onto the couch.

"Well, what the hell do you suggest?"

"I suggest we have his legs broken." My eyes focused on a slick of sunlight on the polished wood floor.

"What?"

"And then you know what I suggest for *you*, you fucking hump?" The floor kept moving in and out of focus as if I was staring at it through unadjusted binoculars.

More silence. Deep nasal breathing.

"I suggest you strap a goddamn catcher's mask to your butt because the next time I see you I'm gonna try to shove that motherfucking electronic watch of yours right up your ass."

"If I *ever* see your face around that diner again, I'm gonna take your fuckin' case an' I'm gonna shove it up *your* ass, you got that?"

"That's a very childish response, Al." My voice was flat, but I could feel my heartbeat in my face.

Al hung up. I was out of a job. Kenny makes a move.

It was goddamn Friday afternoon. That used to be the best time in the week for me. The beginning of the weekend. As high as Monday morning was low. Playground time. Why was it that everybody seemed to have more friends when they were kids than when they were adults? Adults never had buddies. I could have used some company.

The house was freezing. I sat on the couch, the living room phone in my lap. I sat there zoned out until the room was almost dark. I didn't feel like calling La Donna. As isolated as I was it felt like the wrong thing to do, the wrong type of heaviness. My hands were icy and slightly moist. My armpits smelled like coffee grounds. I needed a shower but I didn't have the wherewithal to get my ass up off the couch. It was too cold. I wanted to call Donny but was too embarrassed about last night. I stared at my hand on the receiver, then both hands, the same hands I'd always had. They didn't look thirty years old. I couldn't imagine them getting arthritic, covered with liver spots. They were young man's hands, teen-age hands, finger-popping hands. Maybe I wasn't really thirty. Maybe I wasn't really aging. Maybe the aging process was purely psychosomatic, yeah, and maybe what really got you high was the rolling paper not the dope.

My baby wants space from me, she got it.

I had about $1500 to my name. I was unemployed. I was glad I didn't have to door-to-door anymore, but that's as far

as it got in my head. I noticed the rest of Donny's joints in
the cigar tin on the wall unit.

The job I had before Bluecastle was working with my uncle
doing tax forms out in Queens. It was also an hour's commute
from where I was living, which was with those guys from college. *That* was a disaster. It wasn't a total disaster. At least
they were company. As a matter of fact, we used to have
some pretty good times.

I remember one guy, Alvin, was heavy into jazz. What
were their other names? That place was okay. I didn't spend
much time there, and the minute I started making money I
split, but somehow the bad memories didn't hold up so strong
over time.

But the place had been a dump. Big deal. My joint was as
neat as a pin, but I still wound up playing handball with my
own shit. I wondered if they'd kept that place. It was almost
eight years ago. I had a fantasy of waltzing in and those guys
still in long hair, sitting on pillows, eating wok-fried vegetables
and grooving on Janis Joplin and Vanilla Fudge, as though I
had just stepped out for some smokes. For the hell of it I got
up, got my coat, and got ready to take a walk. I hadn't been
there since the day I left. Maybe I could move back in. I was
jobless. I could use the rent break. Jobless. I kept waiting
for a panic lick, but nothing happened.

I walked over to Ninety-third and Columbus, where we had
lived. The *building* was there at any rate, but the windows
were sheeted over with gray metal and the building entrance
was plastered with posters for long-gone Latino concerts. I
guess they didn't live there anymore.

I was out of a job. That was serious stuff. Come on, Kenny,
let's get heavy here. I walked from Ninety-third Street to
Twenty-eighth Street, worked up an appetite, decided to have a
nice fish dinner. I was eating too much red meat anyhow.
Walked back up to Columbus and Seventy-seventh Street. By
walking I saved a dollar's worth of tokens.

I sat over my bluefish dinner remembering how much I hated fish. Behind me a gigantic plastic trout was mounted on a long oval board. To the left of me two thin faggots, one with a trimmed beard, discussed research grants. To the right, a young couple argued over a mound of steamers who *relatively* speaking had a better backhand, given the fact that she had been taking lessons for six years and he for less than a year.

What I hated most about eating alone in a restaurant was the embarrassment. It was like announcing publicly how fucked up you were. If you're eating alone, you should look for a place with a counter. Eating alone at a counter is less obvious. I'd bought a *Post* so I could at least bury my nose in something. I skimmed the classifieds. After two minutes I was sweating and felt like I was going to cry. I ran my fingers through my hair, tugging at the greasy strands. I had lost my job and I was all alone.

"Are you okay?" The waitress stood over me, her short blond hair wrapped in a blue paisley kerchief.

"No, I lost my job, and I'm all alone."

That took her aback.

"Oh, you poor baby."

"It's true. I just got fired and I don't have any friends. I got fifteen hundred dollars in the bank and that's the size of it."

She touched my arm. "Aw, I wish there was something I could do."

"You can go out with me after work."

"Naw, my boyfriend . . ."

"You can treat me to dessert then."

"Dessert comes with the dinner."

"Well, you can give me extra whipped cream on top. And I'll take it now."

She laughed, I laughed. "Just bring me my extra whipped cream." I turned to the movie page in the *Post*. I started reading the paper backward, skimmed the theater page. Then a whole page of announcements for singles' dances, mainly in Queens and Brooklyn, about half in synagogues. Not on your life. I needed something hipper, faster, looser. I didn't want to score in a house of worship. I needed a bar. A singles' bar. A singles' bar. It sounded like the first good idea I had had all night. A singles' bar. It was eight-fifteen. Early. I passed on dessert and trotted home. Young man. I was a young man. Strong. Tight. White. And ready to love.

I burst into my house like Eliot Ness, threw off my coat, dropped a Barry White and two James Browns on the machine, tore off the rest of my clothes, jumped into the shower and started to prep. No soap. That night I did Vitabath. It left a tangy essence. Organic Apricot Creme Rinse, Shampoo Gel and Conditioner. Three rinses, jump out. I had laid the bath towels on the radiator and they were as warm as muffins. James Brown was shrieking in the living room and I was standing in front of the mirror holding that fist mike, squeezing out high E over C, one shoulder up because *I* had a brand-new bag. *I* was gonna do the Mother Popcorn and *I* was going to a singles' bar where *I* was going to find *her*.

I shaved my face as carefully as if my skin were the turf around the eighteenth hole of a PGA golf course. Slapped Aqua Di Selva on my palms and drew my hands in a wet noose around the back of my neck, behind my ears and did a figure eight across my chest. Baking soda underarm spray. Talcum powder. I ran into the living room, raised the volume on the stereo, ran back into the john to do a twenty-minute hot comb. Into the bedroom where I slipped on white Jockeys. No good. Off they came and on went rust-colored bikinis. They made me look like I had acromegaly of the cock. I checked my front and profile in the full-length for possible paunch. Not a chance. Checked to see if I had a cute ass. Girls always notice a dude's cute ass. I was in business.

All the while I was fighting down a queasy feeling, as if I was about to reenlist or buy the Brooklyn Bridge. In the back of my mind I knew what I was doing, that I was blowing it again. Scared, I was trying to bury my brains by burying my dick. Trying to fuck my fear, but fuck it, I couldn't deal with it any other way. So there I was dressing to the nines and trying to feel like Tony singing "Tonight" in *West Side Story*. It was Las Vegas night in my heart, and I had selective amnesia.

I put on pearl gray continental slacks, a thick wool hot pink turtleneck and my black velvet sports jacket. I took off the jacket and changed the sheets on the bed to crisp cool chocolate browns, turned the reversible fake velvet bedspread from its print side to its solid beige side. Put on the jacket again, went into the kitchen, filled a brandy snifter with a triple shot of Lemon Hart white rum, a squirt of o.j., chugged *that* down for a nice buzz, went into the bedroom, pulled a college anthology of essays on modern theater from a shelf, dog-eared it in a few places, set it on my night table, turned off all but the dramatic lights and I was gone.

I had a nice buzz in the cab over to the East Side. I loved rum. I fantasized about buying a lot of good booze. Scotch, gin, rum, vodka, whiskey. It was good to have a well-stocked bar. A well-stocked bar. That phrase had a nice ring to it. It sounded substantial. Solid. I got off on Second Avenue and Seventy-fifth Street. Dirty Ernie's was supposed to be pretty good. It was set up as a fake English pub. There was sawdust on the floor and a dark-stained wooden chest-high room divider separating the place into a bar—pick-up area and a dining area. There were three tall bartenders — white shirts, thin ties, and towels hanging like miniaprons from their waists. A large color television over the bar.

It was nine o'clock. Too early. There were only two or three women and eight or nine guys. The guys freaked me out. They looked like they came from rural Canada. Pressed chinos, crisp plaid shirts buttoned to the neck, glasses that caught the entire bar, short, almost cowlicked hair. They stood there swaybacked, one hip higher than the other, their

arms folded across their chests. They stared hard across the
barren floor with weird frozen smiles as if girls were going to
materialize out of the sawdust.

It was nine o'clock on a Friday night and those heart-
breakers had been waiting for action for at least an hour.
Them and me. Me in my velvet and continentals. It was nine
o'clock and I was there, too. But I was different. I was
special. They weren't me. No sir. No way. The girls were
blue-ribbon hogs, but in that place any girl became a hot
number. Every woman was the last girl on earth. One chick
had a bare midriff and it seemed as lust-inspiring and pro-
vocative as a bikini in midtown.

For the next hour I sat at the bar, drinking rum and pre-
tending to watch a basketball game which had orange guys
against green guys. People started piling in. I was having
a hard time getting rolling so I continued watching the tube.
A lot of guys watched the tube, leaning against the bar or the
room divider, their drinks tucked under their armpits like
footballs. There was no sound on, but we all watched that
fucking game with a burning intensity like we were politicos
and the screen was flashing election results. I didn't even know
who the hell was *playing*. My elation was taking a bath.
Around me guys swamped girls like pigeons after croutons,
blurting out lines so transparent and tacky that even *I* was
offended. No wonder nobody ever got laid. I watched. I
listened. I was an observer. A girl nearby, the brittle remains
of an almost-melted ice cube floating on top of her half-hour-
old drink, listened politely.

"I'm thinking about goin' back to work with George. You
know, Harrison? I'm tired of Jaggers' crap. George owes
me from way back. He called me this morning but I wasn't
in."

Her eyes darted like mice. A pocketbook dangled from the
crook of her elbow.

A fat girl walked in wearing one of those bright green

phosphorescent chokers that the spades were selling in Times Square. Her neck glowed in the dark. Guys around her were suddenly obsessed with science. Frowned intelligently, opened their come-ons with questions about the chemical properties of phosphorescent paint.

I felt like I was coming down with lockjaw I felt so pulled into myself. I was a walking cave-in. A girl leaned against the room divider watching the game by herself. She was built like a bear but she was alone and if I didn't make a move in the next few minutes I knew I wouldn't make a move all night.

"This place is something else, huh?"

She made a noise.

"This, ah, this is my first time here. I'm, ah, on assignment. I'm writing an article for *Playboy* on sex. You wouldn't *believe* what I can write off as research, hah-hah." What the hell was wrong with me? What slime.

"Oh yeah?" She gazed over my left shoulder.

"Do you, ah, do you like basketball?"

" 'Scuse me." She split.

Who the fuck was she to walk away from me? I got laid more than God. I was deeper than the Pacific. I wouldn't even have *looked* at her outside of a shithole like this. If La Donna were ever to walk into a place like this, they would shit. They would die. She had more class, more presence, was more beautiful . . . If she came through that goddamn door the silence that would fall over this place would be religious. What the hell was I doing this for? La Donna was royalty. I was used to royalty, subtlety, refinement. A night in the sack with me changed women's lives, gave new definitions to the word "desire." On assignment from Playboy — sweet Jesus.

The guy next to me was a hasty shaver. Tiny shreds of toilet paper stuck in festive red clots to his neck and chin.

The girls kept crowding in. I didn't know what to say. I couldn't think. I couldn't think. Everything I could have said sounded so fucking stupid. A pretty girl was talking to two chinks. Piss me off. Talk to me! Talk to me! *Please* don't make me say something stupid. I couldn't take it. Couldn't do it alone.

Every schmuck there had a partner. I needed somebody to laugh and elbow with. Slap palms with after I blew it with a chick by saying I was on assignment from *Playboy*. I needed reinforcements. I needed to pick up a guy first, a friend first, *then* some tail.

The place was now jammed. I went outside, found a pay phone and got Donny's number from Information. Nobody answered.

I walked over to a new place, Fahrenheit's. It had a different layout. There was no dining area, just a bar along one wall, several small tables and a dance area. On a raised platform a goateed guy played a guitar. He finished "Welcome Back Kotter," then jumped into a Mamas and Papas medley.

This place was less crowded; there was more space. No one was dancing. I bought a rum and o.j. A thin, sad-looking girl stared at the singer, her thumb hooked over the top of her drink.

"You know, I've been standing here fifteen minutes wondering what to say, so I'm just gonna say that." I gave her a Mexican bandit grin.

She mumbled something and I was off and running.

"You know" — I winced seriously — "there are so many isolated people here. I can't tell what they want, what they need." I came on like Dr. Kenny's one-man sensitivity clinic. Her arms were folded as if she were cold. I stretched back to the bar to deposit my glass. When I turned back some guy had squeezed between us and was riffing on her like a demon. *Her* fucking loss. That was it. I started looking for a guy.

There were three prospects within ten feet of me. One was picking his nose, the other two weren't. One down. Both the other guys were good-looking dudes. The guy nearest me was my height, slim and blond. The other was shorter, more muscular and dark like me. I liked him better. He was dressed nice — tweed pants, two-tone shoes and a brown turtleneck.

"That guy's fucking horrible," I muttered to him and smirked in the direction of the singer.

He chuckled.

"This guy always play here?"

He shrugged. "I wouldn't know. I never been here."

"Oh yeah? Me neither." The guy sounded Brooklyn despite his Ivy threads and my accent degenerated until I talked like an extra from *Marty*. "Beasts." I grimaced, scanning the women. "All fucking beasts. I'd like to dip their faces in dough and make animal crackers."

"They ain't all bad," he said mildly and I felt like a shit. They weren't all bad at all. He was a better person than me.

"You from Brooklyn?"

"Yeah." He smiled. "You?"

"Manhattan." I made it sound like Brooklyn. "Whereabouts in Brooklyn, Bensonhurst?"

"Bay Ridge, you know Bay Ridge?"

"Sure, my cousin lives in Bay Ridge. You know a guy named Mark Becker?"

He shook his head.

"My name is Kenny." I casually extended my hand. "Kenny Becker." I seemed more nervous introducing myself to this guy than I had been trying to score.

He took my hand briefly in a short shake. "Terry Saperstein. You know something, Kenny? You're right, this guy *is* fucking horrible," he sidemouthed.

I got a weird feeling of comfort when he said that. It was like the time Fat Al asked me what was wrong and called me by my name in the diner that morning. Maybe Terry and I would become friends.

"It's fucking hard to get laid in here. All the fucking girls are in teams."

"Yeah." He smiled.

"It's like the reason girls come here in teams is so each one can make sure the other doesn't have too good a time." I jutted my chin at two pretty girls in dungarees and blazers. "Like those two trombones over there."

I bought another drink. When I finally got my change and turned around Terry was gone.

"Kenny, over here." Terry was sitting in between the two girls, an arm extended to me. He worked faster than the Flash. "Kenny, this is Felice, she's from Manhattan, too!" He offered me the girl with cupcake-sized tits and a Winky Dink smile.

"You're from Manhattan? That's amazing! *I'm* from Manhattan!" I slapped my heart.

"Oh yeah? Whereabouts?" She was a petite blonde, semi-drunk, weaving in place with Arthur Murray dance steps to keep from falling down.

"This place is wild, huh?" I didn't know what else to say. Terry was sitting with Felice's teammate, heads down, rapping intensely and quietly.

"I'm doing a paper for Sosh on how people rap in singles' bars." Felice almost fell against me.

"Oh yeah? Which college?"

"Queens."

"What year, senior?"

"I'm a soph." That meant nineteen. I started one of my death trips in my head again. Nineteen was like my baby cousin. "You in college?" That made me feel better.

"Nah, I graduated."

"Where'd you go?"

"Dartmouth. You ever hear of Dartmouth?"

Felice leaned over and tapped her friend on the arm. "Mary, he went to Dartmouth." Terry made a face. I guess he wasn't getting anywhere. Mary was mousy and unhappy-looking.

"You know Jeffrey Fein?"

"Fein, Fein." I bit my lip and cocked my head.

"He's a senior, he's on the squash team."

"Nah, I graduated three years ago." I winked at Terry, but he didn't know me. He wouldn't have known I was talking out of my ass.

Felice staggered slightly in Terry's direction, smiling at him. Terry returned the smile. Mary glanced away. I moved between Terry and Felice.

"Hey, does anybody remember this?" The guitarist started singing his own lame version of "In the Still of the Night." "Does anybody remember who sang that?" No one answered. A few couples started dancing. It was the Five Satins but I wasn't going to be the putz to yell it out.

"How about this one, who did this? Does anybody remember this? 'Earth Angel.' " Nobody remembered; everybody remembered. Who gave a shit. The people there who remembered hit tunes from 1956 I think would be more into forgetting. Besides, if they were old enough to actually remember dancing to that stuff and were *still* doing *this* scene I don't think they would be into advertising.

The floor was littered with couples.

"Hey!" A drunk, fat guy stepped away from the bar and roared, "Does anybody remember *this?*" He grabbed his crotch with both hands, laughed, turned to leave and smacked his forehead on the doorframe.

"You wanna dance?" That was Felice asking me.

We danced without grinding. I liked the weight of her arms on my neck. I rested a hand on her jutting hipbone, my drink in the other hand. I had a new girlfriend.

"Hold on, one second." I set my glass on the bar and when I turned around she was dancing with someone else. It seemed as if every time I turned my head I got bird-dogged. I felt crushed; what happened to the love that once was ours?

She was dancing with Terry. Mary sat at the bar, angrily scratching her scalp with a long nail.

I was getting ready to split when the song ended. Felice grabbed my arm. I was back.

"Hey, you all wanna get stoned?" she asked. Tricky question.

"Not here," I said, giving Terry the high sign. "Let's all go up to my place."

"Great!" Felice grabbed Mary's arm, too. "Let's all go up to Kenny's!"

Terry gave me a shot on the arm like "Good goin', man." I felt like a team player. Life was great.

Trouble. Mary didn't want to come along. Felice was honor-bound to stick by her friend.

I ushered Felice to the corner alcove between the bathrooms and made a last-ditch plea for a party time.

"I can't, I gotta stay with Mary. You want my phone number?" She rummaged in her bag and whipped out pen and paper.

Back at the bar, Terry was gone. Mary still sat like a geri-atric at a window.

"Where's Terry?" I asked her.

"Home," she muttered, like "Fuck him anyway." For some reason, Terry's splitting hurt the most. I'd been used.

I turned down an offer to go bar-hopping with them.

I walked up Second Avenue, pissed as pissed could be. But I knew. I knew all along what the score was. Even before I showered that night I knew what the fucking score was with that scene.

A phone number. Christ. A phone number. I could have stayed home, got in bed with the Yellow Pages and had an orgy. But screw it. It wasn't my scene anymore. I didn't slave forty hours a week to dress up Friday night, piss away twenty bucks' worth of liver-destroying alcohol all for a phone number. What a goddamned life. All for a phone number, maybe a kiss, a date, a poke, a fuck. Then work Monday with fantasies of cozy weekends in a New England cabin, snifters and turtlenecks by the fire, romance, marriage, planning for some mythical, magical future. Strolling down Saturday night for the Sunday *Times*. It was a fucking mirage. A goddamn public relations lie. A scrap of paper with a phone number. It was whacking your pud or buying a cute blouse in Bloomingdale's and thinking you're hot shit because you know the bartender's first name and are reading all of Kurt Vonnegut and being proud to qualify for a Master Charge and getting sinking feelings in your gut every time the phone rings because you don't know if it's him/her from Dirty Ernie's or your whiny unappeasable cunt of a mother and where the hell are the Valium and all those goddamn young swingers go back, go back, go back every Friday night because maybe *this* week, maybe *this* week. That bastard selective amnesia. That goddamn Las Vegas of the heart. And everybody was getting taken to the cleaners. Going home wearing a barrel. Snake eyes up the ass. Just like me.

I stomped all the way up to Eighty-sixth Street in the cold. The streets were littered with well-dressed singles window-shopping bars.

I stopped at a small bar, not to score but because for the first time that night I needed a drink. The place was called Mr. Natural's. No music, no dancing, a small tight crowd. A four-foot-wide lounging lane ran the length of the bar. The bartender had a longish shag cut. He looked like an Afghan hound. Most of the crowd seemed to know each other. As a matter of fact, I'm sure they did — they probably bumped into each other every weekend.

"You look like a deep thinker."

That came from my right. She was thin and nervous with a narrow head, high cheekbones and suspicious eyes. Her hair was in a permanent like a model in a Lady Clairol ad and she smoked a thin cherry-scented cigar.

"That's exactly what I am, a deep thinker." I rested an elbow on the bar and gave her my best Marcello.

She was a trainee buyer at Altman's, hated it, hated bars, hated her sister whom she lived with on the Upper West Side (Hey! I live there, too!) and never got drunk. I tried one of her cigars. Some guy tried to bird-dog me. She shot him down as I looked away like I could care less. I knew I would score because she said hello to me first. Her name was Kristin.

I grabbed her wrist, tilting her watch slightly toward me. It was eleven-thirty.

"Do you have an appointment?" She smirked.

"Not at all, I just wanted to see what time it was because I've been up since Wednesday." I had no idea why I said that. I just was checking the time to touch her arm.

"Wednesday, huh? You look pretty rested to me." She peaked an eyebrow skeptically.

"That's because I've mastered the catnap like the Chinese. They stay up all night reading, then fall into these intense five-minute sleeps now and then during the day."

"Sounds very Zen to me." She ditched her cigar. I was pretty sure she was goofing on me. Suddenly I felt very tired, as if to back up my Wednesday story. If I wasn't going to score in the next five minutes I would just as soon go home and sleep.

"Oh, I meant to ask you, is your sister older or younger than you?"

"Older, she's thirty-four."

"How old are you?"

"Thirty-one." That sounded hopeful. She had twelve years' desperation on Felice.

"How old are you?" She sounded defensive.

"Me? Thirty-two." I added two years to make her unparanoid. I wanted to ask her to come back with me right then, but I pussied out.

"Are these mainly regulars?" I squinted around the bar, bored with my own question.

"Oh yeah, about three quarters." She didn't look around.

"You come here a lot, hah?" I asked, helping myself to another of her cigars.

"Yeah, usually with my sister. She's home recuperating from visiting our parents."

"Where, in Florida?"

"Nope." She smiled. "New Jersey."

"What, Orange?"

"Elizabeth."

"Well, this is my first time here, which I'm sure you heard before, but it's true." I felt myself shifting into lightweight candidness. "Matter of fact, I wouldn't even be here tonight except I'm totally out of my skull, totally nuts." My mouth felt like it was on automatic pilot, but I was feeling a little better, relaxed, more connected than usual. "You know what I've been doing this week?" I winked. "I've been yelling at my TV, going to peep shows. I went back to my old hangout, from when I was a kid. I've been through a whole bunch of dead-end bullshit this week. A real nowhere week. I also quit my job today." I ran it down like errands. "I've been working six years as a Bluecastle House man, and I just up and quit." I grinned in triumph.

She looked at me admiringly, a slow smile on her lips. "Wow, how does it feel?"

"Good," I said without thinking. "Great."

"Whata you gonna do now?"

I shrugged with more devil-may-care bravado than I felt. "We'll see."

"I wish I had the nerve to quit."

"Hey, just do it. The only way to do it is to do it." I put my hand on hers for emphasis. She moved her thumb against my finger.

"But aren't you scared?"

"Who me? I'm terrified. I told you, this has been some bitch of a week. An unreal week."

"A 'not me' week?" She nodded knowingly.

"A what?"

"Not me. That feeling when you're so out of it you don't even feel like you're living inside your own body. It's worse than a bad mood. It's a nothing mood."

"Oh ho, not me, hah? Yeah, I've been in a 'not me' mood, on and off for many years if you wanna know the truth."

She tapped a cigar on her thumb.

"The best years are over, kid. High school, the guys, the playground, the girlfriends. It was all there. The *passion* was there. I was alive then, not like now. Shit. Now sometimes I want to hold a mirror to my mouth to see if I'm still breathing, but then, then I was really wailin'. I used to have everybody on the floor all the time. I was court jester of the 'in crowd.' They used to call me Kenny the Riffer."

"I hated high school. I was one of those drag-ass depressed girls always schlepping a clarinet case around. We would have hated each other."

"Oh yeah? Well, hey, I don't mean to say I was the king of the school." I was afraid to veer her into a down mood.

"I was real lonely in high school." She finished her drink. I tried to catch the bartender's eye, but he was jammed down at the other end of the bar.

"Well, I was too. I mean on the inside, because I was like a separate person watching myself do my routines. Always. That's loneliness, isn't it?"

She nodded. We were quiet for a while. We ordered another round of drinks.

As I sat there staring at my drink I thought of La Donna singing "Feelings" up onstage, me sitting alone in the Carnegie wanting some girl to touch the back of my head, to slip her hand around me and press her palm into my forehead — my hands, teen-age hands, Donny clutching, grabbing for a mindless riff to save himself from silence. I hoped La Donna would make it. I hoped someday we would be together again. I felt crumpled, deflated.

I started out trying to save Kristin from a down trip and

I wound up dancing alone in my head at a one-man blues bash. It must have been showing in my face because her tone became softer, more personal. I didn't give a shit. I wanted to get laid.

"See, like I said, I had a rotten time in high school. But it wasn't high school. I think the problems with me started a lot earlier. I was brought up in such a way that there was no *way* I could have enjoyed high school. My mother was constantly telling me how horrible a child I was. Once when I was six she came back from church and told me she asked Jesus why, what she did when *she* was a kid that was so sinful that He punished her by giving her *me* as a child, see. I grew up with *that* bullshit, and when my older sister Patty drowned at a beach when I was eight my mother said, 'I wish it was you instead.' So, by the time I got to high school I felt so goddamned nonhuman and hated I didn't have a chance in a thousand."

Maybe La Donna and me would get together sooner than I imagined. I was changing, I was thinking. I could help her. We could both make it.

I latched onto the last few minutes of what Kristin was saying. She sounded like some therapy head. What a big pile of bullshit. She was sucking wind too. I cut her short by grabbing her wrist.

"Yeah yeah yeah, but let me tell *you* something. No matter what happened to you, no matter where you've been, you're here *now,* and *now* is what you got to deal with!" I banged the bar with my fist. "You know, you can spend your whole life thinking about the past and feeling sorry for what happened or didn't happen, but ah, wherever you've been, you're here *now* and here and now are where you're gonna find the things you need. Now, *I'm* hurtin', you're hurtin'. The answer is *here,* not back there."

I ordered two rum and o.j.'s and when the drinks came in thin-stemmed goblets I accidentally broke the glass with the pressure of my fingers, splashing the drink all over me. Luckily I didn't cut myself. They gave me a free refill.

We sat thigh to thigh in the cab headed for the West Side. I felt like a hunter bringing home game, but I also felt angry. I felt frightened. I wanted to bang her brains out.

She made herself comfortable on the couch. I put on the Coltrane album and made drinks in the kitchen.

After ten minutes or so of totally meaningless conversation I brought my arm in a sunrise-to-sunset arch behind her back, caressing the side of her neck. She turned her head to me, eyes down, bypassed my mouth and kissed me under my ear. I leaned back, my hands in her hair. She pressed her palms against my stomach. I tensed my gut muscles. She slid her hand back up to my throat. I slightly disentangled myself enough to move, and holding her by the arms I raised her to a standing position. She seemed unsteady, as if unsure about what I was doing. We walked temple to temple almost in slow motion to my bedroom. Her arm had somehow wound up across my shoulder and it felt unnatural there.

Sliding to the bed we started tongueing and grinding which didn't feel like much because we had all our clothes on. After a few minutes we parted in slow motion and undressed ourselves, sitting back to back cater-cornered on the bed. I purposely didn't look at her undressing, as if that was a sign of my maturity. She didn't look at me. When we were nude we lay back on the bed, on our sides. She slid her thigh between my legs. The first full flesh contact was a rush and I crushed her ribs with a grinding hug. She was flat-chested but long-legged. I slid my hand down her spine, through her buttocks and into her cunt. It was only damp. My finger touched the hard rubber rim of a diaphragm. La Donna used a diaphragm.

"Do you need to put in jelly?" I asked casually, mainly to show her I was hip and experienced with diaphragms.

"Yeah, I guess."

"Nah, I was thinking maybe we should put some in now

rather than at the last minute, you know?" I tried to make that suggestion sound soft and romantic.

"I guess." She went into the living room and returned with a nylon floral cosmetic bag dangling from a loop around her thumb.

She sat on the bed and took out a tube of cream and a clear plastic syringe.

"You want me to do that for you?" I softly offered. I didn't know why we were being so polite. It was like our well-mannered gentleness was a margarine substitute for intimacy.

"No. It's okay." She raised the syringe slightly above eye level, screwed the mouth of the tube into the mouth of the syringe and squeezed, forcing the plunger all the way out and filling the glass with cream. She reminded me of Madame Curie.

"Here at the Will Rogers Institute, our scientists work tirelessly," I announced into my fist. She gave a short, pre-occupied chuckle, then leaned back until her spine was only inches off the bed, and shot up the cream. She sat up and put all the stuff back into her cosmetic bag and dropped the bag on the floor. I reached for her, my eyes averted, and we slowly reclinched. I slid down her body dryly kissing every-thing in my path, nipples, beauty marks, ribs, navel and finally pubic hair. She twisted her legs so I couldn't go any farther.

"I just put in the cream." She winced.

"I don't mind." I gently parted her thighs and got to work. She lay back, eyes closed, a look of discomfort on her face, flinching now and then, finally reaching down for me and making motions to pull me up. I felt unappreciated. I crawled back up her body wiping my mouth on her belly. She rolled me off and went for my prick. She sucked too hard; every once in a while her teeth pinched me. The idea of what she was doing was more exciting than the actual physical sensation and I knew I wouldn't come if she blew me for an hour. I slightly raised my knees; she took the cue and crawled up my body. We kissed, rolled over. I slipped myself inside her, then immediately pulled out. No. This had all the markings of a bum fuck and no. Not tonight. Not after this week. I couldn't take it. She frowned.

"Whoa, listen." I sat up, smiling. "We gotta relax, you think?" I held out my hand as if to touch her, but left it hovering over her thigh. She propped herself on her elbows, her stomach tensing.

"You think?" I smiled harder, but not greasy.

She nodded in tentative agreement. "What do you have in mind?"

"Listen, let's start all over again."

"What do you mean?"

"Let's get dressed and start over again." I shrugged. "Just trust me, okay?" I wasn't sure exactly what I had in mind, but *I* trusted me. I got dressed. She didn't move. "No, it'll be good, it'll be good." I handed her her dress. She slipped it over her head, moved to the edge of the bed and put on her shoes.

"Come here." I sat on the floor cross-legged at the foot of the bed and patted a spot in front of me. Then I got up, went into the living room, threw on the Coltrane again and came back in with a lit joint.

"Just sip it. I don't want no acid trip here. We're just gonna . . ." I nodded and dipped my head. "Nice, like that." I passed her the jay and closed my eyes.

After a few tokes, I reached across to her and held her hand. Okay, Mr. Kenny. Get horny. Get sexy. Think thighs, think lady. Think clothes. Black and slinky and dropping like petals. Think pink. I kneaded her palm with my thumb. I slid my fingers under her dress, letting them rest on the softest part of her thigh. She rubbed my arm with both hands as if to draw me to her crotch. I helped her to her feet, turned her around to face the bed and hugged her from behind, kissing her neck, drawing my fingers down her throat, squeezing her with my arms. Reaching behind her, she tugged my pants down my hips. I unzipped the back of her dress and pushed it down to her stomach by running my hands in a V from her shoulders to her belly. She kept working on my dick, her fingers moving from my balls to the head. I plunged my hands into her bush, pushing her dress past her hips until it dropped to her ankles. She was as stoned as I was. Her two front teeth glistened between her slightly parted lips. She stood on tiptoe and I slipped inside, my arms draped across her hips like a G-string. My lips formed the words "I love you," then they shaped "Wa wa" as if to erase "I love you."

And then we went at it. She held on to my neck, her pelvis pushing against my arms as I kept grinding inside her, running my fingers through her bush, rubbing her clit, slamming her buttocks with my hips until we both fell belly down on the bed. I flashed on the words "class clown." We disentangled to sprawl across the center of the bed. She lay on her back, I slipped myself inside, this time from the front. She sucked in air, ran the soles of her feet up and down the backs of my thighs, and I knew I couldn't last. I was going to pop my wad. She clawed my ass and moaned in my ear and I was a goner. I gave it all I had.

"Oh go!" she shouted, and I exploded, then kept going, kept going more with my hips than with my traumatized prick until she pressed her cunt bone right into me, clamped my ass as hard as she could, slowed me down to short, intense movements, rocking crotches until she started trembling like the vibrations of a train approaching a station. She let out with a roaring gasp. The mattress was shaking like magic fingers. When I finally rolled off, we were both pockmarked with puddles of sweat in the valleys of our bodies and there was a huge wet spot the exact shape of the continent of Africa on the dark brown sheets.

I reached over to hold her face in my hands and kissed her

on the mouth. I felt terrified. Not me. I felt not me. Despite the sweat, I grabbed her, hugged her, my fingers yammering through her hair. I was scaring her. She laughed and tried to get playful, tickling my ribs. I didn't respond. Didn't even crack a smile. Just pressed her to me, my hands on her shoulder blades, my cheek on her jaw, our body heat rising like steam. Not me.

"I'm gonna pee in bed." Pushing me away, she jumped up for the bathroom.

I jerked, remembering the sensation of the fragile glass exploding in my hand. I flashed on sitting in the high school auditorium with a bunch of guys watching some dumb shit movie, *The Yearling, Old Yeller*. It was assembly day. We wore white shirts. I cracked jokes nonstop for the first twenty minutes of the movie. A fat kid in the row in front of me turned around and said, "Do we gotta listen to you all movie?" Snickers. I was so mortified I said, "Yes," and, gray-faced, continued riffing for another fifteen minutes until I could slide into silence gracefully. The snickers were from my friends. I felt betrayed. Lied to. I hated everybody. I felt so alone I wanted to run away, die, make them worry.

I remembered being made to stay after class one day in fifth grade for acting like an asshole in an attempt to entertain my classmates. Everybody filed out at three o'clock, me sitting alone, arms folded across my desk watching them leave, still winking and rolling my eyes at those who were looking back at me on their way out. But the reality was that I felt horrible, an animal in a cage. I expected the teacher to yell at me; instead, she sat next to me in a student's small chair, put her hand on my cheek and said, "Kenny, what are you afraid of?" All I could focus on in that moment was how I never saw a big person sit on one of those small chairs and how my face chilled when she touched me and how I was going to kick fucking Peter Moriarity's ass for woofing on my mother at lunch.

Kristin returned from the bathroom, lay down next to me and started playing with my stomach hair. My impulse was to slap her hand away. It was the most irritating sensation I had ever felt. I wanted her to keep her fucking hands to herself. I needed to sleep. I wanted to grab her face and slowly explain through clenched teeth how fucking badly I needed to sleep. I wanted her out. She would never let me sleep. I had to sleep. She was going to get heavy with me, demand things of me. Off my back. I had to sleep. I would never sleep. Get off my back. I lay in bed rigid. A six-foot stick of dynamite.

She moved away from me, confused. Leave, leave, leave.

"I wonder what time it is?" she murmured.

I raised my head to see over her to the digital. "One-thirty." She exhaled through her nose.

"I think I better get going."

"Sure."

"If I stay out, my sister'll freak."

"Okay."

"You're not mad?"

When we left the house, I felt hollow looking at our half-drained drinks on the floor by the couch.

We had to come back upstairs because she'd forgotten her cosmetic bag.

She lived nin blocks down from me on West End Avenue.

"Listen, I'll call you during the week, okay?"

"Sure." She kissed me.

It was 2:05 in the morning, but I didn't feel tired. My crotch was damp and gummed up with come and diaphragm cream. I was still horny. On impulse I flagged down a cab on West End and went back to Mr. Natural's.

The place was still hopping. I moved cockily through the crowds rapping to this broad and that one but not anybody who was really available. At three o'clock the place had

thinned enough so that I could check out everybody there.
Only two girls left were possibilities. One was talking to seven
guys at once, the other to three guys. I was beginning to feel
desperate. I gravitated toward the nearest girl and increased
her audience to four. She smiled briefly at me and kept
talking. Suddenly bright lights blinked on and off. Everybody
flinched. The shag-haired bartender in white shirt and thin
tie leaned over the bar and droned: "Last call, last call, you
don't have to go home, but you can't stay here."

SATURDAY

I woke up Saturday late, close to ten-thirty. I remembered two dreams: one a nightmare, one a comedy skit. The nightmare was a one-scene deal. I was standing in an arena with two other guys; we were slaves in ancient Rome. Across the arena big-horned bulls snorted and pawed. Between us and the bulls was a wriggling clump of fanged snakes. The bulls were supposed to charge across the snakes to get us. If the snakes killed the bulls we would be granted our freedom. If not, we would be gored to death. The nightmare ended with the sensation of snake fangs flying into my face. The snakes had attacked us before the bulls did.

The comedy was a little easier to take.

I was standing outside a big modern house. It was night-time and there was a party going on inside. It was all women. A dwarf left the house and came up to me. He told me the party was shit because all the women were frigid. It was impossible for a guy to pick up a girl. I stood there thinking it might have less to do with the women's frigidity and more to do with the fact that this dude was a dwarf. As if he read my mind, he said, "I know what you're thinking, and it's not because I'm a dwarf. My friend had the same goddamn problem in there." Then this friend of his comes out to join us. He's also a dwarf. The end.

I noticed the clock and panicked. It was my weekend and I felt like I'd lost precious hours by sleeping. It was my "leisure" time and I was blowing it. *What* leisure time? That's all I *had* was leisure time. I knew I should read the classifieds again, but I couldn't even think about it.

I lay in bed fingering my stomach muscles. I was supposed to do something that day but I couldn't remember what. I wanted to take a shot at jogging, but there was something else. Montauk. That was it. La Donna and I had planned to rent a car and drive out to Montauk. We had meant it to be a mood piece, a romantic, poetic thing like going to Coney Island in the winter, but even at the time we made those plans it seemed ludicrous to me. The romantic sentiment was totally out of sync with the anger and tension we felt around each other. It was her idea so I didn't say no, but I knew it would be a bummer. If you're not happy with each other and you plan a thing like that, all you wind up thinking about is how goddamn cold it would be, what a long son-of-a-bitch ride it would be and the absurdity and irony of the whole gesture itself.

Outside my window, the sun shone colorlessly. It was a bright whitish day devoid of blue, or even gray. I thought of Montauk, that long rocky deserted point at the tip of Long Island whipped by winter wind and bloodless bleached sunlight. In a way the whole trip would be appropriate. Just her and me standing in the deserted cold bleakness right on the edge, the end. Suddenly I felt great relief that she wasn't around anymore. It was over. It really sucked, the last few months. It used to be good, it used to be real . . . in the beginning. There used to be some real emotional feelings, loving feelings, whether we were always fucked up or not; the good feelings were there, the pleasure was there, but now it was really like February Montauk Point and it was over. *That* was over. But people could change. Maybe someday we'd do it up right. Me teaching her singing. She was right, we weren't helping each other just now. We both had a lot of moves to make and they required elbow room. Yup yup.

I fantasized about La Donna coming back. It was very possible. She still had her boots and her sheet music in the closet. As a matter of fact, I would have laid even money on her coming back; those were brand-new boots. She would at least have to make a guest appearance to get her boots.

I turned on the TV and watched *Soul Train*. I still couldn't get out of bed. I didn't know what to do with the day. It was after eleven. I wasn't going out to Montauk but I wasn't getting up, either. It was almost noon. I whimpered in frustration. The fifty dancing kids on the box seemed to be making fun of my paralysis. I leapt out of bed and turned off the TV. Love and ache keep you strong and handsome. I decided to jog. Jogging, swimming and biking were the three best exercises for your heart because the motion and exertion were constant and rhythmic. When I opened my door, the *Post* fell from the jamb and lay headline up on the hall floor.

I trotted down to Riverside Park in sweat pants, long johns, a turtleneck and a hooded sweat shirt. I hadn't run since Basic Training. The day remained colorless. The wind pummeled everything with sudden jerky gusts.

Squatting on my haunches I bounced up and down on the balls of my feet. I spread my legs and stretched right and left, my hands on my thighs. I rested one foot against a car hood and pushed my chest against my knee, then switched feet. I sat on the asphalt running path, held the soles of my feet together in a modified lotus position and jiggled my knees for three minutes. I was stretched, ready. I headed uptown to Eighty-sixth Street. There I would turn around and run down to Seventy-second, a total distance of one mile and one block. I did the nine blocks up to Eighty-sixth without too much trouble, then headed downtown. It was easier than I'd imagined. La Donna kept me going. I felt like a 1930s Olympic Nazi with bulging tendons running for the sun, the snowcaps. Love, heart, pride and youth. New breed. Blond, with visions. La Donna watching and glowing. By the time I got back down to Seventy-seventh Street where I'd started I was dead. The wind was sucking out my lungs, my knees were exploding from pain. Five more blocks. I staggered more than ran to Seventy-second Street. Seventy-second was the end of the path, the end of the park, became a mass of construction equipment, wooden barricades and beyond that the entrance to the West Side Highway.

I was huffing, hands on hips, circling slowly, staring down at the octagonal asphalt tiles.

There was a playground at Seventy-seventh Street and I figured maybe I'd watch some kids play basketball for a while.

It was deserted except for two kids. The wind was too bitter and gusty for ball. One was playing alone. He was black, about twelve years old, a tall stringbean dressed in an apple green warm-up suit with white piping on the legs and arms. He looked serious as he hunkered down the court, gave a slight jump, pumped the ball with bent elbows behind his ears and missed his shot. He missed most of his shots and never smiled. When he pivoted toward the basket I saw the name MELVIN stitched on the back of his jacket. The other kid was a chubby, teen-age Puerto Rican lounging on a bench nearby. Next to his leg was a titanic portable radio. He wore a stadium coat, cuffed dungarees, heavy horn-rimmed glasses and sported the beginnings of a mustache. On his sneakers he'd inked a power fist. He sat there picking his nose and watching Melvin play. The radio was blaring a Joni Mitchell song, and I couldn't think of a more inappropriate sound to hook up with that kid.

Something was pissing me off. I felt this mood of time being wasted. An enraged sadness.

I sauntered under the basket, took one of Melvin's re-

bounds, flipped it up in a half-assed hook shot which went
in and passed it back to him. He gazed at me with that serious
face, accepted my presence because to tell me to split would
require talking and took a jumper which missed. I snagged
his rebound, finger-whistled to the Porto kid and threw the
basketball at his radio. He caught it, started to throw it back,
but I waved him in. He took two steps toward us, thought
better of it and lobbed the ball at me. I threw it right back
at him. Melvin looked away, stood by the pole frowning.

"C'mon!" I waved him toward us.

He shook his head and tossed the ball to me. I bounced
it to Melvin under the basket and he hunched, twisted and
jumped. No basket.

I walked toward the playground exit, passing the kid on
the bench.

"Why don't you play, man?"

"Nah." He smiled and shrugged, embarrassed.

"C'mon, it's Saturday."

"Nah, mah leg is fucked up." He looked away and went
through the motions of rubbing his calf.

"That black dude says you can't play for shit."

He half-laughed and waved me away.

"You gonna let him get away with that?"

He began fiddling with his radio, wishing I was somewhere
else. I felt like I was torturing him, but I also felt like he
was torturing me. Both of them. I left the playground.

Upstairs, I peeled off my turtleneck and sweat shirt and did
my hundred and fifty. For the first time in months my sit-ups
were an exertion. That was from the running. If you're running and doing exercises always do the running first because
that makes the exercises more difficult, and one rule of thumb
around physical development is "No gain without pain."

After a shower I sat down with the *Post* and forced myself
to scan the classifieds. The *Post* wasn't the right paper for that
but they had a few pages full of positions for accountants,

typists, IBM operators — all crap I wouldn't do for full pay pension at thirty-five.

I was feeling really shitty and depressed and a little bit in trouble.

I skimmed other parts of the paper. Thirty-two villagers in Yemen were killed by a marauding pack of wild dogs over a period of ten days; that rated four inches in a corner column on page 32 bordering a three-quarter-page Lane Bryant ad. The President's wife delivered a speech at the University of Akron. A scientist discovered a new cure for hemorrhoids in rats. I was reading with a mixture of despair and boredom, listlessly turning pages with the same energy someone would swish a hand fan with while sitting on a porch in 95-degree weather.

On the page preceding the sports section, I spotted a small, heavily bordered notice:

> Fordham University's two-year-old Pinnacle Program is now accepting applications for the Summer term, which begins May 1. All H.S. grad. adults 21 or over are eligible for candidacy. Credit given for previous college work. B.S. and B.A. degrees granted in all areas of the Humanities, Business Administration and Health Sciences. Students eligible for NYHEAC loans and TAP grants. For more information, call Roberta Lacey at 222–9831, 9:00 A.M. to 3:00 P.M.

My first though was scoring coeds. Then I flashed on sitting in a classroom and learning something. Discussing something. Reading a good book. Shopping for school clothes. September. The fall. Scoring coeds. A diploma. Being a kid again. Dobie Gillis in college. Doing something with myself.

"Pinnacle."

"Yeah. Is Roberta Lacey there?"

"Speaking."

"Yeah. I just read your ad in the *Post* for Pinnacle and I'm interested in applying. What's the story on admission? What's the procedure?"

"Well, you fill out an application, mail it to us, and we'll send you a date to take an exam. Exams are given every Saturday in March."

"Whoa, whoa, what exam?"

"It's a three-hour exam every applicant has to take. It's all reading comprehension — vocabulary skills, written skills. There's no math whatsoever."

"That's no problem. I was Dean's List at Baruch." I felt like a jerk saying that, but I wanted to impress her, inform her that she was talking to a special person, no schlub. "And that's another thing, I already got three years done. Can I get full credit for that?"

"Well, in order to get a degree you have to take at least forty-five credits at Pinnacle, but we give life credits, credits for whatever work you're involved in outside of school."

"I was a door to door salesman." I laughed. "How many credits for that?"

"We would have to discuss it."

I wondered if I could get credits for breathing. "Also . . . I don't have to take Corrective English or Citizenship, do I?"

"It's not that type of program."

I was almost ashamed to be interested in Pinnacle. I was afraid I'd wind up sitting in a classroom with a lot of pencil-heads, dishwashers, beautician majors, "America! America!" jerks. I felt like I would be degraded, would appear weak and unhip.

"It's coed, right?"

"It's open to everyone."

"Yeah? And look, I'm thirty, I'm not gonna be sitting with kids . . ."

"The median age over the last two years was twenty-nine point four. Is that close enough?"

"Hey look, I'm not trying to grill you, you know, but this is very heavy for me."

"Why don't you come in, pick up an application and we'll talk about it, okay?"

"Sure." She had the power to change my life, save my life. "Can I make an appointment?"

"The first time I have open is Monday at two."

"I'll be there. My name is Kenneth Becker."

She slowly repeated my name as she wrote it down.

"Also, I'm gonna be pretty strapped for money. I can get these loans?"

"Eighty-six percent of our students are on loans and grants."

"Yeah? Also, I think I'm interested in English and teaching or something like that. What kind of courses . . ."

"Look, why don't you come in. We'll talk Monday."

"Sure, sure. Thanks a lot. See you then."

I felt like a million bucks. This was gonna be great. I wanted to call somebody, tell somebody. I still needed a job, but I felt like I could move now, really make some heavy moves now. I got up and aimlessly wandered around my apartment. Maybe I would meet some dynamite people. I imagined hanging out in the cafeteria with some guys — all of us unemployed but bright, hungry, going places. Nice-looking women, intelligent, aggressive. Classmates. Classmates.

My phone rang. Pinnacle calling back?

"Hello?"

"Hi." It was a girl.

"Hello?"

"Boy, how quickly we forget."

It was Kristin. Shit. I didn't want to deal with her.

"Oh, hey! How you doin'?"

"Good, and you?"

"Fine. What can I do for you?" I didn't want to tell her about Pinnacle and get involved in a long thing on the phone.

"Nothing, I was just calling to say hello."

"Oh yeah!" I said with false brightness. I didn't know what else to say.

"Actually, I was feeling a little down."

"Huh. What's the problem?"

"I don't know. Nothing."

"Huh . . . Something with your sister?"

"Yeah, I guess, no, I don't know," she whined.

There was silence for a long, long thirty seconds.

"I dunno, I just feel lonely," she said.

"There's nobody to hang out with?"

"No."

"Huh."

Another pause.

"I feel like you're dying to get off the phone."

"No! No! I just woke up. I'm still in dreamland."

"Do you wanna get together?"

"Uh, I can't today. I got to go downtown."

"Do you wanna make a time to get together?"

"Yeah, yeah sure."

"You don't really want to."

"No. I do! I do!"

"I don't feel it. I feel like I'm forcing you."

"No. No, look, I told you I just woke up."

"I feel like you're fucking with my head."

"How am I fucking with your head?" Like I didn't know. Dear God, get me off the phone.

"I don't understand why you don't wanna see me."

"I *do* wanna see you," I complained. "When do you wanna get together?"

"I'm not *stu*pid, Kenny. Are you afraid I'm gonna hurt you?"

That was a laugh. "It's not that."

"But it's something else?"

"I dunno. Look, I'm fucked up. I'm, I dunno, I can't . . ."

"I feel head-fucked."

I was squirming so much I felt like I needed another shower.

"I feel teased. All you talked about last night was how you need people and how you were lonely and how the answers are here and now. What was that, a come-on?"

"No! No! I meant it, but . . ."

"But you just woke up, right?"

I felt like I couldn't breathe. Like I couldn't open my eyes wide enough. I got up with the phone and started pacing, itching.

"I felt like we made a real connection last night."

"We did! We did!"

"Then why don't you want to see me?"

"I do! I do!" I wanted her dead.

"What are you afraid of?"

"I'm not afraid of anything. I just . . . Look, I'm really fucked up. I gotta go." I winced. Please let me hang up. "I'm fucked up."

"Maybe you should think a little about how you fuck other people up."

"Yeah, I'm sorry. I gotta go." I couldn't hang up. We listened to each other's breathing.

"You really suck, you bastard." She hung up. I felt like a bug exposed by someone lifting my rock. I also felt relieved. I didn't want to think about what she said. I didn't want to think about anything. It was one-thirty.

By two o'clock I was in Times Square again. I felt like going down there was the act of a bad boy. It was wrong but I wasn't down there because I loved it, I just didn't know where else to go.

I walked down Seventh Avenue scanning the marquees. I took a massage parlor flyer from some big shivering spade with yellow eyes and huge fossilized fingernails. He wore a stocking hat pulled down almost over his eyes and a green beat-to-shit corduroy jacket that wasn't doing dick about

the cold. His lips were the color and thickness of cocktail
franks. He kept slapping his fistful of orange flyers against
the thumb of his opposite hand and shoving one in front of
every guy that crossed his path.

SOPHISTICATED SISTER

The flyer had a photo of a chick with long hair and big tits
standing nude next to a globe. She was holding an open copy
of *Civilisation* by Kenneth Clark. She had a Barbra Streisand
beak, nipples as big as tops. She was winking at me.

| LUXURY FOR LESS | $10 SATISFACTION COMPLETE |
| NO RIP-OFFS | GIRLS OF ALL NATIONS |

Within the next two blocks I collected flyers from four other
places: My Aunt's Crib, Lady Godiva, Taras Bulba, and Casa
Blo-Jo, each handed out by a desperado scarier-looking than
the last.

There were no good movies to see.

The wind was kicking ass. I hunched down trying for a
no-neck take against the cold and trotted into an Orange
Julius. It was a narrow corner stand with a Formica counter
and a glass-walled view of Times Square. I did up some coffee
and a Drake's Cake, one elbow on the counter, not really
hungry, not really anything. No movies, not hungry. I just
needed some kind of release. I wanted something to happen,
to get off. I was on the lam again. Reaching into my pocket
to pay for my coffee I pulled out Sophisticated Sister. Girls
of All Nations. No rip-offs. Ten dollars, complete satisfac-
tion. There you go. But I didn't think I could swing it. That
scene might be pretty freaky and who the hell knew what
color dick you woke up with next morning. Just to check
out what I would be saving myself from I started walking to
the address on the flyer, three blocks away off Sixth Avenue.
It was a narrow office building jammed between a coffee shop
and a Thom McAn shoe store. In front on the sidewalk was

a stand-up sandwich board like a Danger sign for an open manhole. SOPHISTICATED SISTER — a silhouette of a nude chick with crossed legs lounging in the crescent of a moon. Now I thought that was pretty classy; but still, you never knew, you didn't fuck graphics and the neighborhood was pretty dead.

I stood across the street. I had two choices. I could go home, call Kristin and make like a human being or I could sink from hip deep to chin deep in the bullshit. An angel sat on one shoulder, a devil on the other. Two crew-cut guys walked in together. They were probably sailors because they walked like tough penguins with a side-to-side bowlegged step, elbows out, arms dangling as if they were in shoulder casts. Sailors were the lowest anyhow when it came to that kind of shit. The coffee shop was closed. I pretended I was on stake-out, hidden mike taped to my finger. That was bullshit. The dead nuts was that I felt like a creep because I knew there was no way I wasn't going to go upstairs for a slice of moon pie, and the longer I stood in the cold like a retard the harder it was going to be to head on in, so I hung out the Gone Fishing sign in my brain and walked across the street. Kristin never had a chance. Or, more to the point, I never had a chance.

The elevator opened right into the reception area. A chick about forty, in crucifix earrings and with long dark hair, sat at a counter in front of me. Behind her was a sitting room. Three girls in cheap pastel nightgowns sat chatting on chairs and couches. A Danish modern coffee table centered the room. The walls were wood paneled. It looked like the waiting room of a ghetto dentist. I had been fingering a ten spot for the last half-hour.

"You been here before?" She glanced up from the *Post* and a take-out coffee.

"Uh-uh." I held out the ten, blowing air softly through my cheeks to slow down my guts.

"It's twelve forty the first time, ten forty after that. This is a private club and the extra two dollars is your membership fee." She talked nice and calm and she had the *Post* open to the editorial page. I felt a little safer. I wanted to tell her about Pinnacle. Maybe she was going to be in my class.

"Hey, no problem." I dug out my wallet and forked over fifteen. I got change, a hot-pink membership card and a ticket off a roll like I was going on a ride. I went into the waiting room, my ticket in hand, and sat across the room from an old guy with a humongous belly, his hat on his knee. He scowled, his face red and beetle-browed. He reminded me of Brezhnev. Across from him, a guy about fifty, small and pleasant looking, was smiling his ass off, trying to catch my eye and exchange winks. I walked back to the lady at the desk. "What am I supposed to do with the ticket?"

"Just give it to the girl you want."

I took a seat on a vinyl-back chair and casually checked out what was. A big broad-shouldered blonde with a Frankenstein forehead sitting in a red nightie; a tall, skinny, black broad trudged across the room in a full-length wrinkled white nightgown, one hand on the small of her back and the other clutching cigarettes and a lighter. She had bags under her eyes as if she just woke up and was about to get that first cup of coffee.

And then there was number three, tan, with frizzy orange hair combed out from the brown root center into a halo of corkscrew curls. She had double the beak of the girl in the flyer and it was broken to boot. She wore a pale blue baby doll, which clashed with her hair, and was scarfing down a cheeseburger laid out on greasy wax paper in her lap. A *Daily News* was open on the coffee table in front of her. That was for me. That was real. A fourth girl walked out of a bathroom carefully carrying a plastic washbasin filled with water and vanished around a corner.

From suspended speakers an FM radio station softly played Sam Cooke's "You Send Me." Two more girls walked into the waiting room and slouched into chairs.

"Donna, how was Miami?" the broad-shouldered blonde asked one of the new arrivals, a chubby girl wearing pom poms and an open housecoat over a plain white nightie. They didn't seem like hookers to me. They looked more like ambulatory patients lounging in the common room of a woman's hospital and us guys sitting there were waiting for visiting hours so we could see our wives.

"Miami was nice." Donna did her nails with an emery board.

"What were you down there for, two weeks?"

"Ten days. I just laid on the beach and read. It was nice."

"You look good. You got tan."

"Hey look . . ." My girl tapped the *News* in front of her. "They got a Star Trek store now."

The old smiling guy turned his head from girl to girl as they talked, like he was watching a tennis match. The fat beetle-browed guy didn't move.

"You can buy Mister Spock ears there — aw God my son would love that. He's into Mister Spock."

The girls and the old guy laughed.

"You know, he's got this Mister Spock haircut now. He looks so cute . . . oh, I should take him to this store."

I waited for her to finish her lunch. I yawned as I stood up and wandered over like I was going for a *Sports Illustrated* to kill time. I stuck out my ticket. She wiped her hands, looked at it like it was a parking violation, wiped her lips on a paper napkin and thumbed her nose like a boxer.

Tearing the ticket in half, she put the stub in her purse and rose, motioning for me to follow.

We entered a small room around the corner from the front desk. A double bed was covered with a black drop cloth as slick and shiny as sealskin. A small night table held a dish of foil-wrapped condoms, a jar of Vaseline, Kleenex, a hot comb, a curling iron, Right Guard, baby powder and K-Y jelly.

The walls were the same blond wood paneling as the waiting room. On the wall nearest to me were three brown plastic
coat hooks and an oven timer.

"You ever been here before?"

"Uh-uh."

"Okay, take off all your clothes and I'll be right back." I
stripped down to my shorts and sat on the bed. What if rival
Mafia factions in a war over massage-parlor ownership blasted
this place to shit? What if they stopped paying police protec-
tion and got raided? What if I couldn't get it up? *That* was
the question.

She returned with a yellow plastic basin of water. "Take
them off too, honey." She nodded toward my shorts. I draped
them over my shirt, tensing my stomach for maximum ripple.
She slipped off her nightie. She was a little on the chunky
side with bruised thighs.

She handed me the bowl, and I held it under my cock while
she washed it with warm water and Phisohex. Her hands and
the water felt soft and good. As she washed me I noticed a
chrome-and-red-vinyl exercise bench against the wall.

"Am I supposed to do sit-ups?" I nodded toward the bench.

She laughed. "Nah, that's for in case the guy doesn't want
to do anything in bed . . . then we can say we're doing health
things . . . I don't understand a hundred percent myself." She
put down the basin. "So, what you have in mind?" hands on
her hips.

What did I have in mind? The question stumped and embarrassed me. "I don't know. I didn't think that much in
advance."

"Well, how much you wanna spend?"

"The twelve forty I already spent." Don't get burned.

She shrugged and took the bowl from me.

"Okay, I'll give you a blowjob." She paper-towel-dried
my prick. I didn't think I would come with a blowjob.

"How much for a straight fuck?"

"I can't answer that, honey. That's solicitation. Just tell me how much more you can go for . . ."

"I'll spring for another five."

"We can do half and half without a rubber for an extra five . . . Okay?"

"What's that, sixty-nine?" I didn't want to eat a whore's pussy for free.

"No, no. First I blow you a little, then we fuck. Okay?"

"Sure."

"Pay me first, then we'll get it on."

I paid her and hoisted myself up on the high bed.

"You know, I know Leonard Nimoy," I lied.

"Who?" She frowned, sitting on the bed.

"The guy who plays Doctor Spock. I heard you talking out there."

"Oh yeah?" She didn't seem impressed. I didn't know why I made up that bullshit. Sometimes I embarrassed myself.

"I might have a little trouble getting hard. I'm nervous."

"Don't worry, lotta guys do . . . once they're in they're okay though."

She dipped her mouth to my prick, sucking and flicking the underside. After a few seconds she stopped. "I can't do great head today . . . I had root-canal work yesterday and my whole side is still sore." She tenderly touched the left side of her jaw. "I'll try though." She went back to work. She stopped again. "Ah . . ." She grimaced and brought the plastic basin up to the bed and spit blood into the water. She blew me another thirty seconds, stopping to spit blood two more times. "Okay?" She nodded to me while absently pulling my dick. She went to hit the oven timer on the wall.

"Aw, don't do that." I winced. "I'll be done in ten minutes. I promise."

She shrugged, got on her back and I grabbed my prick to put myself in. "Shit!" she hissed. I froze. I didn't know what I did. She clenched her teeth in anger for a second, then relaxed. "No, no, honey, don't *ever!* put yourself in. Let me do it. Every guy grabs his prick and rams his fist right into me. Every goddamn time. I'm purple down there." She hissed again, gingerly touching herself. My guts were flip-flopping. I felt nauseated.

"Sorry, I didn't know."

"That's okay." She put me in, and as we fucked she kept me in a slight vice with her thighs so I couldn't go in real deep. I was aware of my promise to be ten minutes and felt as pressured as if the timer was ticking. Like a schmuck I tried to put the moves on. She had a lead-lined uterus and I was wiggling and juking, like "Here's something you never got at home." I was arched over her, afraid to lay down, skin on skin. A section of paper towel was clenched in her fist, held near the serrated edges, tensed and ready like the rip-cord of a parachute. I knew the minute I came she would tear it off the roll. Forget it. I couldn't come and I asked her to shift to a handjob. I laid on my back again. She jerked me off with one hand while holding a Kleenex like a screen two inches from my prick to catch the drops. The Kleenex was blocking my view and I tried to watch in a small mirror on her night stand. Through the wall I heard some guy whining, "No, don't *do* that! Then you get me all *excited!* No! That's no good! I *told* you!" It sounded like the old guy from the waiting room. I could tell her arm was getting tired and by sheer will power and heavy fantasizing I forced myself to come.

"The-e-ere you go," she said in a drawn-out steadying tone, like a doctor giving a shot to a scared kid.

"You know, I could never come with a bag on," I mused as I buttoned my shirt. I was nervous and casual at the same time. All my sentences came out with slight blurting inflections.

"You don't ever have to use a bag in this place if you don't want." She slipped on her nightgown.

"If a girl says you do, you go to the desk, she'll change her mind real fast." She brushed her frizzy hair with a nylon brush.

"Yeah, but don't you ever get worried about the clap?" I tried to sound like a Friend of Whores.

"Nah. I've been working this thing four years. I never had nothing. We're supposed to get checked by doctors every week anyhow ... Okay, honey ... see ya ..." She left the room. As I finished dressing I thought about what a real person she was. When we were balling she made little gasps. I didn't know if she was faking or not, but I wasn't the worst screw in the world either.

I started tripping, thinking about asking her out for dinner. That would be wild. I would take her and her kid Doctor Spock. Maybe we would all go down to Miami if things worked out. I sat on the bed thinking of how I could get her alone for a few minutes out there and ask her for dinner. Maybe I could pass her a note. No. I could motion to her at the entrance to the waiting room to come to me at the door. That made more sense. I left the room and headed down the striped corridor to the desk. She was walking toward me with a big goon in tow. He had a shaved head and dirty plaid pants. The type that always sat with spread-out knees on crowded subways. She winked bye-bye and walked past me.

Out in the street three minutes later it seemed like nothing had happened; it was just some movie I saw in a peep show.

I passed a deli and bought a big chocolate chip cookie. A half-hour had passed. I felt like I was waiting for somebody, like I was early for some appointment. I began getting horny again. Near me, a bearded black dude in a skull cap drew a crowd around a hand-painted, six-foot-high chart of the twelve tribes of Israel — each tribe corresponding to a different African or Latin country. He riffed about how the Jews in Israel weren't the real Jews, that Puerto Ricans and Africans were; how Moses was a spade and why it was cool to rip off television sets and Mixmasters from Jewish-owned stores. I was the only white guy, let alone the only Jew, in the crowd.

I stood there listening to this guy's graffiti for twenty minutes. I wasn't heavy into being Jewish, but when it came to this type of shit I could see myself manning the barricades in a second. Jews weren't finished getting fucked over in this world by a long shot. Spades either, for that matter. I flashed on Leonard Wooley, the big, dumb yom from Fantasia, Jackie di Paris, the singles scene. Everybody was getting fucked over. This *world* was a royal screw.

I noticed a movie marquee with an orange-tinted blowup of a nude woman on her back, her neck arched, eyes closed in ecstasy, knees spread and drawn up almost to her shoulders. Her position, the fuck-me look on her face, stopped me cold. Suddenly I realized I was fondling myself. I was standing in the middle of Times Square and fondling myself as if I were home straddling the toilet. I jerked my hand away as if it had grazed something red-hot. What if Kristin saw me? La Donna? The lady from Pinnacle who would then recognize me on Monday? What if . . . What if . . . I felt nailed in my shit, my ugliness, my loneliness. Less than human. Not me. Different from every living, breathing person on the street. "Not me" meant "not human," meant so wrapped up in yourself that the rest of the world is reduced to white sound, background buzz. I reeled down the street burning with horror and embarrassment. I was so wrapped up in my own head, so gone, I was acting like a street schizo. I *was* a street schizo. That was the act of a street schizo. Two hundred people must have passed me while I touched myself. Two hundred people must have registered "degenerate" in their brains. I leaned against a parked car, my hand to my mouth — blown away. I still had a big hard-on. I remembered a cartoon I saw once: a horned satyr lying on a shrink's couch: "Doc, I can't get it down."

I was sprawled out on my bed again scouring the *Post*. On the one hand, I was trying to figure out what to do with the rest of my life, on the other I was trying to handle seven-

thirty. Six o'clock there would be a decent movie on the box.
Tarzan's New York Adventure; rumors abound in the jungle
that Tarzan takes it in the seat from Cheetah, and he has to
leave Africa fast. But I had nothing to do between the movie
and two P.M. Monday. I tried to psych myself up for Monday
and make the time pass with minimum consciousness. I
thumbed through the *Post,* read an interview with a European
ballet star performing at Lincoln Center. The guy sounded
like a yawn, but in his photo he had stomach muscle definition
that made me look like Candy. That was okay. I didn't even
care.

The Drifters were playing at a disco club up in the Bronx.
I was exhausted.

The phone rang.

"Yeah."

"Hey!"

"Donny?" I perked up.

"Yeah. Listen, Kenny, I wanna apologize for the other
night."

"For what?" I felt awake and grateful. "It was *me,* man. I
wigged first."

"Well, we both wigged."

"Yeah, and we *knew,* man, we were just talking about how
we flip out on grass. We both knew, man." I started speed-
rapping.

"Yeah, it was fucked," he muttered.

There was a silence.

"So what you doin' tonight, Donny?"

"Nothing planned."

"You wanna hook up for dinner?" I knew he did. I did.

"Do you?"

"If you do."

"Sure, man."

"Shit yeah, Mr. Donny. We just won't do dope."

"Awright."

"Hey, the Drifters are playing up in the Bronx."

"Fuck the Bronx, man," he said kindly. "Why don't you come down to me tonight?"

"Carmine Street? You're on."

"Good enough. About seven?"

"Yeah. And, Donny, thanks for calling."

"I'm hip."

Rejuvenation again. I lay down to snag a half-hour's sleep, but I felt as though my life had just been saved, and I was somewhat hyper.

"Very tasty, very tasty." I nodded my head in approval at Donny's dump, a one-room kitchenette with a loft bed built about six feet high into an alcove. The walls were painted an atrocious burnt orange. The only part of his studio I dug was a wall-length workbench littered with New York City Housing Department inspection forms. Mirrors surrounded his bed; a poster of James Dean hung over his workbench along with a black-and-white blowup of two rhinos humping. An overhead light made the room seem cold and cluttered. The walls in no way looked as if they had just been painted a few days ago, but I didn't mention it.

"We gonna eat out?" His kitchenette consisted of a three-foot-high portable refrigerator under a stainless steel sink and a two-burner stove.

"Yeah. I figured we'll walk around the Village for a while, go in some place." He pulled on a white cable sweater over his wiry frame, then brushed back his relatively short hair with his hands. He grabbed an old brown bomber jacket and we were out.

We headed down Christopher Street, the main drag of the Village west of Seventh Avenue. The narrow commercial street was popping, jammed with an army of lanky dudes in crew cuts, Levi's, tapered T-shirts under leather jackets. All faggots and all over the place, in couples and groups, sitting on stoops, car hoods, lounging in front of bars, restaurants, boutiques, antique shops. It was like being in a ghetto of all-male Broadway musical dance extras. The mood and the pace of the street were those of a leisurely stalk, like a seduction in an Impressionist painting. Everybody seemed to be strolling, staring, checking out everybody else. Heavy, heavy eye contact.

"Donny, I never seen so many faggots in one place in my life."

"I know." Donny bounced along at my shoulder, his big nose red with cold.

"I've been around here during the day, you know, selling? It's nothing compared to what comes crawlin' out of the wood-work at night here."

"No, it's fuckin' heavy around here at night," he said.

"Hey, you see that? You see those keychains everybody got?" Almost every guy passing us wore a keychain hanging from his belt either on his right side or his left. "See that? That's a code. If they wear the key on the left, they like to take it in the seat, on the right they like to give it."

Donny cocked an eyebrow. "How do you know?"

"I read about it in the *Voice*."

"Sure you did, Kenny." He winked.

"I did."

I wouldn't get into heavy, embarrassing protest. "And those handkerchiefs hanging out of everybody's pockets? All those different colors mean different trips." I pointed to a straw blond Gestapo queen beanpole, who, despite the cold, wore leather lederhosen and construction boots. A red hand-kerchief hung from his pocket, a keychain on his right. "That guy's into getting fist-fucked. Red is fist-fucking. You know from fist-fucking?" I thrust out a fist. "Right up the ass. Up to the elbow. Can you believe that? And if the keys were on the *other* side, he'd be the fist-fuc*ker* instead of the fist-fuc*kee*, you dig?"

"Huh." Donny dug his hands into his pockets. He was chewing gum and every chaw emitted a puff of cold air.

"Christ, man, you wouldn't *believe* what these dementos can get into, *pissing* on each other, *shitting* on each other, *whips,* torture. It's incredible. I think pissing is a yellow handkerchief. I forget the others." I scratched my nose. I was really proud of how much I knew about different New York scenes. I wasn't Broadway Joe, but I possessed a modicum of hipness nonetheless.

"You sure you read all this in the *Voice?*" Donny smirked.

"No, actually, in my secret life I'm the Dragon Lady of Christopher Street. I got more handkerchiefs at home than a haberdasher and more keys than the guy in charge of the Tower of London."

"I dunno, Kenny, sounds like you know a lot."

"Are you serious? What was it, Wednesday? I accidentally walked into a gay bar down here for a drink, I almost died. As a matter of fact I don't even want to eat down here. I'm getting a nervous stomach just walking around."

We took a cab uptown to a steak house on Forty-ninth Street.

"So how's Mr. Bluecastle doing with his housewares?"

We sat down at our table, our plates heaped high with pale lettuce and croutons from a trip to the salad bar.

"You should ask him directly. I'm out."

"Out what?"

"Out a job."

Donny didn't look too shook. "You get fired?"

"You can't fire me. I quit. You know, good-bye, good riddance, et cetera."

"You don't seem too freaked."

"It was a suck job, and guess what I'm doing now? I'm going back to school, man."

"Good! Maybe I should do that, too."

"Well, listen, maybe I'll become a social worker or something. So when the city lays you off after all the buildings burn down in the next riot and there's nothing for you to inspect and you go on welfare, I'll be the guy the welfare department will send around to count your toothbrushes to make sure you ain't getting secretly supported by some garbageman."

"If they would lay me off, I'd celebrate. What kind of school deal?"

"It's this thing called Pinnacle. Sort of an adult ed program at Fordham for people who never finished college or only got a high school diploma. I don't know that much about it. I got an interview at Fordham on Monday." I wanted to play it down. I suddenly felt fearful that Donny was going to do it, too. That he was going to interfere with my new life, cramp my style, pick up my coeds.

"Didn't Vince Lombardi go to Fordham?"

I gave a wild look at the ceiling. "Who cares?"

"What are you gonna do for bread, Kenny?"

"I don't know. I'll get school loans, but I'll need to work anyway. I don't give a shit what I do. I'll wash dishes — as long as I know what I'm shooting for here, as long as I know that whatever I'm doing is temporary and it's over when school is over — I can do it and even feel noble about it. I'm working my way through school." I started feeling excited for the first time since the conversation with Roberta Lacey. "It's a great program, man. They give you credits for what you did already, they give you credits for your work. Shit, man, why don't you do it with me?" There, I said it. "You hate your fucking job as much as I hated mine, right?"

Donny shrugged and rubbed his mouth. His eyes said, "I can't." "I'll think about it."

"Yeah, well, think about it."

We picked at our salads. I felt so good about school I lost my appetite.

"You really gonna wash dishes, Kenny?" He gave a weak laugh that made me think the whole conversation was making him anxious.

"Who knows, maybe I'll manage a peep show joint part time."

"That where you meet your dates?"

"Don't laugh, Donny. It's just about coming down to that. You know what I been doing since I saw you last? Balling my brains out." Half complaint, half brag.

"Shit." Donny paused to chew, his hand in front of his mouth. "When did we get together, Thursday? I scored three times myself since then."

"Are you kidding me?" I put down my fork. "You balled three chicks since Thursday?" The waiter brought over my veal and Donny's scallops. After he left, there was a long pause.

"I didn't say chicks, Kenny."

I laughed. "When then, polar bears?" I scarfed down a veal medallion.

Donny didn't answer; he didn't start eating. He wasn't laughing. My gut sunk. Guys? Fucking *guys?*

"Are you fucking with my head, Donny?"

Donny propped his elbows in front of his meal and tapped his lips with his thumbnail. "It's been a long time, my man." He smiled evenly. "We haven't hooked up in many years."

I sat back, swallowed, and fought down a smile of shock. I couldn't even begin to alphabetize my feelings: embarrassment over putting down faggots, about coming on like an authority, amazement at not picking it up earlier. I imagined Donny kissing a guy on the lips, blowing a dork, taking it in the ass. I just sat there with my mouth open, my eyes focused on a crack in the leather of his jacket — it looked like a river line on a map. My eyes locked, the images shimmering because I wasn't blinking.

"You freaked?" He smiled at me.

I snapped to. "No! No! I mean, yeah! But not, hey, listen, man, I don't care what anybody's into as long as it's cool and they don't interfere with me getting mine."

"Gee, Kenny, that means a lot coming from you." He smirked and started eating.

"Hey, no, Donny, I didn't mean . . . Hey, gimme a break,

huh? Christ." I cringed. "I musta sounded like a real jerk
on Christopher Street."

"Nah." He wiped his lips with two fingers under his napkin. "More like a fucking schmuck."

"Shit, how could you let me go on like that?" I couldn't
help grinning. It was inappropriate but I couldn't help it. A
cousin of mine had died when I was twelve. When I heard the
news I couldn't help grinning then either.

Donny shrugged. "I just didn't think that was the right
place to tell you, you know . . . I dunno . . . I thought it was
funny."

I couldn't stop running through my brain all the things I'd
said. Every time a newly recalled wisecrack came up I felt
like twitching. For some reason this felt many times heavier
than realizing that Donny was a faggot. My eyes went into
a glassy lock again.

"C'mon, eat your veal." Donny jutted his chin at my food,
fighting an amused smile.

"Damn, I remember when I had you on the horn, Thursday
night. I said we'd go out and get laid. That must have felt
weird for you, huh?"

"Nah, I fuck girls too. I was married, Kenny, remember?"

"Oh, yeah, so there's hope for you yet, huh? This is blowing my mind, Donny." I laughed, holding my forehead. "How
do you feel telling me?"

"Relieved." He speared a scallop. "I wouldn't even bother
telling you if I didn't dig you, man. And I was nervous about
it too. Because you threw me."

"What do you mean?"

"Well, at first I figured *you* were gay, man. You're not, are
you?"

"*Me?*" I touched my chest.

"I didn't think so from the way you were talking tonight, but
Wednesday and Thursday I wasn't sure. And when we were
up in your crib Thursday night, it seemed like you were coming on to me."

I dropped my jaw. "What the fuck are you talking about?"

"You know, when you took off your shirt and started doing sit-ups and the like . . . I thought that was pretty crude myself. And then when you went into the bedroom right after — I mean, I'm not stupid, Kenny. I mean, you kept saying how *good* I looked and shit."

That was so not the story that I didn't know how to explain without it coming out phony.

"But I was really doing sit-ups and I was freaking out about La Donna." I started eating to show him it was hardly worth explaining. "And the funny thing about me mentioning that *you* looked so good was that I wanted you to say that *I* looked good. Did you ever hear of fishing for compliments? That's probably why I started doing sit-ups, too. I been workin' out for years and you know I'm insecure like anybody else, man, and you know . . . like that."

"Whew." Donny shook his head, grimly staring at his food. He looked relieved. "That's wild, 'cause I was real pissed, man, real bummed out. I thought you just wanted to ball. See, that's what happens when people don't talk to each other. Everybody gets crazy on their own wavelength. And that's another thing, whether you're straight or gay, man, I'm not interested in coming on to you, you know?"

"I'm that bad, huh?" I was fishing again.

"No, man. Just the opposite. You're in pretty good shape; that's one of the reasons. At first, you know, straights basically look like shit for the most part but, ah, you're not my type and besides, we're friends, man."

"Well, I never," I lisped. *Who's* friends.

"G'head, make fun, dipshit." He smirked.

We buried our noses in dinner.

So my man here swung to the left. Marron. It was a wig, but not a major wig. Maybe because it wasn't that major a wig for him. Also, he didn't want no nut off me. I would've picked it up if he did. So what was the story here? What did he want, friendship? It seemed that way. Suddenly I felt very

nervous, rushed, as if someone had shoved a sixty-page con-
tract under my nose written in Micronesian and was jabbering
at me to read, initial and sign it in blood in thirty seconds.
And you got to be kidding. You're talking to Kenny Watch-
yurstep. Friends. Slowly, slowly.

We ate quietly for a while, only talking to order coffee.

"When did you get into it, Donny?" I asked, hoping that
the question didn't sound like an interview. Trying to main-
tain a light, casual tone like when I asked Mrs. Macready the
age of her mongoloid son.

"What, guys? Not until after my marriage broke up. I
mean, I did shit when I was a kid, everybody did."

"Not me," I drawled.

"Not you," he smirked. "Anyways, I dunno, I used to read
muscle development magazines and shit. A lot of guys start
that way. I bought *Health and Strength* along with the paper.
I was thinking about barbells, barbells, but, ah, I was having
trouble with Barbara, my wife, around sex. We weren't hitting it off. I mean, nothing else was working either, so it
wasn't surprising, but sometimes when we were fucking, in
order to come I would fantasize about being in bed with a
guy, about balling in bed with a guy. And sometimes I jerked
off thinking about a guy. I never had a face and I never
thought of any guy I knew . . . more it was just the idea of a
cock instead of a cunt."

I wanted to ask him to be more specific. What did he do —
take it or give it? I couldn't ask, but I wanted as much bizarre
information as I could get, as if the more aberrations I could
collect on him the less relevant he would be to me, the safer
I would feel around him.

"Anyway, after we broke up I kept the apartment on Carmine Street. I dated some chicks but, ah, nothing. I would
walk around the Village and, like you said, I never seen so
many faggots in my life, and I would peek into all the bars and,
shit, and I knew what was happening, but I couldn't bring

myself. I couldn't imagine picking up a guy and bringing him
home, and the idea of kissing a guy on the lips grossed me
out a lot more than a blowjob, you know? But one night I
was lonely, by myself again, horny. I did some hash and some
Scotch and walked over to this bar, Evans, that ain't there anymore, and you know, I was young, attractive, then. I'm still
considered hot shit. I could hustle still if I wanted. But, anyway, so I'm in there, some guy comes up to me and I'm shitting
pickles, man." He laughed, shaking his head. "He bought me
a drink. I told him my name was Ar-mond Duhaney, can you
dig it? The guy was hip. He knew. He invited me up to his
joint, but I wouldn't. I was too scared, so he drove me home.
We stopped under the highway and he blew me."

"When was this?" There was a court reporter in my head.

"I was twenty-three. Seven years ago. Christ, seven years
ago. I wound up living with that guy for a few months. He
was a real good dude, real tender, understanding. I was considered a catch because I was young and cherry. He was older,
thirty, thirty-one, like us now."

"Please, don't remind me." The line came out phony and
forced.

"After a while I started hanging out at the bars, the clubs.
Guys were hitting on me all the time, but Ron, man, fucking
Ron was always there to make sure I didn't mess around so
I split. You can't do bars and monogamy at the same time.
Oil and water, See, he brought me down there to show me
off. I lived with a few more guys over the years but, ah, I
dunno, I prefer being a free agent, I guess." He glanced at his
empty coffee cup. He wasn't smiling. "And I trick a lot, man.
Sometimes I score every night for weeks, sometimes two, three
times a night. I won't even leave the bar. Depends what kind
of mood I'm in, you know, and I run with chicks, too, man,
now and then."

"You're bisexual." I was showing off. He was blowing me
away. I felt as if I had never known him at all. I also realized

that I'd found somebody as depressed as I was. But I was
going back to school which made me better.

"Donny." I paused as the waiter refilled our cups. "Can I
ask you something? Did you and Maynard . . ."

"Did we get it on?"

"I mean, was Maynard . . ."

"Fuckin' Maynard . . . Yeah, Maynard was gay, *is* gay. He
was like me, though. He didn't know which end was up. One
time we got drunk in the playground one night. I drank too
much and passed out on the bench by the basketball court.
When I woke up my legs were across Maynard's lap and he
had his hand in my fly. I jumped sixty-two feet in the air. I
was so scared I ran home. I didn't talk to him for weeks. And
Maynard, poor Maynard, he didn't know what the fuck was
going on. He was drunk. He . . . I don't think he'd ever done
that before, and we never really talked about it, and you *know*
how tight me and him used to be." He tossed his napkin on
the table in disgust. "It was never the same after that. He
was more scared of me than I was of him. Next fall I went to
NYU and I almost never saw him after that — and I loved
the cat, Kenny. That's how fucked up people are."

I took my cigarettes and offered him one, which he declined.

"Last time I saw Maynard was after I got into guys. I was
into it about six months. I was twenty-four. I went up to see
him in the Bronx. At that time he was married, had a kid
already. He ran his father's record store on Williamsbridge
Road. I walked in. He almost died. It was six years later
and he was still uptight. I was the last person he wanted to see
in the *world,* but I didn't know that because I was so excited
about the new me, and I was looking at him trying to get
across the changes I been through without spelling it out, and
I *knew* that he knew that I knew that he knew blah blah blah
— nothin', man. He didn't wanna know about nothin'. He
was into the family, the kid, the hearth, the home. He was

full of shit and he knew it. I dunno. The next year he broke
up with her and took off for Morocco. I dunno what he's into
now. Candy says he's a travel agent, good for him." Donny
shrugged. "Wherever he's at now, good for him . . . you
know? I mean, fuck it, everybody's gotta live their life the
way they want, the way they can handle it."

"Does Candy know?"

"About me?" He smiled. "Are you fuckin' kiddin' me?
Candy would shit a giraffe."

We laughed and slapped palms. I had enough on him now
so that I could finally relax.

"So what's this thing with La Donna? Who's La Donna?
Gimme one a those." He grabbed a cigarette.

"Who . . . is . . . La Donna. That's the sixty-four-thousand-
dollar question, Donny."

"You break up? I heard you're livin' with her. You're not,
you are, what."

"Well, she walked on me, what, Tuesday? We were living
together eight, nine months. It's *hard*, Donny, it's hard to
make a go of it sometimes. I can't even talk about it anymore,
it makes me sick. *I* make me sick. Maybe I should be a
faggot, then I'd have better luck."

"You want her back?" Donny squinted every time he took
a puff.

"Yes. No. I don't want the bullshit we had, and I would
love to say fuck it. No, I *don't* want her back, but . . ."

I felt tired, bored with my own bullshit. "Awright, you
wanna know what the lick is? The straight poop is that if we
were to go back now I wouldn't want her to sing, to do anything. I would just want her to hug and kiss me full time." I
made a face. "It's shit. I would want her to be my partner in
isolation. Do you know what I mean?"

Donny nodded "sure."

"And sometimes like now I have moments of clarity and I
know it's better that we split — for both of us. No one needs

that crap, but, ah . . ." I shrugged. "I'm a weak person, Donny. I get lonely. When I get lonely my head gets lodged up my large intestine. I don't give a shit about clarity. I just want my baby. I don't care if it kills us both."

We sat there, both of us looking at our fingernails.

"But I'll tell you one thing that's worse than being lonely without her, Donny, and that's being lonely with her. When I'm with her and I know she's pulled out on me in her head, when I think maybe she's hip to me, then I really get crazy. I get horny, of all things, and I wind up chasing her. The more I chase, the more she withdraws, and I wind up feeling like Dracula around sex."

"Why don't you just get laid on the outside?"

"I can't, man. I'm not built like that. I need it all in one place. And I'm not talkin' about romance. Fuck romance, romance is the shits, there's gotta be something else besides romance. I'm walking around with a big friggin' cannonball hole in my guts from romance."

"I'm hip, my man." Donny ditched his cigarette.

"But it feels like it's either nothing, you know, a jump-jerk-and-squirt deal or I get into a year-long scorpion dance."

"It doesn't *have* to be that way, Kenny."

"Yeah, so I hear, but like last night, I picked up this girl, you know, and how do you say to somebody, 'Look, I just want to ball. I don't want to get heavy.' And she starts telling me all these sob stories about her childhood, how she got fucked over by her mother and shit. I *hate* that, man. I *cannot* tolerate people who walk around crying about what is no more, but she's coming on to me with these my mother did this, and my mother did that. I mean *everybody's* got horror stories from back then. Christ, you wanna hear horror stories? You wanna hear bad one-liners? My mother said to me once, 'Don't ever let your father know what type of person you really are 'cause it would kill him.' How about *that* one? I was *seven*, Donny, okay? Both of them. They would always torture me, tell me how I tore out everybody's heart, how they

slaved to buy me toys and clothes, and how I was a little
ingrate, how I would never appreciate it. They used to call
me a little torturer. I had a chronic blink when I was a kid
and my old lady would pull her hair and cry and ask why I
tortured her by blinking like that. See, that was supposed to
stop the blink. And I was a little mope when I was a kid and
was a little depressed — no big surprise but then they would
get on my ass about that. I was torturing them with my moodi-
ness. They would say shit like, 'This room was filled with
sunshine until you walked in like a dark cloud' — real fuckin'
poetry. And that made me even *more* depressed and they
would intensify the torture angle, how I was torturing them
and how they loved me, and *what* could they do to make me
more happy, more human — 'We try *everything, everything!*
We love you so much.' I would freak out and feel like I
wanted to die. One time when I was ten I wigged and started
screaming at my old lady, '*Please, Please,* don't love me so
much, I don't deserve it.' And she looked at me and said,
'You don't want me to love you so much? Okay.' And she
didn't speak to me for ten days. All she ever said to me was
'Drink your milk' or 'Go to sleep.' Whenever I tried to kiss
her goodnight she held the newspaper between us and made
like I wasn't there, and when I got home from school she
wouldn't even look at me until I fucking cracked up. I started
screaming, crying, begging, man, *begging* her to talk to me.
And she says to me, 'Just remember these last few days whenever you get to feel like you don't want me to love you so
much.' So don't fuckin' tell me horror stories about childhood." I lit a cigarette and tossed the burning match into the
ashtray. "And that was called *love,* man, that was in the
name of love. So no wonder I get horny when La Donna
pulls away. That's not horniness. That's nostalgia, man.
That's old-timer's day."

  I spit a tiny dry shred of meat on the tablecloth.

  "Look, the bottom line is, I don't give a flying fuck about
nobody, and that's the God's honest truth. I'm emotional,

sure, but that doesn't mean shit, that's a *style*, man, that's not substance. It's *cold* outside, kid, and it's getting colder every day. You know? And she's right. I don't really care about her. I mean I *love* her and all, but I don't want her to make it now. I don't want her to do anything that's gonna take her away. And I'll tell you something else. I think I'm jealous of her. She's trying. I don't even know what the hell I'm doing with myself. I got illusions about being an English teacher because I like to read. I haven't cracked Book Two since last year. I mean I'm *into* reading, but so big fucking deal. That's a talent about two notches above being a good speller and about half a notch below having a neat handwriting. I'm grabbing at fucking straws here, Donny. English teacher, shit. I feel like a fucking jerk even *telling* anybody that." I stubbed out my cigarette.

I flashed on that first fight I had had with La Donna, when I wound up demanding to pay all of Bossanova's bills. I felt as though I understood why I did that: to control the threat, plain and simple. What a creep.

"So what happened with that girl?"

"What girl? Kristin?"

"I don't know what her name is."

"Nothing. We balled and she split, like that." I didn't mention the phone conversation. It embarrassed me. I lowered my head and made to scratch my hairline.

It amazed me that Donny wasn't jumping on my case. My bullshit seemed as obvious to me as neon. He didn't care about me. Fuck him.

"So if romance, love, don't cut it, what does?"

"Depends on what you call love, Kenny. Can you love anything you don't stick your dick in?"

"Yeah, my country." I laughed. "Lemme ask you something, Donny. In high school, I was okay, wasn't I?"

"Whada you mean?"

"I was in there, I was into things, right?"

"Like what?" Donny shook his head in confusion.

"I mean, I wasn't no depresso, was I?"

"Not any more than anybody else." He frowned.

If I was just like everybody else how come I wound up like I did? Then I thought, as opposed to who? Donny? Candy? Kristin? La Donna? Maybe we all got burned. Maybe to get burned was the nature of "normal."

"And lemme ask you one last thing, Donny. How come, if you were so pissed at me Thursday, you called me back?"

Donny smiled at his hands, then picked up his cold coffee cup. "Because I was lonely, Kenny, and so were fucking you."

I opened my mouth to argue, wound up sighing.

"C'mon, let's go to a movie." I threw my half of the tab down on the table, got up and stretched.

We decided to see *Straw Dogs,* which was playing in one of the dollar-fifty places between Seventh and Eighth on Forty-second Street.

We sat in a packed mainly spade and porto audience, all of us woofing, groaning, laughing and barking at the shenanigans on the screen. The air was choked with grass smoke. We sat in back of two teen-agers. They had joints parked behind both ears. We slouched in our seats grooving more on the audience than on the movie. When one of the villains got finished slapping and raping the blond heroine, a guy behind us drawled, "Ah hopes dat bitch done took her pill *dat* mornin'!" and everybody went berserk.

"Yeah, ah sho hopes she done took her birf control pill." He pushed a good thing too far and someone in front yelled for him to shut up.

"Who gone *shut* me up?" he barked.

"Ah will, me, too, yeah me, too, ah will." A dozen voices from all over the house.

I was proud of myself that Donny's gayness didn't wig me, like a sixties liberal buddying up to a yom. There was also something else going on. He said he wasn't into balling with me, but I assumed that if I wanted to he would. And I sat there thinking about what it would be like to get it on. I'd had fantasies about guys, but I would never dream of coming on to my man here. Other than pure fear, one of the reasons was that I had a hunch that if I did it would make him feel shitty. Like *he* was the vulnerable one, like *he* was the full-time spade, and I was just doing a night in Harlem for a goof. Like it was up to me.

"This is a fuckin' scary movie, man." He knocked my leg with his knee.

"This is a fuckin' scary audience," I murmured into my fist. On the screen four murderous bastards stalked a defenseless couple in a deserted cabin.

"They're comin' after us, Becker, they're comin' after us." Donny laughed and slid farther down in his seat. "Pretend they're coming after us."

"Big deal," I snorted. "I live my fuckin' *life* like they're comin' after me."

"We're in danger, Becker! We're in danger! We're in dangerous Times Square! Dangerous Times Square! Surrounded by dangerous stoned psychotic jigaboos! Ooo, it's so dangerous, Becker!" he riffed, laughing. "Whata we gonna *do*, Becker? Whata we gonna *do*?" He got me laughing. I started to get into his trip, but he was acting weird. And his "Ooo, it's so dangerous" sounded like faggottese to me, I couldn't help it. It was true.

I didn't want to be his friend. I wanted to split right after the movie.

They Died with Their Boots On was on the late show.

"So." Donny hunched against the cold in front of the movie house. People fanned out around us. "What's to be?"

I shrugged. "I think I'm gonna shoot uptown."

"It's only eleven-thirty, where you running?"

"Nah, I'm tired."

"C'mon, Kenny, let's do something. You wanna score some women?"

"Get the fuck outa here." I was embarrassed.

"Then what? I'm up for anything."

"I'm gonna go, Donny."

"Okay." Donny looked glum.

I felt like a shit. "Whata you gonna do, you gonna go home?"

"Nah, I don't feel tired. I'm probably gonna go down to some bars or something." He didn't sound too excited. "You wanna run with me?"

"Whata you mean?" I felt on my toes.

"You know, just see the scene."

"Yeah, and get cornholed by one of your boys?"

"Nah. It's not like that, Kenny. Nobody fucks around with nobody that don't want to get fucked around with. Too many fish in the sea."

"Nah, I'm gonna go home."

"Aw, c'mon, whata you gonna do at home, get in bed and watch TV? Come with me. This'll blow your fucking mind, man. And don't worry about nothing, you're perfectly safe."

"Hey, it's not like that."

"Well, *fuck* clubs then. Let's get something to eat. All I'm saying is, we're having a good time, man. It's still early. I haven't hung out and bombed around in a dog's age, and you neither." He squinted at me.

I was running around all week crying about my loneliness and now when someone wanted my company they almost had to beg for it.

I started feeling sleepy, a panicky sleepy like the exhaustion I felt the night before with Kristin. Donny wasn't going to let me sleep. I would never get to sleep.

I started to waver. I could sleep late tomorrow.

"You still thinking I'm gonna hit on you?" He frowned.

"Hey, no! No!" I really didn't.

" 'Cause if you are, the only thing I'm gonna hit on you with is my foot in your face." He looked like he wasn't kidding.

"You sure those joints are safe? 'Cause I'm serious, man, I don't wanna deal with no psychos tonight." We started walking downtown.

"What makes you so sure they want to deal with you?"

"C'mon, Donny, you know I'm hot stuff."

We hit Christopher Street about midnight. It was freezing outside, but despite the cold the street was so packed it looked as if there were a street fair going on. There were no women to be seen. I was in a totally different head then the last time I'd walked down this street. I didn't feel so contemptuous. And a lot more scared. Donny was in a different head, too, more relaxed, less self-conscious. He barreled along as if he owned the place, staring down any guy who caught his fancy. Me, I was going berserk. My face was set in my "I could give a shit" expression but I felt like somebody was playing jai alai with my brains. I found myself tensing my muscles, flattening my gut. I got totally focused on guys' physiques. I didn't feel turned on, more like competitive. I avoided eyes, but I was sneaking peeks to see who, if anybody, was checking *me* out.

"Okay, Kenny, here she comes, Miss Right."

About ten yards in front of us, a long-haired guy in a leather jacket and white dungarees hooked glances with me and walked slowly past us doing a neck-breaking head turn, his eyes never leaving my face. Donny gave me a shot in the ribs.

"Your first cruise."

"Unbelievable." I laughed. I was pleased. I felt the power of being a cocktease. I thought about some of the "look but don't touch" bitches I had known and at that moment I became hip to the kick.

"Donny, you know that thing about the handkerchiefs? You know, the color signifies your sex trip?"

"No, tell me about it." He laughed.

"Aw, fuck you. Can you imagine if *singles'* bars had them? You know, you go in someplace and a chick's got a white kerchief. That means she'll do anything that doesn't involve touching it. Green, only with guys earning thirty grand or more; blue, fuck no suck; pink, suck no fuck."

Donny wasn't listening. He looked like he was on automatic cruise control.

Grabbing my arm, he dragged me up a few steps toward a heavy oak door. Overhead hung a sign: DANTE'S INFERNO. I put on the skids and pulled him back. "Whoa! What's this?"

We went inside. Heads swung to the door to check out who was making an entrance. I kept my head down and nudged Donny out of their line of vision. The place was large, jammed, designed as a cross between a western and a pub motif.

"Don't fucking move, Donny." I stood there trying to get my bearings. I was more frightened being indoors. "Okay." I calmed down. "But don't leave me." I felt like a kid who couldn't swim hanging on to a grownup in the deep end of the pool.

"It's lightweight, Kenny."

I followed Donny's heels. He was plowing through the chatting, laughing men like an icebreaker.

"Hey, hey, slow down." I didn't like sliding through groups of guys. My hand was casually nailed in front of my crotch. I snagged Donny's jacket. I wanted to slap him on the back of his head for being an insensitive prick.

"Kenny, relax. Jerry!" Donny waved to a tall, thin guy in a striped rugby shirt. Donny kissed him, then introduced me. We shook hands. He looked like some fraternity wimp. I felt a little weird having watched them kiss, but I wasn't gagging either. It just looked stupid.

I stood as close to Donny as I could and scanned the place. Everybody looked collegiate, friendly, definitely middle class, in their twenties, wearing crew-neck sweaters, La Coste shirts

— all-American gay. It felt like a college smoker. The only thing missing was the adhesive nametags. Not very threatening. Soon I even felt brave enough to venture a few feet away from Donny like a cocky yet shaky kid his first time out on a two-wheeler. I turned to make some snide comment to Donny but he was gone.

No good. Alone now, the place took on a sexually sinister shade. I noticed the cruising again. Lots of posing, posturing. I soon had the sense of everybody moving with an underwater rhythm, a slow-motion school of fish — drift, stop, stare, drift. Propping an elbow against the bar I ordered a Tab. Some guy tried to burn me with his stare, checking me out like he was my fucking eye doctor. I looked away, yawned. He moved on. I didn't feel frightened, just wobbly. I didn't feel attracted or turned on to anyone. I didn't even know what I was supposed to be attracted to. I felt like an outsider. As if I had no right to talk to anyone because I didn't belong. A Jew in a church. Across the room several guys leaned against a wall looking bored, showing off their baskets, like someone had slipped crowbars down the front of their shorts. They were like chicks with big tits in low-cut dresses in singles' bars.

"Kenny, where'd you go?" Donny came up to me at the bar.

"What do you mean, where'd *I* go?"

"I thought you found somebody."

"Get bent. So what's the story here, it's like a singles' bar."

"Yeah, I come here when I feel like being sociable, when I just wanna hang out and talk."

"But it's really easy to get laid here, right?"

"Yeah, I guess, but there's heavy competition. The best guys go fast. And I'll tell you something, the final trip here is just like anyplace else. Everybody's looking for that one person. Straight, gay, no difference. You fuck this one, you fuck that one, but in the back of your head . . ."

I was feeling pretty good. I was hanging out in a gay bar, being cool, having an intelligent conversation.

"You wanna check out other places?" Donny asked.

"Sure."

Once we hit the street I started ogling a middle-aged woman with her husband.

"See that kid over there?" Donny nodded toward a blond, crew-cut runaway looking seventeen years old, smoking a cigarette and sitting on a parked car. "He lived with me for two weeks."

The kid's back was to us. Most of the guys passing by gave him a heavy cruise. He didn't look up.

"Is that good?"

"Is what good?" Donny turned up the collar of his bomber jacket.

"That he lived with you for two weeks."

"It was good for him." Donny put his hands in his pockets and rolled his shoulders.

We moved in a westerly direction toward the river. There were fewer stores, fewer lights, a lot of warehouses. Two guys passed us dressed from head to toe in black leather. In addition to keychains, handcuffs dangled from their belts. Donny didn't even blink. I blinked enough for a Morse code dictionary. At the end of Christopher Street we turned up Eleventh Avenue, which could have been a set for *On the Waterfront*. On our left was the river, rows of deserted piers and warehouses and armies of trucks parked for blocks under the gloomy shadow of the elevated West Side Highway. On our right were gay bars sprinkled among beat-up factories, meatpacking docks and trash-filled lots. The only sounds came from the sporadic, speeding rumbles of overhead highway traffic. I noticed a chunky guy dressed in leather with a blond Nazi flat-top pissing in a lot. His dick was profile to the sidewalk.

"Shit, Donny, where you taking me?"

"It's all bullshit, Kenny. Just hang in there."

Occasionally a low-flying taxi zoomed between the highway pillars on the cobblestoned street and rocked to a halt in front of a dimly lit doorway as anywhere from one to five guys in motorcycle leather erupted from the back seat and vanished behind a club door.

"This is the other end of the spectrum." Donny glanced around. "But it's not as scary as it looks."

"Oh, yeah? Tell it to the marines."

"I'm sure the marines already know." He ushered me into the Stockade. From the outside the place looked closed. The shades were drawn and I couldn't hear any noise from the street.

The minute we walked in I realized we'd landed on another planet. I started wigging. I was scared. No lie. The place was huge, high-ceilinged, cavernous, with a sinister glow as if the color black emitted its own tint of light. Music boomed, pounded, exploded. The place was mobbed with giants in leather, shades, chains, shaved heads, boots, Fu Manchus. It was a cocktail party in hell. Grim dudes with crook-necked vulture postures stood motionless against walls. Suspended from the ceiling were straps, harnesses and assorted metal and leather objects which looked like they might be used for either torture or training race horses. I felt like any second someone was going to come up and hurt me. Donny led me to a clear spot on the wall and we stood silent across from a forty-foot bar over which hung an enormous American flag at one end and an entire Harley Davidson at the other.

"Snort this." Donny passed me a gray metal inhaler, his thumb over the tip.

"What is it?"

"Just snort it."

"Hey, fuck you just snort it! What is it?" I was so tense I couldn't even look at him.

"It's amyl, man, it's lightweight."

"Everything's fuckin' lightweight with you, Donny. I'm startin' to think *you're* a little lightweight, you know?"

"You scared, Kenny?" He didn't take offense.

"No! No! I'm used to walking in on the Luftwaffe and the Hell's Angels, man. This is everyday shit for me!"

"Kenny." He touched my arm. "Just relax for a second, look around you, check out some of the people here." He nodded in the direction of a guy my size. "Take that dude. How much you think those threads set him back?"

The leather looked brand new, custom tailored.

"A yard?"

"Try two. Two hundred dollars' worth of leather and chrome, man. Now who can afford that kind of dough? You get what I'm drivin' at?"

"Whata you mean?"

"I mean the guy's probably some lawyer, a professor. Whata you think, those are his everyday clothes? They get that shit in *boutiques,* man, joints that take Master Charge. Just look around you, man. Don't look at the leather; look at the faces. This is an upper-middle-class scene, Kenny. I guarantee you if everybody had to empty out their wallets right now I'd have enough American Express cards to wallpaper my apartment."

I scanned the joint. Some guys didn't look like they were bullshitting, but a lot did. Under a lot of motorcycle hats were a lot of kick-me faces, baby faces, scared faces, wrinkled faces. There were spindly legs and potbellies. It was as if the Junior Chamber of Commerce had dropped acid and threw a Walter Mitty party. But not all of them.

"So what we're saying here, Donny, is that half these guys are doing Disneyland in their heads."

"Shit, yeah, the tougher the front the bigger the pussy."

"Yeah, but some of these dudes look like they'd be into sucking out your eyes through a flavor straw."

A short weightlifter wearing a gray Godspell T-shirt cruised by like a battleship on patrol.

"Well, that's the trick here. You got to figure out who's into what before it's too late. That's some of the kick, too, the danger. Just stay away from the loners, the guys who aren't so dressed up. Everybody's trying so hard to come on like street punk or working-class badass. It's all fantasy. I know one kid who ran into his father here, for Christ's sake."

I leaned back trying to tell who was into what. Donny was ducking and weaving, grooving with the music. I couldn't pick out any songs on the track. They all blended from one disco riff to another. Donny passed me the inhaler again. I took a five-second snort and the back of my head took off for California. The music took on echo chamber proportions and I couldn't hear myself laugh even though I knew I was halfway to hysteria. Donny held out his hand for a slap, grinning and grooving. The music was a bouncy bitch. My neck and ears were burning with piping hot cherry red blood.

"What the fuck is amyl anyhow?" I laughed.

"Heart attack medicine." He staggered backward clutching his heart in a mock seizure and I almost fell to the floor. We could hardly hear ourselves over the disco.

"You're a sick man, Donny."

"Ain't this place a groove?" We stared at a huge scary dude with a shaved head, shaved eyebrows, no shirt, riding pants, knee-high boots and a diagonal leather SS strap slashed across his naked outrageously pectoraled chest. He slid a finger to his second knuckle up his nose. We started laughing so hard I began to retch.

"Oh, fuckin' Donny, you're in trouble." I gasped for air.

"Kenny, man, I think he likes you."

"Not me, man. You the Jew with the schnoz. He wants to fist-fuck your beak, man." The amyl was wearing off.

"Hey, later for this room. They're all posers in here. I want to show you the back room, you game?" Donny winked.

"Shit, let's go." I was still laughing as I followed Donny to the rear of the bar.

At the archway we were charged a buck to go any farther. We rounded the arch into another bar with maybe a hundred and fifty guys standing in a twenty-by-thirty area — nominally a dance floor. The only light was reflected off a movie screen mounted overhead. In the movie two Boy Scouts crammed what looked like a five-pound salami up the ass of a tenderfoot. Donny bulled his way toward the center of the cluster. I didn't want to follow, but I wasn't hanging out by myself, so I moved through the crowd in a mild panic, my forearm clamped in front of my groin like a police bar. I kept my eyes trained on chests, found three square inches of space and planted myself.

I stood rigid, packed in on all sides, staring at the screen. The crowd was dead silent; faces were stony. There was some kind of movement in the crowd, but I couldn't figure out where. As my eyes adjusted to the darkness, I noticed that some guys were jerking each other off. A few had slipped to their knees and were giving head. Fuck that. I wanted out. I couldn't move. The crowd had me hemmed in. Donny was nowhere to be seen. I started pushing. I felt like everybody suddenly decided to move in the opposite direction and I was bucking a tide. A hand brushed my cock. That was it. I was gone. I made it through a hundred guys in two seconds. I stood on the edge of the pack, sweating. Teeth and shirts glowed ghostlike under an ultraviolet light I hadn't noticed before. I stared into the mob. Donny emerged.

"Kenny, where'd you go?"

"Fuck you."

"Hey, relax, anybody grabs your joint, just push their hand away."

I flashed on a Jacques Cousteau film I once saw where a diver in a shark cage tapped the noses of inquisitive sharks. Donny plowed back in. Screw it. Back in I went. Somebody brushed my joint. I pushed his hand. He went away. I felt a rush of power. Pricks blossomed out of flies like speeded-up nature films. I started to gawk. A short bald guy was desperately grabbing at every cock in sight — getting slapped away, like some creep trying to grab a slow dance at a mixer and getting shot down by every girl.

Against a wall I saw Donny, his arms behind him, gazing

at the screen. A big dude approached him, his broad back obscuring Donny from my view. I could see Donny's face over the guy's shoulder. Donny briefly glanced at him, then returned his attention to the movie. I had never noticed that look on Donny's face. It was one of power. Control. Hidden talents. Suddenly I realized I didn't know him. Donny Goof-off. There was a lake in his face, a deep lake of other things, other hungers, hardnesses. There was more to him than met the eye. More to everything than met the eye, and I didn't god-damn like it. The guy made some movements with his arm, then began jerking his elbow back and forth in short, rapid strokes. Donny looked down momentarily, then back at the movie. I shoved out of the crowd to the same wall I'd run for earlier.

I stood there staring into the snake pit and all I could think about was finding a caption for the picture. If the disco music hadn't drowned out the nonstop shuffling of feet and a few sporadic groans or grunts I probably would have jumped out of my skin.

"Hey, man, you keep getting lost." Donny reappeared.

"Nah, you know how I am at social gatherings. I'm shy."

"Unbelievable, right?"

"I saw some guy in there with his fly open. I would have passed him a note but I didn't want to embarrass him."

"Kenny the Riffer." Donny chuckled, wiping sweat from his eyebrow with the curl of his wrist.

"That's me." I smirked. "The grim riffer."

"Let's take a walk." We left the Stockade.

"You get done?" I tried to make the question sound casual.

"I got done, I did somebody — the whole shot."

Getting done didn't seem too bad, but doing somebody made me jump back. I imagined Donny on his knees in front of some guy. The image was too much and I changed chan-nels. I no longer noticed the leather boys as we walked along the black street. They were there, but they didn't stand out so much anymore.

"How you doing, Kenny?"

"I'm good, I'm good. I got done, too."

"You did?" Donny stopped abruptly.

"Shit, yeah, I got blown by a one-legged dwarf in a motor-cycle jacket. I never knew sex could be like that."

"Seriously, Kenny, how you doing?"

I didn't know how to answer that question. All I could do was come up with one-liners. I wasn't tired anymore, and I wasn't shocked. Maybe numb, but the type of numb that came out as "oh yeah? what else is on this planet?"

"I'm just taking it all in, man. It's very bizarre, very bizarre. What time is it?"

"About two, two-thirty. You want to try one more place?"

"Why not." I had my immunity, and I knew I was going to shake Donny after the night anyhow.

Donny walked me over to a new place. The Garrison. We walked in and ba-boom! Sodom and Gomorrah. *Hundreds* of guys slammed and barraged by lights, jungle disco, nudity, heat, dungeons, come and sweat.

He pushed me through to the bar. Inches from our drinks and hands a young Spanish go-go boy, wearing construction boots and a gem-studded leather ring around his cock and balls, was strutting, prancing, mincing, twirling. Six of these nubile pubites danced around like that. Above their heads hung knotted, heavy ropes and wooden perches. They swung and flipped over the bar. They hung upside-down from the perches, flexing their assholes, the expression on their faces pure Mae West. The disco pound was ear-shattering. A half-dozen large, dance-hall reflecting balls threw wild fragments of colored light like shrapnel against the floor, the walls, the paralyzed faces in the room and finally leapt up to the ceiling. The heat and packed flesh were unbelievable. On raised platforms, two ash-gray spades with the most finely chiseled musculature this side of the Alvin Ailey dancers twisted and contorted to music from outer space. One was nude except for a cowboy hat and a cock ring, the other was draped in chains. Above the pounding thunderlust shrieked a nonstop trill — a cross between a tropical bird and an ambulance siren. At first I thought it was coming from one of the go-go boys swinging wildly upside-down on his perch. I didn't know. I couldn't tell. Maybe it came from me. The walls.

Donny was standing next to me at the bar, ignoring the dancers but intensely scanning the mob.

"This is incredible, Kenny. This is the wildest! You gotta get into it! You gotta get into it! You can't *watch* it! You gotta get into it!" He was sweating like death and looked half-gone with excitement. Suddenly he grabbed my wrist and pulled me through the crowd.

"Feel the excitement, Kenny! Feel it! This is where it is!"

"This is where *what* is?" I tried to wrench my hand free but his grip was cemented with his intensity. I was stumped for a funny answer to my own question. I was riffed out. He scared me. Donny was gone in his eyes and wouldn't have heard me anyhow. He didn't even know I was trying to get loose from him. Crazy son of a bitch. In a way I was glad he was acting like this. With every moment I felt more and more distant from him and safer by myself.

He yanked me into the back room. Once again it was cluster-fuck-suck-snake-pit action under the flickering lights of two West Pointers reaming each other's assholes on a movie screen. The crowd was so tight I was gulping air. We plunged into a catacomb. Musty brick, crumbling, moldy, utter blackness. I could see shadows. People on their knees.

Donny had disappeared somewhere deeper into the darkness. I moved out into the back room. In front of me, a guy in Jockey shorts was getting blown. Older men clustered around the action, watching, heads to one side, hands behind their backs, as if they were observing a chess match in the park. In a corner an enormously fat middle-aged man masturbated — his face to the wall. A kid buried his head into somebody's buttocks and his glasses dangled on one ear. Cocks and mouths.

I moved into the crowd to break through to the front room and immediately got stuck. Movement was constant yet nobody went anywhere. I was dripping wet, stretching my throat for air, like a prehistoric animal trapped in a tar pit. I could see the dancers over by the bar spinning and swinging. On the fever-pitch disco track some spade chick came in waves, the heavy, relentless brass section stirring up images of piledriver dicks. I was dying from the heat, drowning in invisible come. I was turned on. Motherfucker, I was turned on. I was thinking pussy but I couldn't exactly ignore where I was. I tore through the crowd to the relatively free space of the front room. I cooled out, calmed down.

At the bar I grabbed a drink, then another. Staring at the go-go dancers, I tried to feel turned on again. Nothing. I felt pissed. Like a kid having a great time playing pinball then suddenly the machine jams. As my anger angled toward depression, I got hit with the absolute silence of the place. Despite the music, the trills, the lights, the dancers, the crotch violence, there was a total silence. I scanned the front room. Not one conversation. Eyes clicked and roamed like radar blips, but everyone was alone. La Donna. I wanted my baby. My mommy. I needed her. I loved her. Don't give me this *time* shit. There *was* no time. I was hugging myself. We could work it out. Hug-crush love blows away all the bad air. I wanted her so bad I would gladly cut it off in the morning for just one more night. Turn priest, nun, anything. Donny popped out of the crowd and crashed into me, laughing and panting.

"Whew! Awright, lemme just cool off here so I don't get pneumonia, and we'll blow this popstand."

He seemed calmer now.

"I go fucking berserk in this joint, Kenny, you know? I get everything out here. It's like a gym for me, you know what I mean? I walk around all week like I got bees in my head and I just blow it out here. You okay?" He was breathing like a six-day bike racer at halftime.

"You know, Donny, I was just thinking, despite all the dead-end stuff I was talking about between me and La Donna, I do feel that if I'm gonna change then La Donna is the person I have the most potential stuff going with and so I shouldn't throw the baby out with the bath water."

"Oh yeah?" He ran his forearm across his face. "C'mon, let's split. I'm fuckin' exhausted."

We flagged a cab. He started nodding out, his head resting against the window.

"Fuckin' Kenny, man." His eyes were closed. "I had more fun tonight, man, than in the last five years, thousand years." Eyes still closed, he extended his hand for a slap. "Maybe we'll go to college together, man. Go back to college."

I felt like punching him in the face. Fun. What fun. That was like the descent of man in there. Dissociated jerk-off. But as the cab rolled on and Donny nodded out, his hand still extended limply for a slap, I flashed on doing amyl and laughing our asses off, grooving on *Straw Dogs* in the yom palace, our heads down heart to heart in the restaurant.

I didn't want to be alone. I needed company. The thought of going home, whacking off and going to sleep was unbearable. I felt like asking Donny if he wanted to snag something to eat in an all-night diner. Doing a recap of the night over coffeeand. Buddies. Forever buddies. No. Not tonight. Enough was enough. Suddenly I felt furious. I felt deep hate like an asthma. I felt like there was a con man in the cab. I couldn't turn my head in Donny's direction. I needed to get out, to get laid, to find some soft bitch and do it to death. I wanted to get off again in the worst way. Dump Donny and get some slash. A thought hit me and took my breath away like a suction pump in my lungs:

Go back! What? Go back! Suddenly my heart started pounding enough to make my eyes pop out of my head. I can go back to the Garrison! What? No! Yes! Go! You can't! I can do anything I want! I wanted to go back and have someone pop my nut. I wanted to stand against a damp brick wall and have an anonymous mouth suck my dick. Dear God, was that the end or what? You can't do that! Whata you mean, I can't do that? Half the goddamn place was wearing kneepads!

"Stop the cab."

"Huh?" The driver craned his neck to the rear.

Donny blinked and rubbed his eyes.

"Stop the cab, right here. This is good."

"Kenny, what's happening?" Donny tried to shake the nap from his face.

"I know this chick in this neighborhood."

"Becker, it's four in the morning!"

"It's cool." I got out and leaned my head inside the window. "She's just getting off work." I extended my hand inside the cab. "Be good, Mr. Donny."

Donny gave me a tentative slap.

"I'll be in touch."

I staggered back to the Garrison. I couldn't see straight. I was totally torn. My heart was pumping Kool-Aid. My hard-on was going up and down every ten seconds. This was evil. This was bad. I was ripped between a terror and an excitement that I didn't understand. I didn't even know where I was. One block from the Garrison I grabbed a cab, gave the cabby directions. He looked at me like I was nuts.

"You wanna go one block?"

My face turned red with shame. I felt ugly and slimy. I was being the baddest bad boy in the world. But I was still turned on. Maybe that's what the turn-on was all about.

If Mommy only knew.

I was a dead man so I couldn't die, had nothing to lose. I could plunge in fire, make mudpies out of my shit and eat it. The kick was so intense I felt it rise like a tide past my teeth to my eyes. I was like the Invisible Man . . . invincible.

The cabby was staring at me over his shoulder. He threw the meter and, one arm across the top of the front seat, cruised to the Garrison. He turned to me, the look on his face one of amused contempt.

"Hey! I didn't say here! I said Eighteenth and Eleventh, but I didn't say here." I was covered with a sweat as thick as butter.

He smirked. "Okay, which corner you want?"

"By the gas station." I pointed to a deserted garage that had been closed a good six hours.

He sighed, drove fifty more feet and turned off the meter.

"Not everybody's a faggot, you know." I dropped a dollar and slammed the cab door.

I went into a phone booth by the blacked-out gas station and pretended to make a phone call until the cab was out of sight. My lust had died in seconds. I felt like a schmuck. Disgusted, heartsick, and exhausted. I didn't give two shits about a blowjob. I just wanted to get away from Donny. Buddies in a diner was scarier than solo in a snake pit. My life. My fucking life.

I moved toward the Garrison knowing I couldn't get it up now with shin splints. As I walked through the door the music was just as loud as before, the reflecting lights just as chaotic, but I felt immune to the barrage. Jujuba the Nuba was up on the stage again. Coated with a protective fluid, he was in flames. Nude, glistening, he passed two torches across his crotch, around his ass, his thighs — blue flames like ceremonial wings danced on his arms. Caps of fire wavered on his fingertips. I ordered a gin and tonic. It felt sweet and heavy in my stomach. I walked out.

There were half a dozen cabs parked in front discharging and boarding passengers. I wanted to fall into one, but I was embarrassed to take one right there. I didn't want some guy checking me out in his rearview mirror. I walked east to Sixth Avenue and grabbed a Checker uptown.

SUNDAY

When I crawled in it was sunup. I felt like a vampire beating it back to his coffin in a race with the daylight. I headed straight for the bathroom, dropped my pants to my shoes and started beating off. The weak sun filtered in through the heavy leaded snowflake patterns of the window, bathing the room with a strange illumination — like the lighting in a Rembrandt painting. I crouched over the bowl like a ghoul throttling my meat, my brains a speeded-up film of pussies, cocks, assholes, mouths, faces, places, music, hair and groans. My kneecaps were trembling like overworked generators, my elbow flaming with cramps. I lost my balance and almost fell face first into the wall. I caught myself on the sink, my feet trapped by my pants, and shoved myself upright.

My dick was throbbing, my lungs ballooning, my forearm charleyhorsed.

I pulled up my pants, sunk my hands into my front pockets and stared at the floor. "Oh man . . . Oh man."

My skin was crawling. I felt infected, filthy. I stepped out of my clothes, jumped into the shower, then jumped back out before hitting the faucets. It wasn't time for a shower. I felt like I needed to sweat more, to pump some of the shit to the surface. If I took a shower right then it wouldn't have felt like anything.

Grabbing my barbell, I slipped on my sneakers and lay out on the living room floor, my bare ass on a pillow, my feet jammed under the couch.

I hit fifty without even blinking, without even breathing. Kenny makes a move. Kenny makes a move. What a joke. All my moves were frauds, to get out of things, not *into* them, to disentangle, to clear the boards of whatever pathetically little there was for me. Cleaner. Neater.

One hundred came and went. I couldn't even feel my stomach tense. I could do it for hours, it was comforting. I started doing them faster, gripping the weight tighter.

I passed one twenty-five like a downhill train. The weight felt like a feather. Faster. Banging the iron on the floor with every downstroke, smacking my forehead into my kneecaps on the upstroke. Even anytime *I* wanted more, anytime *I* wanted to get close, I was gone. I blew charge and retreat at the same time.

At one fifty my breath came out of my mouth in soft chugs. My stomach knotted a little and there was the slightest clammy sprinkle of sweat on my back and chest. The pain was baby-sized, soothing.

At one seventy-five I tossed the weight aside to pick up speed. I started grunting.

What's the difference? I wasn't a kid anymore. I was a man. An adult. What was done was done.

Two hundred. My stomach was so tight it felt as if it were floating to my knees under its own power. Baby Mississippis rolled from my armpits. I held onto my hair, jerking my neck forward.

Bullshit. Hypocrite. Bullshit. Weakling. Bullshit. Mind-fucker.

I started shouting "Huh! Huh!" with every sit-up. My lower back was red-hot.

Teacher! Teacher! Teach who! With what! I was a fucking ding-dong salesman circle-jerking pussy-chaser. Teacher.

La Donna. My mind clicked off. I rolled with the pain, my fist trembling in my hair, nausea jumping for the catch in my throat. Every sit-up took hours.

"Hunhnh!" My teeth were grinding, my face a black pocket of blood, my thighs rippling, my gut stretched and wrenched.

Two hundred and fifty. Every time I dropped I banged my head on the floor. My prick was twitching from the inside, that crazy unreachable itch that made me want to squeeze it like a tourniquet. I couldn't loosen my fingers from my hair. They knotted on me like rigor mortis.

Fifty more. Fifty more. I couldn't breathe in too deep. My diaphragm was surrounded by pulled and cramped muscles. I collapsed on my back, closed my eyes, grit my teeth and let it rip.

"One! Two! Three! Rrrr! Nnnn!" I was snarling like a lion, my eyes unfocused. "Bastad! Bastad!" Pumping hard. Ripping myself apart. I was crying. Banging my head on my knees and crying. I couldn't stop. "You bastad! Bitch bastad!"

"Twenty-one cunt! Twenty-two cock! Bastad!" Grinding my teeth, I couldn't breathe. I didn't have the wind to cry anymore. I froze at twenty-six, my head stuck between my knees, my fingers snarled in my soaking hair. I growled and retched, spitting on the floor between my trembling legs.

I was dead. I sat naked on a bench with other dead people in what seemed like a waiting room. I knew I was dead because my skin was the color of uncooked chicken — that and because a note was fastened to the skin on my chest with a long pin, and it didn't hurt. I couldn't read the note. Nobody talked. We were all dead.

My eyes snapped open. I was sweating. I felt light-headed with terror. The digital read four-twenty-eight. Sunday afternoon. I started whimpering. Stop the clock. Eat the clock.

The clock was eating me up. Eat the clock. I jerked my head and my neck flamed, my midsection flamed. I couldn't get up. I was trapped. Paralyzed. I rocked my head to help myself breathe. I was alone. Dead. I wanted someone to help me.

Slowly I rolled out of bed. I couldn't stand up straight. The best I could manage was a hunched-over old man's walk. Dead man's walk. I was high on fear. I staggered out of the bedroom like the mummy going for a victim and headed for the living room phone. I had to call someone. Anyone. Emergency. Who? Who? Who. Madame one-and-only. La Donna. But I couldn't. She said ... She needs ... But I'd changed. This last forty-eight hours had come around the horn like forty-eight years. I'm changed. I'm patient. I'm wiser. I can give like a bastard. I collapsed on the couch and picked up the receiver.

La Donna, this is Kenny. Don't hang up baby look I know what you said but I've been through the wringer and I've straightened out.

I dialed her number, listened to the crackling of the line before the first ring.

I've learned so many things, can share so many things, we're both on the move, both growing. The phone rang three times. Each ring sounded like a human voice. By the fourth ring the tension started to dilute. I cradled the receiver under my jaw and stared at the descending reflection of winter sun on my wall.

Hold on. Of course she's not home. She's at the showcase. Should I, shouldn't I.

No contest.

Downstairs, the dying light had an unrealness to it that enhanced my weird, trancelike state. As the cab floated toward the East Side I kept touching my biceps as if to make sure I really existed.

I briefly debated buying flowers for her, but I figured after the showcase they might be misconstrued as for a funeral. The show was at six. They didn't even care enough to give them a respectable starting time.

After I walked into the bar area I did a quick scan. No La Donna. The Mad Russian was at the bar, but I didn't recognize anybody else. I decided to go inside the cabaret. It would probably unnerve her to see me beforehand.

I sat at the same table as last week, in the back, in the dark. Maybe she changed her mind and copped out. It didn't seem likely. The place was three-quarters full. It was ten of six. I should have gotten the flowers. I felt very calm even though I wasn't sure what the hell I was doing. I kept running movies in my head of our contact to come. Rushing into my arms. Slapping my face. Laughing and kissing me. Walking away from me. Slugging me. Hugging me. Crying. I kept thinking that whatever would happen would involve crying. Win, lose or draw there would be tears.

A half-hour later the emcee came on stage. A different, more subdued guy.

First was the duck-talk kid, then the Russian. The audience was hooting and yowling. Two-hundred-pound Annie Akins came on in a fringed miniskirt and a cowgirl hat and sang "Oklahoma." They had her leaving the stage in tears. I didn't even hear La Donna's name called. It seemed like all of a sudden there she was in front of the mike in dungarees and a floppy turtleneck.

Even though I knew she couldn't see past ringside, I slouched down against the wall and casually covered my face with the bridge of my hand as if the spotlights were on me. If I could have done it without anyone noticing, I would have belly-crawled out of there as though I were under fire in basic training. The piano player hit the first few notes of "Misty." Eyes glistened and mouths were slightly open in anticipation of big yuks coming up. I zeroed in on two heavyset middle-aged guys in expensive suits. One guy wore a star sapphire pinky ring, the other had a cigarette going. The one with the ring had small dagger teeth. They were giving her the once-over.

"Loo-ook at me-e."

They semismiled. One nudged the other, whispered. I fantasized jumping up and doing flamenco on their faces.

"I'm as help-less, as a kitten up a tree."

I imagined them doing a Pat and Mike on her, a salt and pepper. Her begging for more, them switching ends. Cigarettes and hundred-dollar bills.

Somebody coughed to my right. I wheeled my head so fast I pinched a nerve at the base of my neck. If anybody wanted to heckle I'd pounce. I swear I'd pounce. Nobody heckled. My neck burned.

"With my heart-rt in my han-nd, I get mis-ty, calling your name."

I scanned the crowd like a prison spotlight. Laugh, somebody. Just giggle. I felt as taut as the top knot of a shillelagh. She was looking away from me. She was playing to ringside, to the curtain, to the piano player. Nobody laughed. I made myself sit back and tried to relax a little. She wasn't bad. Not great, not bad. But "not bad" wasn't good enough. She wasn't going to make it in a million years.

The audience applauded for real. It wasn't hysterical applause, and there was a mood of slight disappointment in the room because she was no clown show. She smiled and slightly dipped her head in acknowledgment. She looked happier than I had seen her in months. I wanted to feel relieved and happy for her, but I felt somewhat deflated, like when that suicidal girl called in to the talk show to say she was "okay now." I felt sad. Bullshit. I didn't feel sad. My jaw felt sore. I was grinding my teeth for I don't know how long.

La Donna, run for the hills. She smiled in my direction. I looked at her eyes; she couldn't see me. She didn't know I was there. I tried to think what she ever did to me that was so villainous that she deserved my "love." I put my hand in front of my face again and stared at my shoes. I imagined myself a crack running back, the sixth Temptation, a lean stud, a hungry hawk. My shoes.

When I looked up again, Ronnie Landau was singing "September Song." The chubby kid wasn't that bad, except his voice kept breaking into sobs like a cantor every now and then. He got some nice applause too. More power to him. Next was a professional comedian named Frank Allen who, I must admit, was very funny. Very few people can make me laugh.

I finally left the club at seven-fifteen.

I took a cab home. Halfway through the park I panicked. I felt an agonizing sensation of time wasted, love wasted. I felt terrified of my loneliness. Terrified of my apartment. My haunted house. I had the driver drop me off by a phone on Columbus Avenue.

I was struck again by the limbo weirdness of a winter Sunday. It was night now. And windy. The streets were as empty as if an air raid drill was in effect, the storefronts were black mouths. Six blocks of traffic lights turned green for the benefit of one car. I dropped a dime and dialed La Donna. Hung up before the first ring. But what about *me?* What about *now?* What about this goddamn twilight zone street? I had to make a call, make a connection. Who? La Donna, Kristin, Jackie di Paris, Little Flower, Donny. Glue nose. Blue shoes. Red lips. Swivel hips. Cheeseburger George. Donny. What list. What friends. Donny. Donny.

"Hey, Kenny, what's shakin'? How'd it go last night?"

"How did *what* go?" I was so relieved to hear his voice I didn't even say hello. I had just said *"Donny!"* when he answered, like "Gotcha!"

"The chick."

"What chick?" I couldn't even concentrate on the words. I just wanted to drink from the sounds of a voice.

"The chick you jumped out of the cab . . ."

"Oh. Oh." That bullshit felt like sixty-three years ago. I had to play through the lie. "It was okay."

"So what's up, Kenny?"

Do you want to have dinner? Do you want to be my friend? Do you want to save my goddamn life? What if he never goes away? What if he hits on me? What if he doesn't want to be my friend? What if I die holding the phone? I pretended I had a gun pointed at my head.

"You wanna have dinner, kid?"

"Sure, where?"

Where. Where. American Three Brothers Greeks China.

"American Brothers?"

"Where?"

"Three Brothers?"

"Where's that?"

"By me up here . . . I'll go down there, okay?"

"Kenny, whata you talking about? You wanna go to Victor's?"

"Sure, sure." Yeah, Victor's, Victor's.

"What time you wanna meet?"

"Time?" I glanced at a bank clock, but I couldn't concentrate on the numbers. A haze of ragey urgency cut my visibility.

"Time?" I repeated. "It's seven-thirty."

"C'mon, stupid, I know it's seven-thirty. What time you wanna eat?"

I frowned as I stared at the clock. It could have just as easily been the control panel of an F-104.

"You wanna eat about nine, Kenny? How about nine, does that sound good?"

"Nine?" I repeated in a daze.

"You need more time, we can eat at ten."

"Hold on," I mumbled. I rested the receiver against my neck and drummed my fingernails on the metal phonebook shelf. An empty bus came gliding and rocking by on the night-time street.

"No." I breathed deep. "Eight. I'll meet you there at eight."